# Down the Garden Path

Colleen Price

Library and Archives Canada Cataloguing in Publication

Price, Colleen, 1987-, author
 Down the garden path / Colleen Price.

ISBN 978-1-927507-44-5 (softcover)

 I.Title.

PS8631.R5234D69 2018 C813'.6 C2018-902918-8

I would like to thank everyone who helped me with this story, both reader feedback as well as the editing.

# CHAPTER ONE

*August 1, 1865*

A horse snorted nearby just about causing Leah to drop her skirt as she jerked back to reality. Leah managed to stop herself in time and avoided getting the hem of her skirt wet. She looked up from the fish to the shore. There by the water's edge was a man sitting on a horse. Leah felt the flush of embarrassment start to creep up her neck to her face and she tried to swallow it back down. She wanted to disappear under the water and stay there until this stranger had gone away, but since he had obviously been there watching her for several minutes Leah knew he was not likely to just ride away. Sliding under the water and ending up soaking wet would just embarrass her even further, if that was possible.

"Where did you come from?" Leah blurted out before thinking first.

"That way," the man answered pointing towards the trees. Leah did not recognize him immediately but there was something a little bit familiar about him, so she figured he might have been at some social event she had attended since he lived so close but she had attended many community gatherings with her father and he had spoken to many people at them.

"How long have you been standing there?" Leah asked as the man lowered his hand.

"A couple of minutes," the man answered, "I was curious as to what fascinated you so."

Leah studied the man. He was maybe a year or two older than her seventeen years. Leah guessed him to be about the same height as her father had been before he had gotten sick. The man's brown hair was only long enough to be able to curl at his forehead and around his ears and it looked soft and perfect for running fingers through. Leah could tell the he was fairly muscular even from a distance and he had a more solid build than Randall's skinny frame. The man smiled, but his smile did not seem to be mocking Leah or her current situation. Instead there was warmth in it that made Leah's stomach flutter.

"Fish," Leah's response came out in one rushed breath, "I have been watching the fish." Leah tried to expand of her explanation, but somehow the man on the horse was leaving her a little flustered. She thought about going back to the bank and putting her shoes and stockings back on but realized that would show even more bare leg so she did not move.

"I see," the man replied. Leah was not sure how to respond so she stayed silent.

"You are Leah Winsand, are you not?" the man asked.

"I am," Leah answered, "But I do not know who you are."

"Caleb Morley," the man said.

Leah tried to remember what she knew about the Morleys. Hilary mentioned them occasionally, but Leah's mother never talked about them. It was strange that Leah's mother did not talk about them because she was usually very vocal about others and their behaviour, especially if the gossip was juicy.

"Nice to meet you," Leah said as she started back towards where her shoes and stockings were. As she got into the shallower water she lowered her skirt to cover her legs, but without getting it wet. Leah found her petticoat stuck to her wet lower limbs. She barely avoided tripping and falling into the water before she finally reached the shore.

"I am sorry I interrupted you," Caleb said. He had walked his horse around to where Leah was standing.

"I should get back to my father," Leah said as she picked up her shoes and stockings. She figured she could walk as far as the garden and put them on once she had closed the door.

"How is your father?" Caleb asked getting off his horse, "He has not visited lately."

"My father visits you?" Leah was surprised as she turned to look at Caleb.

"He and father get together to discuss the issues of the day and their annual deer hunt," Caleb answered, "Father invited him a couple weeks ago to discuss this year's plans but never received a response."

"Father is sick," Leah looked down at the grass and tried to not let emotion into her voice. The tears were too close to the surface and would come easily if she let them.

"What is wrong with him?" Caleb asked.

"The doctor does not seem to be able to figure it out. No one else has gotten sick so it is not contagious but that seems to be all anyone knows," Leah answered.

"I am sorry to hear he is sick," Caleb said. Leah looked up into to his eyes and saw sympathy in the brown depths. She found herself wishing Caleb would take her into his arms and tell her it would be okay. Leah quickly pushed the thought away. Caleb was a stranger and nothing would be okay as long as her father was sick.

"The doctor is not even sure if father will survive, because sometimes he is doing better and sometimes he looks close to death," Leah blinked back the tears that tried to spill onto her cheeks. It would not be good to cry about her problems in front of a stranger.

"He will come through," Caleb said as if sensing her distress, "Your father is a strong person."

Leah nodded, but she was not sure she believed him. She was starting to feel tired and did not want to do anything more embarrassing in front of this stranger who was made her feel nervous and yet in a strange way comfortable.

"I should get back," Leah said, "He has probably woken up by now." Leah turned and started for the hedge before Caleb could say anything more. He did not say anything, but Leah could feel him watching her.

Leah had gone only a few steps when she started to feel dizzy. Closing her eyes she shook her head to try and clear it. When she opened them again she found the world was spinning faster. She closed her eyes again. Leah thought she could feel strong arms surround her before she blacked out.


Caleb caught Leah before she hit the ground. He lifted her up. Caleb looked at the open door in the middle of the hedge, where Leah must have come from, but it looked too far to be useful. Instead he carried her around the fish pond and into the shadow of the trees. Caleb gently set Leah down on the grass. She did not wake up.

Caleb studied her. Leah's pale face was flushed, probably from too much sun. Her hair was falling out of its bun causing a halo effect around her face. Leah's brown hair had a touch of red in it, which Caleb was sure she had inherited from her father. Caleb remembered how bright her blues eyes were when she had looked up to find him sitting there. He had been sorry when she had lowered them in embarrassment.

Leah's light blue dress brought out both the traces of red

in her hair and the bright blue of her eyes. It was also a marvel to Caleb how a simple dress could look so good but since she already seemed embarrassed he had not said anything for fear she would think he was teasing her. Most women of his acquaintance would have been upset to find that he was watching them without indicating his presence and since he did not like to be subject to a sharp tongue Caleb had not found any of the young women around that he wanted to court. But Leah had been embarrassed by his presence, not insulted. His father definitely would not mind if Caleb courted James Winsand's daughter, since they were old friends, if Leah was willing. Caleb brushed back a loose hair which had fallen in Leah's face.

Warrior had wandered over to where Caleb and Leah were. He stopped in the shade and nibbled on the grass. He snorted once to remind Caleb the ride was not over. Caleb got up off his knees. He took out his handkerchief and headed for the pond. He soaked it in the water before carrying it back to where Leah lay. He placed the wet cloth on her forehead. Leah started to stir.

# CHAPTER TWO

Leah became aware of her ankle was resting on something prickly. She moved her leg but the sensation did not go away. Leah slowly opened her eyes but she really did not want to do so as the light caused her head to hurt. She found herself lying in the shade of the trees on the other side of the lake from where she had been. A horse neighed nearby. Leah sat up a little bit at a time. The man, Caleb, was coming toward her from the lake with something in his hand, while his horse was standing a few feet to Leah's left.

Leah felt like sliding back into the blackness rather than deal with feelings of being overheated and tired. She reached up a pushed the hair back out of her face. Leah found her face and head radiated heat. I cannot be sick, Leah thought, aside from being tired I had been fine. As she rose still further Leah did find herself suffering from waves of nausea, but she forced the sensations down. The thought came to her mind that she may have caught whatever was killing her father, but she quickly dismissed it. Her father's symptoms were much more severe than the mild ones she currently was feeling. Also she had been by his side for months without as much as a cough. It was probable just the shock of finding out what her mother had planned for her, Leah decided.

Caleb reached Leah and offered her his handkerchief which had been soaked in water. Leah accepted it and pressed it to her face. The water was refreshing against her skin.

"You passed out," Caleb said, "Probably too much sun. You will recover quickly if you just cool yourself down with the damp handkerchief and rest for a few minutes."

Leah wanted to ask Caleb a question but found her throat was dry. Instead of asking the question Leah laid back down again. Caleb took the handkerchief and went back to the lake. He came back a minute later. Caleb brushed Leah's forehead with the handkerchief and down the side of her face.

Caleb went back and forth from Leah to the lake a few times before Leah tried to sit up again. This time Leah did not feel as tired.

"Feeling better?" Caleb asked as he handed Leah the wet handkerchief again.

"Somewhat," Leah answered. Leah pressed the material to her neck and felt the water run down into her dress.

I cannot believe I passed out, Leah thought, and needed all this help from a stranger. I should get back to the manor before I do anything more embarrassing, but I am still tired.

Leah gave the handkerchief back to Caleb and started to get to her feet.

"I can give you a ride to your home," Caleb offered. Leah hesitated for a moment, but realized the only other way to get there was to walk.

"Thank you," Leah said, "I just need to get to the door in the hedge. The rest of the walk is in the shade."

"Very well," Caleb said. He helped Leah up on to his horse before climbing up behind her. Leah felt all the nerves come alive where her back touched Caleb's chest. Caleb reached around her to pick up the reins causing the nerves in Leah's arms to come alive. Leah found herself holding her breath and forced herself to breathe. Riding with Caleb, Leah felt like she was safe from the rest of the world, but she also was scared of these new sensations which were making her extra aware of Caleb.

Caleb stopped his horse near where Leah had passed out and got down. Leah instantly missed him being behind her even as she was trying to figure out why he had stopped. Then she saw him pick up her shoes and stockings. Caleb offered them to Leah. She accepted them with shaking hands. Leah hoped Caleb would think the shaking had to do with too much sun and not to nervousness over his closeness.

"Thank you," Leah said, her voice came out as a hoarse whisper.

"You are welcome," Caleb replied. He got back up behind Leah. Leah stopped herself from leaning back and relaxing into Caleb's arms.

The hedge and door came too fast for Leah. Caleb stopped his horse and got down. He helped Leah down. On the ground Leah did not let go of Caleb's hand as she looked up at him.

"Thank you for your help," Leah said looking into Caleb's eyes. She could not identify any of the emotions in those brown eyes, but there was something there she wanted to stay and explore with him.

"You are welcome, Miss Winsand," Caleb said. There was no mockery in Caleb's eyes instead it was like he felt a similar connection.

Leah slowly let go of Caleb's hand. She turned and walked to the path. Leah started to close the door before looking back. Caleb was still standing there watching her. With regret Leah closed the door the rest of the way.

Caleb shook his head to snap out of the daze. He had met plenty of ladies, what was it about Leah Winsand made him want to take her in his arms and never let go? Maybe it was the look of surprise and then embarrassment when she noticed him. Many of the ladies Caleb knew probably would have invited him to join them. That type of behaviour had always repelled him.

Perhaps what attracted Caleb to Leah Winsand was the sadness in her eyes yet he sensed she did not want comfort. Even though she was hurting and tired her stubborn streak was not going to let her be wrapped in his arms and told white lies. Though the idea of taking her in his arms made Caleb's arms twitch as if someone had lit the nerves on fire. The same went for his lips when he remembered how kissable hers looked.

Caleb shook his head again in hopes of clearing it of distracting thoughts. He mounted Warrior and started back across the field toward the estate. Mother and Father were probably having tea and wondering where he was. Warrior had only gone a couple steps when Caleb decided he was not ready to head home and perhaps be asked questions about his afternoon. His parents would not really notice if he did not show sometimes his rides took him to visit other people. Caleb directed Warrior towards the far end of the field and let him run. Warrior was happy to run so Caleb let him figure out where to go.

When Leah Winsand was talking about her father being sick her expression had reminded Caleb of James Winsand's expression one evening he had showed up unexpectedly for supper. Caleb had been twelve-years-old and his parents had not been expecting anyone. So when there was a knock at the door they were surprised. Caleb remembered his parents welcoming James into the dining room. They did not ask him why he was there or what happened, even though Caleb could tell there was something wrong. Instead Caleb's parents had tried to make James laugh and forget all about what was worrying him. Caleb remembered the night fondly because he could not remember another time when he laughed so hard.

The expression of sadness and tiredness had disappeared for the night, but Caleb had seen the lines they had worn into James's face the last time he had been over for supper. From that unexpected visit it took Caleb five more years to understand James had been running away from his wife that night. Caleb had not understood why James had gone back to his wife, or why he stayed there all this time. Now that Caleb had met Leah he thought he understood why James went back. Caleb found himself wanting to go back to the door in the hedge and see if Leah was still there, but he figured it would not be a good idea besides maybe she would come out to the meadow again tomorrow. He hoped she would come out tomorrow.

Leah stood there staring at the door. After a moment she heard Caleb ride away. The thought came to open the door and see how far he had gone, but Leah brushed the thought away. It seemed foolish and Leah was not even sure why she wondered about him. It should not really matter to her how far away from her Caleb was. He was a stranger to her. Leah turned from the door and took two steps along the path. She found the gravel of the path bit into her bare feet. Leah stopped and pulled on her stockings and shoes. When she was finished she got to her feet as she wondered why she had forgotten she even had them in her hands. Shaking her head Leah started back along the path.

As she walked Leah tried to remember which way she had come and also remember how to get back to the door. Leah was not quite sure why she did this. She would probably never come back out here especially with all the plans her mother had for her life. Leah shook her head hoping the thought would go away so she could enjoy the walk back through the garden, but it seemed lodged there. Leah sighed and let her mind drift. It brought up two brown eyes Leah thought should have been mocking her, but they had not been. Those eyes seemed to push away any worries about her mother and made Leah relax. She longed to feel those strong arms around her again. Her fingers itched to run through that brown hair to see if it was as soft as it looked.

Leah came to the statue in the clearing. She glanced up at the lady. Something about the lady made Leah stop again, but Leah could not figure out why. It disappeared before she could grasp it. After a moment Leah turned and left the clearing. The path continued its twisting and Leah continued trying to memorize how to get back. In the next clearing Leah stopped at the fountain. She scoped up handfuls of water and drank. The water felt nice on her throat and where it splashed on her dress. Leah drank until she felt better. Then she stood up and continued through the hedge maze.

When Leah caught sight of the manor she slowed her pace. If her mother saw her then Leah knew she would be in trouble. If Melissa saw her Leah knew she would get a lecture about the grass stains on her dress. Leah came out of the hedge maze and started up the lawn. No one came out to greet her or lecture her. Leah sighed with relief. She walked across the lawn and went to the French doors. Leah opened one part of the way and slipped inside. It was quiet. She glanced at the clock. According to the clock she had only been gone for two hours, which was good because it meant her mother would not home for probably another hour.

Leah moved towards the hallway. When she heard footsteps Leah moved out of direct sight of the doorway. Roger walked down the hallway towards the kitchen. Leah saw he was carrying a tray. Once he was passed and his footsteps were softer, Leah went to the hallway and looked out. No one was there, but she could hear voices coming from the kitchen. Leah stepped into the hallway and headed the opposite direction from the kitchen. She got to the stairs and went up. At the second floor she hesitated. If Roger was taking food back to the kitchen it meant Leah's father was awake. She wanted to visit him. She turned to start down the hallway when she caught sight of herself in the mirror in the hallway. Her face was flushed, her dress disheveled and her hair waved around her face where it had come out of the bun it had been in this morning. Leah turned around and headed up the stairs to the third floor. She went into her room. Melissa must have still been in the kitchen gossiping with the cook, because she had not been up here since Leah had left. Leah closed the door behind her before heading to her wardrobe to find a clean dress.

When she had washed up, changed her clothes and redone her hair, Leah left her room and went back to the second floor. She went down the hallway to her father's room. Leah stopped at the doorway. Her father was sitting up in the bed reading a book. Roger was not there. Leah studied her father for a moment. There was a little more colour in his face than when he had gone to sleep after lunch, but he was still very pale. He was also very skinny. The hands turning the pages on the book seemed almost skeletal. Leah remembered a short time ago when they had been full and warm. Leah swallowed the tears which tried to choke her.

Leah knocked on the doorframe. James looked up. He smiled at her as he beckoned her to come in. Leah smiled back at him. James did not close the book but just pushed it off his legs and to one side. Leah entered the room and went to the bed. She placed a bookmark in the book and put it on the table beside the bed.

"How are you feeling, Father?" Leah asked as she sat down in the chair beside the bed.

"Better," James answered, "The nap did me a whole lot of good. What have you been doing this afternoon? You look tired."

"I went for a walk in the garden," Leah answered.

"How is the garden?" James asked, "With this warm weather it must be doing well."

"The flowers are in full bloom and the grass is starting to look like it needs watering," Leah answered, "It is all beautiful."

"That is good. Perhaps if I feel well enough tomorrow I can sit outside for a while," James said, "As long as the warm weather holds out."

"That would be nice," Leah said.

"So, what did you and your mother argue about this time?" James asked.

"She wants me to get married," Leah lower her gaze to her hands. She found she could not look at her father for fear he would get angry with her as well. She knew her father supported the idea of marriage and would go along with that part of her mother's plan for Leah's life.

"And what is wrong with getting married?" James asked.

"I am not ready to get married," Leah answered. She glanced up at her father. She found he did not appear to be angry, just tired and a little bit sad. It was the same look that came across his face whenever marriage came up. Leah had never figured out why he looked so sad and tired, especially since he believed marriage was a good thing.

"Your mother just wants to make sure you will be taken care of," James said, "With this illness I could die tomorrow or next week or next month and your mother knows it will be a difficult time. If you are married there will be someone to support you and help you move on with your life. Your marriage was coming whether I am sick or not. You are seventeen and many of your friends are already married. It will all be okay. No one is sure they are ready to get married, but they end up happy at the end of it anyway."

"Yes, Father," Leah said. Once again her eyes were on the backs on her hands. She could not look up at him and let him see the fear gripping her at the thought of being forced into marriage; especially with the groom being Randall.

"How are lessons?" James asked.

"They went well," Leah answered without looking up.

"It will be all right," James said reaching out his hand to take Leah's. Leah raised her eyes to his. He smiled and some of the light that she had formerly been accustomed seeing in him reached them.

"It might not seem like it now, but everything will turn out all right," James said. Leah nodded, but she did not believe it. It felt like a lie to make her feel better. The only way everything would be all right would be if her father was not sick and her mother was not planning out her life. Leah forced all the negative thoughts to the back of her mind.

"Yes, Father," Leah said.

"Roger forgot to bring my writing stuff from the library when he brought me the book," James said, "Will you get it for me? Maybe we can figure out where the princess in the story is going."

"Yes, Father," Leah said. She turned and left the room. She went down the hall to the library. The door was left open. Leah went in and over to the desk. All of her father's writing supplies were on top of the piles of books he had chosen from the shelves.

Maybe someday he will be well enough to come back and finish reading all of these, Leah thought as she gathered up all the writing supplies in one pile. Of course, he claimed there are always more books to read and more stories to write when he had finished the ones he was currently working on.

Leah picked up the pile and left the library. She went back to her father's bedroom. James was still sitting in the exact same position as when Leah left. Leah placed the pile beside James on the bed. Then she sat down in the chair beside the bed. James sorted through the pile until he found the last page he had been writing upon. Then he carefully set up his pen and ink.

"Now, where was I?" James asked as he peered at the page, "Ah, yes, the princess was lost in the woods and she had stopped at the stream to have a drink."

"And the witch was following her," Leah said.

"Right," James said. He picked the pen and started to write. As he wrote he told Leah the story.

CHAPTER THREE


Melissa opened the kitchen door enough she could see there was no one inside for the moment. She slipped inside and hurried through the kitchen to the hallway. There she slowed down to her usual walk. From the sound of things Roger and the cook were discussing the arrival of the Lamberts in the store room.

"Why are the Lamberts back again?" the cook asked there was some desperation in her voice.

"Because Lady Winsand invited them over again," Roger answered without any kind of emotion.

"Their visits would not be so bad if Lady Winsand did not expect everything to be perfect for them," the cook said, "She has threatened to fire me because a small drop of gravy on the edge of her plate the last time they were here. And the time before it was-"

"I know," Roger cut her off as irritation entered his voice, "If it was not for Lord Winsand and Leah needing us, I would suggest finding employment elsewhere."

The cook was quiet and Melissa decided she did not want to hear anymore. She continued on her way.

Melissa went down the hallway and up the stairs. On the

second floor landing she heard Lord Winsand's voice. He was telling Leah more of his story. There was a time when Melissa would listen in and dream about a prince to come and rescue her, even though she knew it was impossible. Now she did not listen because she had found a man to fulfill the part of the dreamy prince. He was good looking with his crooked smile, hazel eyes and amazing touch. Sure, he smelled like horses, but it was better than the cook's helper who smelled like someone had tried to boil him in oil. Before she met her dream man she had been lovers with the cook's helper. Fortunately, they had parted as friends when she moved on. The only problem with her current lover was he did not work for Lord and Lady Winsand; which meant he had to come to Melissa, and they could only meet at certain times. And there was always the hazard of being caught by Roger or the cook when trying to sneak out or sneak back in.

Melissa continued up the stairs to her room. It was a closet beside Leah's bedroom. It had room for a small bed and a trunk for her clothes. It was not much, but it was better than the hut where her parents lived. She had her own bed and clothes were of better quality than the rags she used to wear. Melissa checked herself in the mirror that she had gotten when Lady Winsand had renovated her rooms. She had to take out her hair and put it back up. It had gotten mussed up out in the garden, where she met her lover. Today they had gone into one of the branches of the hedge maze rather than just behind the door. It turned out to be a good idea because there had been other people in the maze. As it turned out they had found a patch of grass they could lie down where the gardeners had already tended and left. They had agreed to meet there from now on. Melissa glanced at the clock. It was just about time for Leah to get ready for supper. Melissa did one more check in the mirror to make sure she did not look like she had been out of uniform before hurrying out of her room.

Leah was relaxing in the chair and letting herself get lost in the story of the princess and the witch. In her head she was the princess and usually the prince was faceless, but today the prince looked a lot like Caleb Morley. He looked far more handsome in the white shirt with the top buttons undone and black pants the prince in the story wore. The only other character who truly had a face in the story was the witch, who lately had taken on the appearance of Leah's mother.

The prince was so gently and loving towards the princess in the story, though there were few scenes of romance between them. The last time Leah had sat and listened, she had paid more attention to the scenes where the prince was rescuing the princess, but today she could almost feel the touch of the prince's hands when he brushed dirt off the princess's face. She was the one the prince picked up and carried because she could not walk across the narrow bridge made from a downed tree that was the only way to reach the other side of the river. Leah could feel the strength of Caleb's chest and arms as he ran with her through the dark forest. She was swooning in his arms at the sight of the dragon, but he protected her with his shield at the first blast of fire. Caleb made sure she had a good grip before swinging both of them across the canyon.

There was a knock at the door, causing Leah to come back to her father's darkened room and away from the safe embrace of Caleb's arms. She looked up to see Roger standing in the doorway. James stopped speaking and put down his pen.

"It is time to get ready for supper, Miss Winsand," Roger said, "Melissa is waiting for you in your room."

"Are we having company?" James asked.

"The Lamberts are coming to supper," Roger answered.

"Were they not here just the other night?" James asked.

"They were," Roger answered, "Lady Winsand seems to

enjoy their company."

"You better go get ready," James told Leah.

"Yes, Father," Leah said as she stood up. She left the room and headed up the stairs to her room.

After Melissa helped Leah getting dressed for supper, Leah stepped out of the room and to the top of the stairs. She was just about to head downstairs when there was a knock on the front door. Leah stepped back out of sight but from where she could still see. Roger must have been waiting because immediately he appeared to open the door.

"Good evening," Roger greeted the Lamberts as they stepped inside.

"And remember you must help a lady with her chair," Lady Lambert's voice was shrill and loud as she spoke over Roger as if he had not been there at all, "Of course, make sure you pay attention to which piece of cutlery you pick up this time. I was horrified last time when you used your dessert fork for the roast." Leah was amazed she had not heard Lady Lambert before the door was opened.

Lord Lambert had been the first inside and was taking off his coat while ignoring the lecture his son was getting from his wife. Lord Lambert and his son shared similarities in appearance. They were both tall and thin with long, narrow faces. However, Lord Lambert's face was drawn and lined as if he was constantly tired and frowning. Randall's still had some youthful vigor but lacked any spark to make it interesting. Lord Lambert's red hair was disappearing from the top of his head, some of it by thinning and the rest by going to white. Randall's hair was bright reddish orange but it lay limply against his head as if uninterested in its surroundings as its owner. The only difference between father and son was Randall's eyes were green to match his mother's eyes, while Lord Lambert's eyes were a dull brown.

Lady Lambert was wearing a dress to match the green of her eyes. The dress had gold coloured highlights and trim.

The brooch at her throat was the same one she always wore with its black silhouette on a white background surrounded with gold setting. Lady Lambert's blonde was piled up properly with not a strand out of place. In all, she was the pinnacle of the latest fashion as if that overcame her shrill voice and complete lack of tact.

Lady Lambert looked like she would have continued to lecture Randall if Leah's mother had not come into the hallway, not that Randall appeared interested in anything she had to say. He looked instead like he was trying to figure out the solution to a difficult mathematical question without the benefit of pen and paper, but he always looked like that. Roger took the Lamberts' coats.

"Good evening, Jennica," Lady Winsand said. She spoke as if she had not interrupted Lady Lambert's lecture or that there had been one. Aside from her hair being brown and her dress being dark red she matched Lady Lambert exactly in fashion sensibility.

"Good evening, Vivian," Lady Lambert replied, "It was wonderful to receive your invitation."

"I am glad you could make it on such short notice," Lady Winsand said.

"We would not miss it for the world," Lady Lambert said. The ladies led the way into the drawing room. Lord Lambert and Randall followed behind them like two forgotten dogs trailing behind their master. Roger closed the front door of the house before heading off to the kitchen.

The Lamberts had been invited over for supper for the last three days in a row. Leah figured her mother believed Leah and Randall needed to spend as much time together as possible as if he was more likely to ask Leah to marry him if he was around her constantly. Leah doubted frequent visits were going to increase the chances of Randall doing anything unless his mother specifically directed him to propose. As far as Leah could tell Randall only noticed people if they started the conversation with him and only if it was on religion. Randall had only ever read one book and it happened to be about religious controversies of the medieval church before the reformation. He had memorized this outdated tome like a parish priest memorized the Bible. Leah did not care to discuss this subject and found when she was forced to converse with Randall he repeated himself a lot. It did not help that Randall's favorite book was considered a waste of shelf space by anyone who had heard of enlightenment or even those who followed doctrines of the Anglican Church.

Leah stepped back into sight of the door and went down the stairs. When she reached the second floor she went down the hallway to her father's room. He was still sitting up and writing. Leah knocked on the door frame. James looked up and smiled at her.

"You look beautiful," James said as he looked over her person.

"Thank you, Father," Leah said.

"But you should be downstairs helping your mother entertain the guests," James said.

"I know," Leah said, "But I wanted to make sure you are all right." Leah entered the room and went over to the bed. "I hate how much time you are left alone."

"I will be fine," James said, "Now, quit worrying about me and go enjoy being with other people. It is good you and your mother are socializing despite my current circumstance. Roger will bring me some supper and I will eat. Meanwhile you need to enjoy supper and stop worrying. It makes you old before your time."

"Yes, Father," Leah said. Her smile did not quite reach her eyes, though for her father she tried. Leah kissed her father's cheek before turning and leaving the room. She went back down the hallway to the stairs. Leah stood at the top of the staircase which would take her to the front hallway. She could hear her mother's voice as well as Lady

Lambert's voice coming from the drawing room. The tones even without the words made her want to go back up to her room and not come down until the Lamberts had gone home for the night.

Leah took a deep breath and started down the steps. Once at the bottom she walked into the sitting room. Lord Lambert and Randall stood up when she entered. Lady Winsand and Lady Lambert remained seated. Randall stepped toward Leah while Lord Lambert returned to his seat.

"Good evening, Miss Winsand," Randall's tone of voice suggested he greeted her out of obligation or rather to please is mother than any want to start a conversation.

"Good evening," Leah replied. She kept a similar tone out of her voice. She sat down in the chair across from the settee Lord and Lady Lambert were taking up. Randall plopped down as if he had not the strength to stand unless his mother was pulling his strings. The conversation between the two ladies had not stopped with Leah's arrival and it continued completely uninterrupted. Neither of them bothered to greet Leah who sat quietly and wished herself somewhere else. It only took seconds for her mind to do exactly that.

Leah day dreamed she was in one of her father's stories. She was the princess sitting here in a long flowing, white dress and was in very real danger of being bored to death by her evil mother, who was once again dressed in the black attire of a witch. Her evil companion was also dressed in black and had the golem as her familiar sitting at her side. The honour bound knight did nothing because he had been taught not to interrupt someone when they were speaking, not to mention the weight of his armour had to be pinning him to his chair. Then Caleb rode into the room on a black horse. He was wearing the colours of the opponent to the honour bound knight. Unlike the honour bound knight his lighter armour was gleaming in the light and he wore no helmet. His sword was out as if he was ready for anything which might come at him. The evil mother and her companion stopped talking to start throwing spells at him. Caleb ducked the ones he did not block with the shield on his wrist. Urging his horse forward Caleb advanced into the room until he was beside where Leah was sitting. She got to her feet and he pulled her up on to his horse while protecting them both from the spells. Then he spurred his horse out of the house. They rode away from the estate with the witches following them and headed for the kingdom where Caleb was the prince. Once there the king, who looked a lot like Leah's father, demanded they be married immediately. They immediately rode to the wedding chapel, where a priest was waiting. There Caleb got down to the ground before helping Leah to her feet. They went up to the altar only to have her evil mother and her mother's companion arrive through the church door. Leah ended up cowering behind the altar with the priest as Caleb fought the witches. He looked really good in battle. Finally the battle ended and Leah got out from behind the altar. She ran into his arms.

Caleb was just about to kiss Leah when Roger came into the room to announce supper was ready. Leah stopped herself from sighing at the interruption. No one seemed to have noticed she had been day dreaming. Lord Lambert had been paying attention to the women's conversation and Randall was staring at one of the paintings hanging on the wall with his usual pained look on his face. As Roger left the room all of them stood up and followed him into the dining room. Randall helped Leah with her chair before sitting down in the one next to her. Lord Lambert did the same across the table for Lady Lambert. Roger helped Lady Winsand with her chair, which was the head of the table since James's chair was empty.

The salad course was already on the table so once everyone was settled they started to eat. The conversation from the drawing room continued. Randall dug into his food as if it was the only thing in the room worthy of his interest. Leah sat there and followed all the rules her mother had taught her about behaving in company. Since the day dream from the sitting room was gone she concentrated on eating and pretending to look like she was listening and interested in the conversation.

Once everyone had finished the salad course Roger came in and cleared away the plates and forks. He took them to the kitchen before bringing back soup bowls. Roger placed a soup bowl in front of each person. Then he went back to the kitchen and brought back the soup tureen. Roger started with Lord Lambert and moved around the table from there.

While she was waiting for Roger to finish dishing up Lady Winsand's bowl of soup, Leah took a sip of water and put her glass back. As she was bringing her hand back to its proper position in her lap Leah's soup spoon got caught on her sleeve and it slipped off the table and on to the floor. Leah bended down and picked it up off the floor. As she was straightening Leah's head hit Roger's arm as he was bringing the soup tureen to serve her. Somehow Leah managed to hit the right spot on Roger's arm so the soup did not end up on her or Roger, but flew through the air and ended up in Randall's lap.

The conversation came to an abrupt halt and the stunned silence of those first seconds seemed to freeze everyone just where they sat very much like statues that can do nothing but gape in horror at some atrocity. Roger was the first to snap out of the shock. He got some towels to help clean up Randall's pants. Lady Winsand was the next to snap out of her daze. Her face started to turn purple in anger over what her daughter had done. She only regained control with the memory of her guests. Then the Lamberts snapped out of their daze chaos broke out. Leah used the confusion to slip out of the dining room.

Leah dashed out to the hallway and ran up the stairs. At the second floor she paused and thought about visiting her father, but decided against it when she thought about having to explain why she left supper early. Instead she continued up the stairs to her own room. Once inside Leah locked the door behind her. She rested against it a second as if to keep the memory of what happened out of her mind before she straightened up and went to the window to assure herself that the world has not been destroyed as a result of her clumsy action.

The sun was getting close to the horizon and giving the world a pinkish light. Leah looked over the garden and tried to trace her path through the hedge maze. But she could not figure out where the door was and every time she restarted she ended up at a different spot. If she was in the maze Leah was sure she could find her way back to the door. Maybe she would try to go out there tomorrow if her mother did not find some way of torturing her for the soup incident. Leah's eyes moved above the hedge maze to the field lying beyond it. The setting sun gave the grass the look of gold and the light reflected off the lake. It looked so inviting, but Leah knew she would never get passed the tumult downstairs to go out there before it was completely dark.

I wonder if Caleb will be out riding tomorrow, Leah thought. If it had been Randall out there today, he probably would have thought I was an air-headed child who does not know enough to get out of the sun. That was how I behaved but Caleb had not mocked her or chided her. He had helped her. She had even seen the want to hold her and tell her everything would be all right. But he had not done it. Leah was thankful Caleb had not taken her in his arms and told her that lie. She probably would have broken down in tears and an embarrassing situation would be made worse. Still she did feel like she missed a chance to be held by him. Her body seemed to crave his arms around her, which was utter foolishness, so, were the thoughts of his lips on hers and her body molded to his.

Leah shook her head before sitting down on the widow seat. She leaned her forehead against the glass. As if I did not embarrass myself enough this afternoon I had to do more of a thorough job this evening, Leah thought. Maybe she would get lucky and Randall would not have anything to do with her after tonight. After all who wants a wife who will cause the servants to spill soup on your person? Randall probably wants a wife who is perfect at being a lady, who needs nothing from him except a name. I am not that lady, Leah thought, and I never will be no matter how Mother tries. I wonder what Caleb wants in a wife? Leah let her mind go that direction. Does he need one who will be the perfect lady, or would he mind one with a few flaws?

The sun touched the horizon. The world took on a magical quality Leah could not remember noticing before this moment. It again seemed to issue the invitation to come out and enjoy it. Leah sighed because she knew there was no way she would ever get passed her mother.

"I wish my life was not so flawed," Leah whispered against the glass, "I wish I was happy again." Leah closed her eyes and felt the tiredness of the day wash over her.

# CHAPTER FOUR

She was unsure of the time when Leah opened her eyes again. She listened for any noise outside her room that suggested her mother might be there and did not hear anything so she went over and opened the door a crack to listen.

"It was wonderful to have you over tonight," Lady Winsand's voice came clearly up the stairs, "And I am sorry for what happened. She is usually not like that."

"It is all right," Lord Lambert's voice answered, "These things happen."

"Of course," Lady Winsand's voice sounded like she was agreeing with him only to be polite but she would otherwise explain to him accidents do not just happen, at least not during a supper she was hosting.

"We will accept your invitation to join you for supper another time," Lady Lambert's voice was a friendly as it ever got, like she was already putting the incident behind her.

"We will see you then," Lady Winsand said.

"Good night," Lord Lambert said, "It was a good meal."

"Thank you," Lady Winsand said, "I hope you have a

good night as well."

"Good night," Lady Lambert said. For a moment there were no sounds and then Leah heard the door close. She quickly closed and locked the door again before returning to the window and pressing its coolness against her cheek. She knew the conversation she overheard meant her clumsiness had not solved her marriage issue as she had hoped. The cold feeling against her check calmed the heat of her embarrassment as she thought of what happened.

Leah lifted her head from where it was resting against the glass once the last of the light disappeared from the horizon. The room was dark because she had not bothered to light the lamp when she had run to her room, which might make hiding easier if her mother decided to come upstairs and forced her way through the door. Leah held her breath as she listened to see if she could hear what her mother was doing. Nothing, no footsteps, no angry mutters, nothing beyond the familiar sounds reaches her ears. Leah sighed with relief when no one came up the stairs.

Leah looked out the window. The moon was not out yet, but she could see a few things by the light coming from downstairs windows at the back of the house. She looked across the field. There were a couple of lights from approximately where Leah guessed the Morley Estate was. She wondered what Caleb was doing. Whether he was getting ready for bed or sitting up visiting with someone. Leah shook her head. Why was she suddenly so obsessed about a man she had met only that afternoon and may or may not see again?

Her stomach growled. It told her salad was not enough to satisfy it for the night. Leah thought about going downstairs to the kitchen. The cook had probably gone to bed already, but Roger would still be up. He would let her get something to eat, especially since he knew why she had gone into hiding for the night. But she would have to be very careful to avoid her mother.

Leah stood up when she heard footsteps on the stairs. They sounded like her mother was coming up the stairs and the rhythm of the footsteps suggested her mother was angry. Leah froze and held her breath. She hoped her mother would just continue up the stairs to her own room and not stop. The footsteps stopped outside Leah's door. The handle rattled a little as Lady Winsand tried to open the door. But finding it was locked she make no further effort to open it.

"Then starve in there," Leah heard her mother mutter, "We will talk in the morning. I have other things to do." Lady Winsand's footsteps retreated down the stairs. Cautiously Leah went to the door of her room and opened it. She looked out. No one jumped out at her so she stepped out of her room and closed the door. Leah heard Roger's voice and then something that sounded like the front door opening. They must have stepped outside because their voices were much quieter Leah went to the top of the stairs and looked down. The front door was partly closed. Without stopping to think or even consider what would happen if she got caught, Leah headed down the stairs trying to make as little noise as possible. She hurried down the stairs and then along the hallway. Leah stayed out of sight of anyone outside until she reached the kitchen then she went across the hallway to the kitchen door with speed. No one had come back in, so Leah felt safe when she got into the kitchen.

As she figured the cook had already gone to bed. Melissa was not there either. She had probably found Leah's door locked and had gone to bed. Roger, to Leah's surprise, was putting the last of the dishes away from supper.

"Your mother is very angry with you, Miss Winsand," Roger said, "It would have been better if you had not left the dining room."

"I could not face the embarrassment," Leah replied,

"Because of me Randall received hot soup in his lap. He might not be very smart, but he did not deserve that."

"You will have to get over your embarrassment quickly," Roger said, "Your mother has invited them for supper a couple days from now. Then you will have to face them again."

"They are coming back so soon? I would have thought they would be afraid of further accidents," Leah said.

"Your mother calmed them down and assured them such accidents were uncommon," Roger said.

"Not as uncommon as they should be," Leah muttered. Roger finished putting the dishes away and was starting to prepare a tray to take to James.

"Everyone has times when they are clumsy," Roger said, "It is not usually a permanent condition."

"Just one Mother believes can be cure by being locked in a room for days at a time," Leah said as she looked around at the empty counters.

"If you are hungry is some food in the pantry," Roger said.

"Thank you," Leah said.

"Things will get better," Roger said as Leah started towards the pantry.

"When?" Leah asked as she turned to look at him.

"When you least expect it," Roger answered. Leah shook her head as she opened the pantry door. She stepped inside. Once she was there the door closed most of the way leaving only a small space through which Leah could see into the kitchen. The small space was also the only source of light. Leah thought about finding something to prop the door open, but decided she did not need the light. Leah glanced back into the kitchen and saw Roger start to put together a tray of soft foods for her father's late night meal. Leah went to the back where the light was starting to get scarce. She found some cheese and leftover bread wrapped up in a cloth on one of the shelves, where either Roger or the cook had left it for her.

"Roger," Lady Winsand's voice came from the kitchen. Leah turned to look. She could see her mother was standing in the kitchen, but her mother did not see her and was not looking in her direction. Leah did not dare move nor do anything that would make a noise and attract attention. If her mother found her in here scrounging for food she would lock Leah in her room until just before supper with the Lamberts.

"Yes, Lady Winsand," Roger said.

"I need you to check the fire in the drawing room," Lady Winsand said, "I think there is a problem with the grate."

"Yes, Lady Winsand," Roger said then left the kitchen. Leah watched as her mother took out a bottle from her pocket. After taking the cork out Lady Winsand put three drops into the cup on the tray to go up to James. Then she put the cork back into the bottle top before tucking it back into her pocket. She left the kitchen and Leah could hear her go down the hallway.

"The grate is fine, Lady Winsand," Roger's voice came from the hallway.

"Then I will go off the bed," Lady Winsand said. Leah thought about moving, but it was as if her mind as unwilling to allow her physical moment until it understood what she had just seen. As her mother's footsteps went toward the stairs Roger entered the kitchen. He picked up the tray and left the room with it. Leah wanted to stop him, but her mind was slowly at processing the thought of what she had just seen and by the time the words came to her lips he was gone. She stood immobile for several minutes before she crept forward. The footsteps for both Leah's mother and Roger went up the stairs until Leah could not hear them.

Leah stepped out of the pantry and staggered the few steps to a kitchen chair. She sat down on it and set the food on the table in front of her. Leah did not feel hungry anymore. In fact, she felt nauseated. Fear crept up Leah's spine as all the implications of what she had just witnessed came into her mind. Questions started to fill the space instead. Who could she tell? Who would believe her? Who could do anything about it? Why was her mother doing this? What was really in the bottle? What else could it be besides poison? Why would her mother want to poison her father? Was that what was causing his illness? Did the doctor know what it was? Was the doctor in on it? If it was poison, why was her father not dead already? Could she tell Roger about it? Could he do anything about it? Was there anything Leah could do to stop her mother from killing her father? Her father had been doing better recently, could the bottle have a cure in it instead? A cure her mother did not tell anyone about?

Leah opened the cloth and set out the food. She mindlessly ate some of the bread and cheese. When she ate what little she could she wrapped it back up. It took another several minutes before Leah could stand up and put the food back where she had found it in the pantry. When she had finished, Leah left the kitchen and headed up to her room. Leah walked the distance in a daze. She almost did not hear her mother's door open in time, but she did manage to duck out of sight before her mother saw her. Her mother went into the empty bedroom next door to hers, which she used to store any clothes she could not fit in her wardrobe, and closed the door behind her. Leah started up the stairs again, but went faster this time. She got into her room and had closed the door before she heard the door to the room open again. Leah locked the door to her room. She stepped back from the door as if she was scared her mother was standing on the other side and was getting ready to attack. The door to the room beside her mother's closed and the sound of Lady Winsand going into her own room could be heard. Leah stood still for several minutes until the shaking had diminished enough her hands would work again.

Leah changed into her nightgown and crawled into bed. She curled up on the bed and covered herself with the blanket. Leah stared at the ceiling above the bed because her mind was too busy trying to figure everything out that it was not going to let her get to sleep any time soon.

Leah stared at the ceiling with her thoughts in turmoil. She wished someone would come and make everything better. Thoughts of Caleb came to mind, but she banished them. He was a stranger and did not know what was going on. For all her fantasies there was no prince to come and rescue her from her life. Her father might have been able to make everything better, but that was before he got sick. And now he had been sick for so long Leah was not sure he would ever fully recover from it. She just hoped he survived it.

The manor went quiet as everyone settled in for the night. Finally the only noises Leah could hear were the creaks and groans of the building. Leah was so used to them she hardly noticed them, except when the noises matched her thoughts.

She was not certain how long she had been lying there staring up into the dark when she heard Roger's footsteps on the stairs. Leah knew Roger was just checking on her father. Roger's footsteps went along the second floor hallway. It was quiet for several moments. Then Leah heard Roger's footsteps retreating in the other direction at a much faster pace.

The footsteps got quieter as he went downstairs but she did hear him call out to someone. And then Leah could not hear what was going on. She found her breath catching in her throat and fear paralyzing her. Her father must have taken a turn for the worse. There was no other reason for Roger hurrying anywhere at this time of night. The impulse to get up and go to her father was almost too much, but Leah stayed where she was. What if her mother came to see what was happening? Since Leah was not certain anyone would believe what she had seen earlier but she didn't trust herself not to just blurt it out and who knew what her mother would do if she found out Leah knew about the poison.

Leah wrapped her arms around the pillow, hoping it would provide some comfort. It did not, but there did not seem to be much that could. Leah hoped her father would survive this. He had been getting better maybe when he was strong enough she would be able to tell him about what she had seen but she certainly didn't what to tell him news that would cause him to get worse if he had another setback.

Leah heard Roger's footsteps come back, but he did not go up the stairs this time. It sounded more like he was waiting by the front door. He has sent the groom for the doctor then, Leah thought. Should she go out there when the doctor arrived? Should she tell the doctor she believed her father had been poisoned? Would he believe her? Would the rest of the neighbourhood know by the end of the day?

Leah knew what the gossip would be like and did not want to live with the ensuing scandal. Most of the neighbours knew her father was sick and that was enough. She knew it was not the doctor, but the doctor's wife who was the person spread most of the gossip about his patients. And the doctor is unlikely to keep the news of a poisoning from his wife especially considering her father's social status. No, it would not be good.

The thoughts tumbled through Leah's head made sleep impossible. Time crept past so slowly that when she heard someone at the door Leah thought she should be able to see the sun rising. It was the doctor's voice Leah could hear. Then Roger took over talking as two sets of feet were on the stairs. Roger was telling the doctor Leah's father was doing much worse now than he had been all day. The two men went down the hall. Then she could not hear either of them, though she tried.

It was several minutes later she hear the two sets of feet in the hallway.

"Another attack," the doctor's voice was clear, though quiet.

"What should be done?" Roger's voice was much quieter.

"Has anything helped?" the doctor asked.

"Not that I can tell," Roger answered, "Usually he gets better and then another attack hits making him worse. Then he starts to get better again."

"Give him plenty to drink and get him to eat if he can," the doctor said, "I will see if I can figure out what is causing the attacks."

"What else can you try?" Roger asked.

"I have written away to another doctor whose opinion I greatly respect about this puzzling case," the doctor answered, "I expect his reply within the week. If this case stumps him then I am not sure what to do."

"I hope an answer turns up soon," Roger said.

"How are the rest of the family?" the doctor asked.

"Lady Winsand is the same as she usually is," Roger answered, "And Leah is spending a lot of time sitting with her father."

"She has not been sick?" the doctor asked.

"Worried, yes, sick, no," Roger answered.

"Hopefully my colleague will have an answer," the doctor said. The voices started to get softer as the men moved farther away.

"I hope so too," Roger's voice floated back to Leah.

Leah rolled on to her side and curled up in a ball. Please make everything all right, she prayed.

Melissa listened to all the noise. She had been planning to go out to the garden to see her lover, but there was too much going on in the house. It sounded like Lord Winsand had taken a turn for the worse, which meant he was not going to get better soon and she could not sneak out without it being noticed. She would explain her absence to her lover tomorrow.

Thoughts of her lover drifted through her mind, as Melissa changed into her nightgown. The feel of their bodies intertwined on the grass in the shade of the hedges. His lips on her skin. The rough hands brushing the hair out of her face. The smouldering way he looked at her after they made love.

Melissa wished she had a window in her small room. Then she could have made a rope out of sheets and snuck out that way. They would never have missed her. Leah was locked in her room for the night. Lady Winsand would not come out until morning. Roger would not have bothered Melissa. However, she would be caught up in the emergency if she tried to go through the house. Melissa would have to explain why she was not there tomorrow when she met her lover. They would make up for the missing each other tonight.

CHAPTER FIVE

*August 2, 1865*

Leah opened her eyes to a room filled with sunlight. She got out of bed feeling like she had not gotten any sleep at all. Leah's mind was still replaying the scene with her mother and the bottle in the kitchen. It all seemed as fresh as the moment it happened. Leah tried to push it away until she could figure out what to do about it, but it did not want to go anywhere. Instead it stayed at the center of her thoughts and made her feel sick. Sighing Leah found some clothes for the day and got dressed. Since the door was still locked Melissa had not come in this morning. Leah shrugged off the thought and put her own hair up. She was not sure she wanted to see anyone until necessary. It took Leah a few more minutes than Melissa would have taken to put up her hair, but it did not look any different. When Leah was done, she went to the door and unlocked it. Melissa was nowhere to be seen. Leah stepped out of her room and headed down the stairs. She stopped at the second floor and went down the hallway to her father's room.

The door was open and Leah could see her father lying

in the bed with his eyes closed. He looked ghastly pale and if possible thinner than yesterday. If his chest had not moved every time he breathed Leah would have believed he was dead. Leah tiptoed into the room and to her father's bedside. His eyes moved beneath their lids in his sleep, but she had not disturbed him. Leah took his hand in hers and gently squeezed it.

"Do not go yet," Leah whispered, "I need you to stay." A tear slipped down Leah's cheek. She brushed it away with her other hand and tried to hold in the rest of her emotions. Leah lifted her father's hand and kissed it before placing it back at his side. She could hear Roger's footsteps coming down the hallway. She wiped away the other tears that had gathered beneath her eyes. Roger came into the room. He was carrying a tray with mug and a bowl of broth.

"Your mother is waiting in the dining room for you to come for breakfast," Roger said as he set the tray down on the table beside the bed, "You should go down before she gets even angrier."

Leah nodded before turning towards the door. She stopped at the door and looked back at her father. He looked like he was barely holding on. Leah stepped out of the room quickly before any more tears came uninvited. Her steps down the hallway towards the stairs were like five-year-old dragging their feet. Leah stopped in front of the mirror in the hallway. The eyes looking back appeared to be sad and tired, but it did not look like she was trying not to cry.

Leah took a deep breath and slowly let it out. She did this twice more before starting down the stairs. She went straight to the dining room. Lady Winsand was already sitting at her place at the end of the table. She was impatiently waiting for Leah. Leah sat down in her own chair and kept her eyes on the table. Her mother did not say anything, but the tension in the air could have been eaten for breakfast.

The cook brought in breakfast. She set a plate in front of Lady Winsand and Leah.

"Where is Roger?" Lady Winsand demanded.

"Checking on Lord Winsand," the cook answered.

"Then next time we will wait until he is ready to serve us," Lady Winsand said.

"Yes, Lady Winsand," the cook said before retreating back to the kitchen. Leah waited until her mother started to eat before picking up her spoon.

Leah spent the meal looking at her plate and concentrated on eating. She pushed away any thoughts that came into her head for fear of any emotions showing up on her face. Leah forced herself not to speed through the meal.

After Leah and her mother were finished eating Roger came and collected the plates. Once he had gone into the kitchen Leah stood up to go get ready to go to lessons.

"The Lamberts will be here for supper tomorrow night," Lady Winsand's voice could have frozen a lake, "If there are any accidents I will lock you in your room until you can go through a week without knocking things over. Do you understand me?"

"Yes, Mother," Leah said. She had not turned around to look at her mother.

"Good," Lady Winsand said, "And if Randall asks you to marry him you will say yes."

"Yes, Mother," Leah said. Leah escaped from the room before her mother could say anything further.

Leah went back upstairs. Melissa was waiting with Leah's coat. Melissa looked like she was going to say something, but after seeing Leah's face decided against it. Leah accepted her coat and slipped it on before going back down the stairs to the front door. Leah went outside. The carriage was not there yet so Leah sat down on the steps and waited. She tried to stuff all her emotions and fears into a box so she could concentrate on the rest of the day. They did not want to go, but she slammed the lid on them.

It was ten minutes before the carriage came down the drive. Leah stood up when she saw it. The carriage stopped in front of the steps and the door opened. Leah climbed inside. She sat down on the seat beside Hilary Whitelaw and across from the twins, Margaret and Meghan Kenley. Hilary's black hair looked like it had been put up in a hurry with some tendrils having escaped and her hazel eyes contained their usual seriousness. Today her dress was brown and dark red while emphasizing how much of a woman she had changed into over the last couple years. The twins had their blonde hair done up perfectly and looked exactly alike. Their blues eyes were a similar shade as Margaret's light blue dress, which complimented Meghan's pink dress. Aside from the colours of the dresses and the beauty mark just above Margaret's ear, the twins would have been the perfect reflection of each other. Once the door was closed the carriage started moving.

"Good morning," the twins said in unison.

"Good morning," Leah said.

"How was your evening?" Hilary asked.

"I heard Randall was invited for supper last night," Margaret said.

"The rumour is he is supposed to ask for your hand," Meghan said.

"There are worse matches," Margaret said, "At least he has a title."

"With money and a large house," Meghan said, "So you would be looked after."

"Meg! Peg! Stop it!" Hilary said, "Between the two of you, you will make him sound like a king, not the idiot he is."

"Well, since she does not have much choice in the matter," Margaret started.

"We might as well point out the good side of marrying him," Meghan finished.

"So far she has not even had a chance to tell us how she is without pestering her whether the rumour is true or not," Hilary said.

"So," the twins turned to Leah, "Is it true?"

"If he is supposed to propose he has not done it," Leah replied carefully.

"There, now can we move on to other things?" Hilary asked. Leah was grateful for the change of subject. The twins spent the rest of the carriage ride repeating all the gossip they had heard since yesterday. Even Leah found herself laughing at some of it. For Leah it felt good to be some place where the worries of home seemed so distant.

After lessons Leah sat there for several minutes after everyone else had started moving towards the door. Hilary also stayed in her seat. Once the room had cleared somewhat Leah and Hilary got up and started toward the door.

"I was wondering if you would like to come for lunch," Hilary said, "Unless your mother has plans for you today."

"I think Mother is eating lunch with the Lady Milburn, so I can come for lunch," Leah said.

"Wonderful," Hilary said. They left Mrs. Travers' house. There were several carriages waiting for girls. The Kenley twins were getting into the one that had brought the four of them. Two other girls climbed in behind the twins. Once a carriage was full it moved out of line and headed down the drive. The Whitelaw carriage was at the end of the line. Since the line of carriages was not moving very fast Leah and Hilary walked the distance to the carriage. The driver saw them coming and got down to open the door for them. He helped them both inside before closing the door. Leah sat across from Hilary. A moment later they could hear the driver climb back into his seat. Then the carriage started moving. Leah stared out the window at the passing scenery. She felt Hilary study her. Then Hilary turned to look out the other window without asking what was bothering Leah. They rode without speaking. Leah did not mind at all.

The carriage was about half way to Hilary's house when Leah could hear the sound of horses coming up behind the carriage. Hilary peered out the window. Leah turned to look out the window Hilary was. The horses came along side and started to pass the carriage. Leah watched as Caleb Morley and Percival Spencer rode by. A smile came to Hilary's face as she watched the two men ride passed. She stuck her head farther out the window to watch them for a few moments longer. When she could no longer see them Hilary brought her head back inside. Leah smiled a little to herself as she went back to watching out the other window.

When they arrived at the Whitelaw Estate the carriage slowed and then stopped in front of the steps. The driver climbed down and then opened the door for Hilary and Leah. He helped them down before climbing back up. The girls went into the house. Hilary led the way through the manor. They passed through the drawing room and the dining room but Hilary did not stop until they arrived at the doors to patio. The doors were open and Leah could see there was a table set up just outside for them. Hilary and Leah went out and sat down at the table. The table was only set for two.

"Mother and Father went to London yesterday and are not supposed to be back until Sunday," Hilary said. The butler came out with a pitcher in his hand and poured each of them a glass of juice. As he went back inside Leah took a sip. It tasted wonderful with how hot the day was. It might have even relaxed her if Hilary was not back to studying her.

"You never did answer how your evening was," Hilary said leaning towards Leah, "And with the look on your face this morning something must have happened."

"When I got home from lessons yesterday Mother was

waiting to talk to me," Leah said, "She told me I was going to marry Randall and he was supposed to be proposing soon. She said when he proposed I was to say yes."

"So, the twins were right about that," Hilary said.

"I cannot think about getting married and I told Mother that, but she acted like Father might as well already be dead." Leah blinked back the tears threatening to come. She had been successful at keeping them in so far, she was not going to start crying now. "We yelled at each other until she left to go for tea. I do not want to get married but she is not willing to understand that."

"Being married probably is not that bad," Hilary said, "However, being married to Randall is not something I would wish on anyone. What did your father say about you getting married to Randall? Or was he well enough to talk to?"

"He told me I was going to get married soon anyway," Leah answered.

"And the groom being Randall did not bother him?"

"I did not tell him that part. Father was doing better, but he still is not well. I did not want to worry him more than necessary. And he was worse again this morning."

"You need to tell him it is Randall your mother wants you to marry. He loathes the Lamberts and does not like Randall. He could save you from the horrible match your mother is making."

"Mother does not listen to him anymore; to her he is already dead. She is just waiting until everyone else realizes it."

"Did Randall propose? Or was he even over for supper?"

"He was invited over for supper as well as Lord and Lady Lambert. But he did not propose, if that was the plan."

"What happened?"

"I am clumsy."

"Leah, what happened?"

The butler brought out their lunch. Leah took another sipped of her juice as she tried to keep the tears from spilling out. Once the butler was gone Hilary looked at Leah expectantly. Leah took a bite of her sandwich to give herself a minute to finish composing herself.

"I bumped Roger as he was serving the soup and the soup ended up all over Randall. I escaped to my room after that. And now Mother is furious with me."

"I think being a klutz saved you from having to accept Randall's proposal," Hilary was trying to keep the laughter out of her voice with only partial success.

"It was not helpful enough, because Randall and his parents are supposed to be back for supper tomorrow. Mother told me if anything happens I will be locked in my room until she is sure it will never happen again."

"You need to talk to your father before supper tomorrow otherwise you could be dooming yourself to an unhappy life married to Randall." All laughter was gone from Hilary's voice this time, in fact, worry had started to creep in.

"I do not want to worry him, especially when he is so sick."

"I have met your father, he would rather you were happy if it killed him."

"What is your news? You rarely invite me to lunch unless you have some kind of news."

Hilary gave Leah a look that said she knew Leah was trying to change the subject. Then Hilary's face went from worried to glowing with joy.

"Percival Spencer asked Father for my hand in marriage."

"And what did your father say?"

"He said yes, of course."

"Congratulations, you have been trying to get Percival's attention for a couple years."

"I have had Percival's attention for a couple years. He was just too scared Father would turn him down. I kept telling him just because his parents are dead does not mean he has anything to be ashamed about. It is not like he is penniless or without a title. Finally he got up the courage. I think it had something to do with his friend Caleb. They went out riding one day and the next he was ready to ask Father."

"Any date for the wedding?"

"I want it as soon as possible, but Mother wants time to plan it and invite everyone. I am not supposed to tell people, but I wanted you to know."

"Congratulations, I am happy for you. At least one of us has something to look forward to."

"You need to talk to your father, he will do something."

"I will try."

"That other thing I wanted to tell you was I received a letter from Selena yesterday."

"What did she say?"

"She will not be coming home. She wishes us both well and says she will pray for us, but she cannot face her parents and family members."

"What will she do then?"

"She said she was preparing to join the convent, that she feels lead under the circumstances to remain there. If she is as happy about staying there as she sounds I would say it is a good thing."

"I hope she is happy, she deserves happiness after everything that has happened to her."

"I was going to write back to her and tell her my good news, but I think I will wait. Hopefully, I can tell her how you managed to escape marrying Randall."

Leah's eyes shifted from Hilary to her almost empty plate.

"And if I do not manage to get out marrying Randall?" Leah's voice sounded almost like that of a small child.

"Then I will ask Selena to pray harder for you," Hilary said. She reached out her hand placed it over Leah's hand. Hilary squeezed Leah's hand.

CHAPTER SIX

When lunch was over the Whitelaw's carriage took Leah home. Back at the manor Leah found her mother had gone off for tea. Leah checked on her father, but found him still asleep. He still looked closer to dead than alive so Leah kissed him gently on the cheek and left without disturbing him. Since Leah did not see her she figured Melissa was back in the kitchen gossiping with the cook. Leah stopped in the library and picked up the book, she had been reading, off the table and looked at it. Then she looked out the window at the sunny landscape beckoning her. The sun looked as welcoming as stirrings of hope that Caleb would be out riding today leap into her mind. Leah put the book back on the table before going up to her room. She put her hat back on and went out the French doors. No one stopped her as Leah walked across the lawn to the hedge maze.

Once at the hedge maze Leah took one glance back to make sure no one was watching. Not seeing anyone Leah turned back and headed into the hedge maze. Without thinking about it Leah started to run. She ran passed all the landmarks she had memorized on her way back yesterday. Leah felt like she was running away from her mother, her mother's poison, and thoughts of Randall. She remembered how inviting the field looked from the library window and how she wanted to come out here to forget all her worries even if Caleb choose to be elsewhere. Those thoughts gave her a burst of speed.

It was not long before Leah came to the door leading to the field. Leah stopped to catch her breath. Somehow she felt like the door was closer than it had been yesterday. Leah shook the thought out of her head. It only felt that way because she had run today instead of wandering to it and she had known where she was going this time. After all she had gone through both clearings to get here and her breathing was heavy.

Finally getting her breath back Leah pushed the door open. The same scene from yesterday greeted and welcomed her. A breeze had the grass waving and the sun reflected off the lake. It was like they were saying they missed her and were glad to have her back. Leah glanced back, but the path seemed to repel her rather than invite her to go back. So, she turned back to the field and stepped off the path on to the grass. Leah walked down to the lake. The breeze blew across the water causing waves and preventing Leah from being able to see the fish.

Leah took off her stockings and shoes. Then she sat down on the edge of the lake and put her feet into the water. Today her dress was only hiked up to her knees so if anyone came passed there would be a lot less to be embarrassed about. And she was hoping for a certain someone to pass. With the brightness of the day Leah was glad she remembered her hat today because it made the sun's glare less harsh. Leah rested her elbows on her knees and her chin on her hands. Closing her eyes Leah relaxed fully intending to enjoy the afternoon whether Caleb made an appearance or not.

She had only been there ten minutes when she could hear and feel a horse walking towards her. Leah could smell the horse as it stopped nearby. She opened her eyes and looked up at the horse. Caleb was sitting on the horse. He looked as good as the memory Leah had kept in her head from yesterday, maybe even better. She could still see him as the knight coming to her rescue and felt her heart start to beat faster. Leah shoved those thoughts aside and hoped Caleb could not see them reflected on her face.

"Good afternoon, Miss Winsand," Caleb said.

"Good afternoon," Leah replied.

"You seem to be fond of this fish pond," Caleb commented.

"I find it calming out here," Leah replied. She went back to looking at the lake. Caleb got down off his horse and sat down in the grass beside her. But he did not take his shoes off or put his feet in the water. He was quiet for a moment. Leah snuck a glance at him, but could not read much in his face. She went back to looking at the lake.

"How is your father doing?" Caleb asked after another minute.

"Worse than yesterday," Leah answered. She found the tears threatening to come once again and tried to blink them away. The emotions she kept pushing back rose to the surface as if they had been waiting to explode. Leah tried again to put them back in the box where she wanted them to stay. But something seemed to be stuck when she tried to slam the lid.

"I am sorry to hear that," Caleb said. The compassion in his voice made all the sides of the box crumple to dust.

"I think my mother is poisoning him," the words burst forth from Leah in a rush. She wanted to cover her mouth with her hand or reach out and put the words back, but she felt frozen. The box was gone and things were spilling out seemingly beyond her control.

Caleb did not immediately respond. Leah felt water on her hands and realized she was crying. The tears she had been holding in for months were flowing. To Leah everything became a blur of tears and trying to take a breath. Caleb wrapped his arms around her and pulled her to his chest. She sobbed into his shirt.

Leah felt she should pull away, she should not be falling apart, and she should not be crying into Caleb Morley's chest. This sort of behaviour was not proper for young ladies and she needed to get herself together. But there was nothing she could do to stop the tears. After fighting with herself for several minutes, Leah gave in to the overwhelming emotions and allowed herself cry.

Caleb looked down at the lady in his arms. If it had been any other lady he might have murmured words of comfort and tried to sooth whatever caused her to cry. But with Leah Winsand he had seen in her eyes the depth of emotions that were causing the tears. These were not the tears of a lady who tore her favourite gown, but tears of sadness, fear, tiredness, and grief. These tears had been denied for too long and there was nothing that could stop them now they had started. All Caleb could do was to hold her and let the tears flow until they were all out.

Caleb's nature wanted to help her as he had helped others who had come to him with their problems but something deeper made him want to kiss her tears away and tell her he would make everything better. He could take her away from her mother to where she would be safe. Caleb knew a few places where she would never be found. It would not be the first time he helped someone in need of a place to hide from their problems. Her father could join her there, if James wanted. It would solve their problems until they could come up with a better solution. However, Caleb doubted Leah would accept such an offer. His instincts told him that she may not know what to do about the situation, but she was not going to run from it.

No, Caleb was not going do anything as foolish as suggesting Leah run away from her problems. Instead he was going to have to come up with some other way of helping, because he had to do something to help her. It would require some more thought.


It was a while before the tears slowed and Leah found herself able to breath without gulping. She found it felt nice in Caleb's arms so she did not move. Leah just sat there and tried to calm down.

"I am sorry," Leah's words came out as a scratchy whisper.

"You needed to cry or it would not have happened," Caleb replied. He offered Leah his handkerchief; she accepted it and used it to wipe her face. Neither one said anything for several minutes.

"What did you mean you think your mother is poisoning your father?" Caleb asked finally breaking the quiet.

"He was doing better yesterday evening," Leah said, "He even talked about getting out of bed and spending some time outside. Then yesterday night I was in the pantry looking for something to eat because I missed the main course of supper. When I heard Mother come into the kitchen, I was in the pantry with the door part way close and I saw Mother put something into Father's drink and this morning he looked barely alive. She acts like he is already dead and not just sick. I do not know what to do about it." The tears started to well up again. Leah used Caleb's handkerchief to wipe them away.

"Perhaps I can help," Caleb's words seemed to surprise him. Leah felt her heart do a flip as if Caleb could be the knight riding in to her rescue.

"How? How can I do something without making a bigger mess? My father would not want a scandal." Leah asked. Even she could hear the want of something to give her hope in her voice.

"I am not sure," Caleb answered, "But I will think of something. But you are right Lord Winsand would not want a scandal." As much as he sounded unsure of his own words somehow they brought hope to Leah's heart. She closed her eyes and rested against Caleb.

Could this man, who was a stranger yesterday and barely more than that today, really help solve this problem? Leah wondered. She was not sure anyone could help with her problems but something within Leah told her to trust Caleb.

After a while Leah opened her eyes. Caleb let his arms fall away as she straightened by and moved away from him. Leah put the handkerchief into the lake and rinsed it out. Then she used it to wipe her face. She did this a second time before sitting back down beside Caleb.

"Are you going to be all right now?" Caleb asked.

"I think so," Leah answered. Sitting there her body seemed very aware that he was sitting right beside her and longed to be back wrapped in his arms. But Leah tried to push those thoughts to one side.

"I know you are going through a lot at the moment but I was wondering if you would like to go riding with me tomorrow afternoon," Caleb said. Leah managed to stop herself from just blurting out yes and that it would be wonderful. She let the other thoughts coming into her head finish forming.

"I would, but I do not have a horse," Leah said," We only have the horses that draw the carriage and the one Father rides, which I don't dare take."

"You can borrow one of ours," Caleb said, "We have several horses that you can pick from."

"Then certainly I would like to go riding," Leah said.

"Then I will meet you at the door in the hedge after lunch," Caleb said.

"I will be there," Leah replied.

"I am expected at home," Caleb stood up, "Would you like a ride back to the hedge?"

"Thank you for the offer, but I am not quite ready to go

home," Leah said.

"Okay," Caleb said, "Then I will see you tomorrow." He mounted his horse.

"See you tomorrow," Leah said. Caleb smiled at her before turning his horse towards the forest between the lake and Morley Estate. Leah watched him go. She wished she was with him, if nothing else but to be in Caleb's arms again. Once the trees blocked all sight of him Leah turned her eyes back to the water.

Leah found her heart was singing with the prospect of going riding tomorrow though she knew it had been years since she had been on a horse. There was one small part of her brain saying she would probably end up doing something embarrassing, like falling off the horse. But that part was being drowned out by the singing. Even the heavy burden of worry seemed to be lighter with thoughts of tomorrow in Leah's head.

If her mother knew about riding with Caleb, Leah knew she would be locked in her room until the day she was supposed to marry Randall. The idea someone other than Randall might court Leah probably had never entered her mother's mind. Or at least Leah did not feel like her mother had given it any thought. But Caleb had shown up in Leah's life like a knight out of one of her father's stories and she hoped he could help her. Leah decided it would be best if she did not tell anyone about her seeing Caleb just in case word got back to her mother.

Feeling better Leah put her stockings and shoes back on. She stood up and headed back across the field to the door. Before going through it Leah glanced back over the field. It seemed to be inviting her to stay.

"See you tomorrow," Leah told the grass, lake, and sunshine. Then she went through the door and closed it behind her.

Melissa lay there in Haines's arms. She knew she would

have to get back to the manor very soon if she did not want someone to come looking for her. Leah would not bother to ask for her for she liked to be alone. But Roger might come looking if she was gone too long, or he might send the cook's helper. Either way she did not want to be found naked in the arms of her lover lying in a clearing in the hedge maze. But right now she was not ready to move. Many men would have already put on their clothes and left, but Haines was willing to lie here with Melissa as long as she wanted.

Not long before Melissa had heard the door to the field close and someone going down the path towards the house. Melissa assumed it was the same person who had come from the house and had opened the door before leaving it that way for a while. Since Roger, the cook, the cook's helper, and Lady Winsand would not likely come this way, Melissa figured that it was Leah. She always seemed to be trying to run away from her problems. Usually Leah just ran away in her head but with Lady Winsand's insistence Leah marry the lump called Randall Melissa did not blame her for trying to physically run away. Melissa figured Leah should find some man and elope. It would better than running through all the things that were wrong over and over in her mind. The worries of her father and mother were making Leah look years older than she was. If it lasted too much longer someone might mistake her age and then Randall would be the only one willing to marry her. Melissa was glad she was just a servant and invisible to Lady Winsand, but to continue as such she would have to get back to the house soon. With a sigh Melissa started to get up so she could get her clothes. Haines took her wrist gently to stop her from moving.

"I should get back," Melissa said. Haines tugged her to him for a kiss. The kiss brought Melissa back down to lie beside Haines and caused her to forget about heading back inside.

Back at the house no one greeted Leah as she entered nor did anyone seem to be searching for her much to her relief. Leah went up the stairs to the second floor. She stopped briefly to look in the mirror, but she did not look as bad as she feared she might after all the crying. Leah headed down the hallway to her father's room. The door was open and she could see he was propped up with some pillows; though he still looked very close to death. He looked up at her before she could knock on the door frame. Leah's father smiled at her as he gestured for her to come to his side. Leah stepped into the room and went over to the chair next to the bed. She sat down.

"How is my daughter this afternoon?" James asked in a hoarse whisper.

"Still worried," Leah answered.

"Everything will turn out all right, you will see," James said, "Despite what you have seen between me and your mother marriage is not a bad thing."

"I guess it is just the thought of being married to Randall Lambert that has me upset and worried," Leah replied.

"Randall Lambert?" James asked. He sounded like he was trying to remember who that was. Leah was sure he could not have forgotten who Randall was since he had hated the Lamberts for as long as Leah could remember. She was never quite sure why, but it had always been there.

"Mother told me that I am supposed to say yes when Randall Lambert asks me to marry him," Leah answered, "And according to the Kenley twins he is supposed to be asking me anytime." James looked puzzled for a moment and then he seemed to come up with the solution.

"As I said, everything will turn out all right," James said.

"Yes, Father," Leah said.

"Now, how about you bring me what I wrote yesterday?" James said, "You can read it to me and we will see if it needs any editing done to it."

"Yes, Father," Leah said as she stood up. She left the room and went into the library. Gathering the writing supplies off the desk she went back to her father's room. After setting herself up in the chair beside the bed, Leah started to read the story to her father.


When supper was over Leah went up to the library. Sitting down in the chair she picked up the book she had been reading. But she could not concentrate and various thoughts from the day clamoured around in her head. Her father being worse, but still telling her everything was going to be all right. Hilary being excited by her own news and telling Leah that somehow the situation she found herself in would all work out. And Caleb being not sure how, but promising her he would do what he could to help her anyway. Leah knew life was not one of her father's stories. The prince did not ride in and take away the damsel in distress to safety before locking the witches in the dungeon but she wanted it turn out that way. Leah closed her eyes and let that dream wash through her mind. The image of her happily ever after looked nice but Leah also knew deep down it was not real. With a sigh, Leah opened her eyes and focused on the pages of the book.

After a page, Leah's mind started to drift. She remembered the feeling of safety and comfort she had felt being in Caleb's arms. There was also the feeling of warmth and strength of his chest where she had cried into it. His closeness had made blood rush to places she had never noticed before. Leah remembered the feeling of never wanting him to leave and of wanting him to take her away from all her problems maybe even eloping. Leah shook her head. Even if Caleb was willing, which she was not sure he was, there was her father. He needed her and she could not leave him alone with her mother.

Leah's mind switched and could see her mother dressed

up as a witch and stirring a cauldron of smoking liquid. The smoke formed a skull and cross bones before drifting to the ceiling and floating with the rest of the horrors up there. Her mother cackled as she stirred the brew again before taking out her little bottle. She filled it before putting the cap back on it. Cackling some more, she hid the bottle away. The knight in armour broke down the door and charged the witch. Before the knight could reach the witch, she threw a spell at him. His love for the princess was so strong the spell deflected off him and turned the witch's pet raven into a rope. Then knight used the rope to tie up the witch and opened the window for the breeze to disperse her other spells.

Soon the witch was banished and the knight rescued the princess from her tower. Only then did he remove his helmet and the princess could see that her rescuer was Caleb Morley. He gave her a swoon worthy kiss before putting her up on his horse and riding away from the tower.

The book dropped to the floor, but Leah did not notice as her eyes closed with the memory of being in Caleb's embrace. Her arms slipped around her as she focused on the feeling of safety that he brought her.

# CHAPTER SEVEN

*August 3, 1865*

Leah woke up to a pain in her neck. She opened hers eyes and looked around. She was still in the library, where she had started to read a book after supper. But now there was morning light coming in the windows. For some reason neither Melissa nor Roger had woken her and directed her to her own bed. The pain was just her neck stiff from sleeping in a strange position. The book she had been reading when she fell asleep was now sitting on the floor. Leah stood up and stretched. She picked up the book off the floor and placed it on the table beside the chair. Leah stretched again before leaving the library. She went up the stairs and into her room. Melissa was already waiting for her with her clothes laid out. Leah dressed and then let Melissa do her hair.

When Melissa was finished Leah went downstairs. In the dining room Roger served Leah immediately because her mother was still asleep and no one would be joining her.

After Leah had eaten breakfast she went up the stairs to

the second floor. She went down the hallway to her father's room. Through the open door Leah saw her father was sitting up and drinking out of a mug. Before Leah could knock he looked up and smiled at her. Leah smiled back as she stepped into the room.

"How are you this morning?" James asked.

"Well," Leah answered, "How are you feeling?"

"Better than yesterday," James answered.

"Good to hear," Leah said.

"Should you not be off to lessons?" James asked.

"Soon," Leah answered, "I had lunch with Hilary yesterday."

"What news did she have?"

"Selena is going to stay at the convent."

"It is understandable after everything that has happened to her."

"And Hilary is engaged."

"Who is the lucky man?"

"Percival Spencer."

"They are well matched. What took him so long?"

"According to Hilary, Percy's fear of her father's displeasure."

"Well, it is a good thing he got over it or he would have missed his opportunity. It is probably a debate among those who gossip as to how he won her."

"Hilary's parents want to keep the news quiet for now. I think she told me because she was so excited she had to tell someone. The announcement will probably be next week after her parents return from a trip to London."

"Then we shall not tell anyone else until the formal announcement. The wedding will be one not to miss."

"It shall be." Leah only manages half a smile.

"What is wrong?"

"Mother has invited the Lamberts for supper tonight."

"Do not worry about the Lamberts. Go to your lessons and have a good day."

"Yes, Father," Leah kissed her father's cheek before leaving the room. She went up the stairs to her room. Melissa was not there, but she had left out Leah's coat and hat. Leah put on the coat and hat. Then she went back down stairs to the front door. Leah opened the door to see the carriage coming up the drive. She waited at the bottom of the steps for it to stop. When it did she opened the door and climbed in.

"Good morning," Hilary said.

"Good morning," Leah replied.

"Did Randall propose?" Margaret asked.

"I did not see Randall yesterday," Leah answered.

"Perhaps it will happen today," Meghan said.

"Why rush him?" Hilary asked, "It is not like anyone would actually want to marry him."

"He is supposed to propose to Leah," Margaret said.

"But she can turn him down," Hilary said, "A proposal does not guarantee anything, especially since I doubt Randall has asked Lord Winsand for Leah's hand."

"He has not asked?" Margaret looked confused.

"It sounded like he had permission and everyone is just waiting for Randall to propose," Meghan said.

"Roger is not likely to let anyone disturb Father," Leah said, "Not while he is so sick. As far as I know Randall has not talked to him, nor is he likely to if anyone is given a choice. And that has more to do with Father's health than Randall."

"Which means," Margaret started.

"When Randall proposes," Meghan said.

"There may not be a wedding," Margaret said.

"Because your father could stop it," Meghan finished.

"Now we have settled that rumour," Hilary said, "What other gossip is out there today?"

"The invitations for Edwina's wedding are out," Margaret said.

"Marian was caught with the stable boy, again," Meghan

said.

"Lord Nortand is heading for London without his wife," Margaret said.

"Which means her lover is moving back into her bed," Meghan said.

"Has anyone figured out who Lady Nortand's lover is?" Hilary asked, "Or does he hide in her room not to be seen by anyone else?"

The twins go quiet for a moment as they think about the question. Leah let a small smile come to her lips as she turned her head to look out the window. Trust Hilary to stump the twins, Leah thought.

"Someone must have," Margaret said.

"Otherwise how would they know he exists," Meghan said.

Leah could hear hoof beats coming up behind the carriage. She looked out the window to see several people on horseback riding passed the carriage. They were boys probably on the way to their own lessons. Leah felt her heart beat a little faster as she remembered Caleb had asked her to go riding with him this afternoon. She hoped lessons would go by quickly, but the afternoon would go by slowly.

Caleb was eating breakfast when his parents came into the dining room and sat down. John brought them breakfast before withdrawing.

"Good morning," Lady Morley said.

"Good morning," Caleb replied.

"What are your plans for today?" Lady Morley asked.

"Probably go out riding this afternoon, other than that not much." Caleb answered.

"Is Percy going with you?" Lady Morley asked.

"No," Caleb answered, "He is spending the day with Hilary Whitelaw."

"Has Percy gotten around to asking Lord Whitelaw for his daughter's hand in marriage?" Lady Morley asked.

"What do the rumours say?" Caleb asked.

"That Lord and Lady Whitelaw are in London to arrange a marriage for Hilary with one of those young, outspoken politicians they like to talk about so much," Lady Morley answered, "But I doubt that is true. Lord and Lady Whitelaw's opinions on marriage get more and more liberal every time we talk to them. They would be okay if their granddaughter wants to marry the stable boy."

"Considering the inbreeding of the nobility in some countries, letting the occasional stable boy in is not necessarily bad thing," Lord Morley said as he reached for jam to go on his toast.

"My point was that it is unlikely the Whitelaws would arrange a marriage for Hilary," Lady Morley said.

"That tradition does seem to be disappearing," Lord Morley opened the book he had brought with him.

"Besides, I am sure Lord and Lady Whitelaw can see that Percy was meant to be with Hilary," Lady Morley said. Lord Morley nodded as he started reading.

"That has not stopped Percy from being nervous about asking for Hilary's hand," Caleb said.

"Perhaps when Lord Whitelaw gets back you can talk Percy into it," Lady Morley said, "An autumn wedding is just what we need this year."

"Their wedding would make three weddings this autumn," Caleb said.

"The invitation to Edwina Lavern and Curt Erland's wedding showed up yesterday," Lady Morley said, "Who else is supposed to get married?"

"Rumour is Randall Lambert is supposed to propose to Leah Winsand any day now," Caleb answered. Lord Morley snorted as he looked up from his book.

"That match will only happen over James's dead body," Lord Morley said.

"Lord Winsand has been sick for a while," Caleb said. The look on Lord Morley's face changed from incredulousness to concern.

"An illness would explain why he has not been around for supper in a long time," Lady Morley said.

"It is not good," Lord Morley said, "With James sick, who knows what Lady Winsand is up to."

"I doubt she is that bad," Lady Morley said.

"The stories James used to tell would make you shutter in horror," Lord Morley said.

"Then why did he marry her?" Lady Morley asked.

"His parents arranged it after Leanne Dalen was thrown from a horse and died," Lord Morley answered, "He met Lady Winsand at the altar where they exchanged vows."

"And that is another argument against the tradition of arranged marriages," Caleb said.

"Do not be too set against them," Lord Morley said before going back to his book.

"Why?" Caleb asked.

"Because your father has an agreement for you to marry someone," Lady Morley answered.

"What? Who?" Caleb asked.

"This is not the right time to discuss it," Lord Morley said.

"And when is the right time to discuss your plans for my life?" Caleb asked.

"There are a lot of ifs to the agreement," Lord Morley said, "I am leaving things open until it is the right time to discuss it." Lord Morley gave Caleb a look informing him the subject was closed for discussion before going back to reading his book.

"I was planning to spend the day with the horses," Lady Morley said, "But I have an invitation to go visiting."

"I will be out in stable," Caleb stood up. He left the dining room.

He did not stop until he got to the stable. Haines was nowhere in sight, nor could Caleb hear him. It was too early for Haines to be in the rose patch so Caleb figured he was probably still asleep. Caleb went over to the stall where Warrior was. Warrior greeted him by sniffing for treats. Caleb smiled.

"You know me," Caleb took out an apple and offered it to Warrior. Warrior took it out of Caleb's hand without even nibbling on Caleb's fingers.

"Sometimes I think if I do not bring you a treat every morning you would shun me," Caleb patted Warrior's neck. Warrior was too busy chewing on the apple to respond. Caleb picked up the brush and let himself into the stall.

"I am beginning to think parents were made to keep a person on their toes," Caleb said as he started brushing Warrior. Warrior ignored him. "I thought I knew where my life was going and what was expected of me and then my father makes some comment which sends all my set plans to the four winds. Like marriage, before this morning I thought they were waiting for me to find someone I loved so I could marry her and be happy. And then this morning my father says he has an agreement with someone about who I am to marry. But now is not the right time to talk about. I turned nineteen two months ago now and many of my friends are either married or engaged. Should my father not have told me about this agreement before? And what did he mean by too many ifs?" Caleb paused but Warrior made no move to answer the questions.

"And why did this subject only come up now that I think I found someone?" Caleb continued, "If this had all come to light last week it might not be such a problem. I would not have gone riding yesterday near the fish pond in hopes Leah Winsand would be there. I would not have promised to help her. And I would not have asked her to go riding with me today."

Warrior snorted in disbelief as Caleb's words.

"Say what you want," Caleb told him, "But I am not the type of man to go after women if I know I am taken or if they are. And now my father has decided to let me know I am with great probability taken, I have a pair of beautiful, blue eyes haunting my dreams and keeping me up at night. How is a person supposed to deal with the resulting mess?"

"You got woman troubles?" Haines's voice came from outside the stall, "Or are you just talking to your horse for fun?" His head popped up above the stall door. Caleb glanced at him before going back to brushing Warrior. Haines's brown hair was in need of a haircut and there were bits of straw in it. There was also several dirt smears on his face.

"I am stuck between a marriage and the possibility of love," Caleb answered, "With no idea what my father's plan is as far as the marriage goes."

"Why not have both?" Haines asked, "It is not uncommon among unhappy marriages for either side to find happiness with other partners. Shelley has been telling me all about various nobles who don't keep to their wedding vows."

"Is that what you talk about while you are in her bed distracting her from her chores?" Caleb asked.

"I don't dally any lady who is not willing," Haines said, "And if she don't want to be distracted she'd tell me."

"After taking a wedding vow, I could never go off and be with another woman," Caleb said, "Even the thought of it feels wrong."

"Then you got a problem," Haines said, "Maybe you can explain the situation to the girl you might be seeing."

"She is facing enough problems without me dumping anything more on her," Caleb said, "And before you suggest I talk things over with my father I will tell you now he refuses to discuss this any further at the moment because he claims it is not the right time."

"Then you are stuck until you can do one of the two," Haines said, "Either that or you can run off with the girl and solve all your problems. Unless, of course, her problems have to do with her husband then everything gets a bit sticky."

"I know she is not married," Caleb said, "Her problems revolve around her father being sick, probably being poisoned."

"Being poisoned, eh?" Haines said, "Any idea by who?"

"His wife," Caleb answered.

"Ouch," Haines said, "When you nobles get into trouble you really get into trouble. The most trouble I've ever been in was the one day that I had to hop into my pants as I went out the back door because her husband was coming in the front."

"Did the husband find out?" Caleb asked.

"Don't know," Haines answered, "Had to skip town later that morning for being caught stealing breakfast. Won't have done me any good to know anyway, just be more trouble."

"No wonder you are willing to give advice on how to get into trouble," Caleb said, "You never learned how to stay out of it."

"Course I learned how to stay out of it," Haines said, "If it weren't for this gimped leg and your parents' willingness to let me look after the horses I'd still be running from the law somewhere. Once you have lost use of part of your leg you learn to avoid trouble."

"Does the cook know you have been stealing potatoes to make the rotgut you sneak out to the rose patch to drink?" Caleb asked.

"Nope," Haines answered.

"Then you have not figured out how to stay out of trouble," Caleb said, "But I will take your advice under consideration anyway."

"If there anything I can do to help, all you got do is ask," Haines tipped his cap before limping off to start his chores. Warrior tossed his head as if to say, do not mind him he does not know what is good for you. Caleb laughed.

CHAPTER EIGHT


The house was empty when Leah arrived home from lessons, which meant she ate alone in the dining room. When Leah went upstairs after lunch she did not see Melissa, so she thought Melissa assumed that she would spend the afternoon reading and had gone off to the kitchen to gossip with the cook. Leah stopped at her father's bedroom and looked in. Her father was asleep. He still looked awful so she figured it was better not to disturb him. Leah went up to her room. In her room she changed into clothes fit for riding. Then Leah made her way back downstairs as quietly as she could. She successfully avoided meeting anyone as she made her way through the house. Once outside she walked across the lawn to the hedge maze. When Leah was out of sight of the manor she broke into a run. Nothing was going to come between her and going riding with Caleb today. It was as if her sanity depended on it.

Melissa stepped out of the kitchen door in time to see Leah disappear around the first bend in the hedge maze. Being as quiet as she could Melissa followed Leah into the hedge maze. She stayed a turn behind the crunch of feet on the gravel path. Leah was headed for the door to the field. When Leah took the last turn that would take her to the door, Melissa went straight until the next turn. This one led to the grass clearing. Haines was already there, but he was listening by the hedge. He waved for Melissa to keep quiet. She did as she joined him by the hedge.

When Leah reached the door she stopped long enough to catch her breath. It felt like ten minutes before she could breathe properly, but it was probably only one. Leah opened the door. Caleb was standing there beside his horse. The field of grass might have been as inviting as it was yesterday with the lake shining in the sunlight calling to her, but the only thing in the field that had Leah's full attention was Caleb. Leah smiled as she stepped out and closed the door behind her.

"Good afternoon, Miss Winsand," Caleb smiled back at her.

"Good afternoon," Leah said. She noticed Caleb's horse was the only out there. Caleb followed her gaze to the horse.

"I was trying to figure out which horse you would prefer to ride, but I forgot to ask you what level of experience you have had with horses so I figured it might be better if I took you to the stable," Caleb answered, "Then you can choose the one that fits your experience with horses. Otherwise you may not enjoy the ride as much."

"That does make sense," Leah said. She went over and Caleb helped her up before getting up behind her. Caleb directed the horse away from the door and across the field. They went passed the lake and into the trees. In the trees the horse needed very little guidance to go along the path. Slowly the trees thinned out and the path led them into a well-kept garden. Leah looked around. It was a flower garden with paths going through it in various directions. In the centre was a fountain shaped like a child pouring water out of a jug. Then there was the lawn with the stable to one side of it. At the top of the lawn was the manor. It was at least as big as the Winsand Manor, though to Leah it did not look like it had been built in stages like the Winsand Manor had been. The Morley Manor looked like someone had been careful and deliberate in building it, whereas the Winsand Manor had been built small and added to as the various owners decided they needed this room or that one.

The horse was well trained to keep to the one path that led straight to the stable. As far as Leah could tell Caleb was not directing the horse at all. When they arrived at the stable, Caleb got down before helping Leah down off the horse. He wrapped the reins around a post that stood by the door of the stable, but it looked like the horse could wander off if he had wanted to. Leah followed Caleb inside the stable. No one came to meet them and aside from the horses there did not seem to be anyone in the stable. Caleb did not seem worried or even to feel this was unusual. He just headed for the stall he wanted.

"There are about five horses I can offer to let you ride," Caleb said leading the way. He stopped in front of one stall. "This is Princess. She is a little snobbish, but the attitude is only a front. She really is a good horse."

The horse was a pretty, dark brown. Leah reached out and touched the horse's neck. The horse raised her head as if the thought of Leah riding her was beneath her.

Caleb continued on and Leah followed him. He stopped in front of a stall with a black horse.

"This is Blackie. He is gentle and does what he is told," Caleb said. Leah reached up to pat the horse's neck and he lowered his head for her. Caleb went down to another stall farther along. Leah followed him. This one was a light brown horse.

"This is Daisy. She likes to stop and munch on flowers if given the chance," Caleb said. Leah reached up and

Daisy sniffed her hand before letting Leah pat her neck. Caleb crossed to the other side of the stable and stopped in front of a stall holding a brown and white horse. Leah went over.

"This is Chester. He will let you ride him, but usually it takes him a while to warm up to people," Caleb said. Leah reached up but the horse backed away from her hand, so she followed Caleb to the next stall.

"And this one is Jewel," Caleb said. The horse was black with white on its nose and stomach. "She is getting old, but is good for an inexperienced rider."

Leah reached up and patted the horse's neck. Jewel just kept munching on the grain in her mouth as if such an everyday occurrence should not interrupt her lunch. But she watched Leah as if she was prepared to be ridden if that was what Leah wanted.

"Which would you like to ride?" Caleb asked.

"It has been a while since I have ridden so I think I will ride Jewel," Leah answered.

"Okay," Caleb said as he opened the stall. There was a side saddle in the stall, he just took it down and put it on the horse. Jewel stood there patiently. When he was finished Caleb walked the horse out for Leah. There was a mounting block just outside the stall Leah used to get on Jewel. Then Leah directed Jewel to follow Caleb outside she accepted the order like she was used to taking orders from Leah. Leah remembered the horse from lessons had taken a while to get used to her and would not have taken such an order immediately from an unknown rider. Caleb got up on his horse and started in the direction they had come from. Leah followed him along the path through the garden and through the trees. When they were on the field and clear of the path Leah moved to ride beside Caleb.

Leah thought it felt wonderful to be out riding. I wish Mother would let us keep more horses, Leah thought, out here, on this horse, I feel like it has not been five years since I was last on one horse.

Leah encouraged Jewel to go a bit faster. Jewel was willing. Caleb kept pace beside Leah. There was another group of trees at the far end of the field. Leah figured she could get there without tiring Jewel out. Leah told Jewel to run. Caleb seemed prepared when Leah urged Jewel faster. He fell a little behind, but had his horse moving at a similar speed.

To Leah being on a running horse in a field felt like being flying. All worries, fears and restrictions were a forever away. She felt like she could spend all day riding a horse and, if possible, at this speed. It was hard for Leah to believe that something as simple as horseback riding could make a day better. Though going horseback riding with Caleb was the best of all worlds, Leah thought as she glanced back. He was still there and appeared to be having as much fun as she was. She was sure that if he wanted to he could pass her, but he chose to stay beside her.

Once Jewel reached the trees she slowed down as if the trees were the finish line. Leah let Jewel lead as she continued at a slower pace. Caleb followed behind because the path through the trees was not wide enough to ride beside Leah. When Jewel reached a clearing Leah stopped her letting Caleb catch up. Caleb stopped his horse beside Jewel.

"Have you ever thought about being a jockey?" Caleb asked, "I do not think I have ever seen Jewel run so fast."

"No," Leah answered, "I have not been on a horse since I took lessons and Mother would never approve of it."

"Your father would?" Caleb asked.

"He would keep more horses around if he knew," Leah answered as she climbed down of Jewel and let the horse wander over to the pool of water.

"More horses?" Caleb asked as he got down off his horse.

"Mother does not ride and sees no point in keeping

horses around," Leah answered, "So, we have the horses for the carriage and Father's horse. Though Mother would try to get rid of Father's horse if she thought she could."

"From the stories of hunting trips I would say selling your father's horse would be difficult," Caleb said, "My Father complained once that it was half wild."

"That is the reason Mother has not sold Father's horse. The only people the horse allows around him is Father and the groom," Leah said. Leah and Caleb walked a little ways from the pool and sat down in the grass.

"Your groom must feel over worked with how many horses you have," Leah said.

"Not really," Caleb answered, "He has help. My father gave control of the stables to my mother after they were married. So any free moment she likes to be out there with the horses."

"It must have rubbed off on you."

"I was practically raised out in the stables. I was riding before I could walk."

"I am surprised that there was no one in the stables while we were looking at the horses."

"Mother was invited to tea by one of her friends and the groom is known for taking long breaks from his work."

"That does not sound good."

"If he is needed everyone knows he is sitting on the bench in the middle of the rose patch having a drink. He has been told that if he does not get the chores done he will be fired. So far he has kept up with those. And with other people spending time there it has not really been a problem."

"Mother would have fired him just for drinking, whether he could keep up with his chores or not. But then she would have fired our groom already if he was not needed to take care of Father's horse."

"Does your mother have a problem with horses?"

"No, she calls having horses and grooms a waste of

money. She likes to have things certain ways and spending as little money as possible while still maintaining the required lifestyle is one of those things. If it was up to her Father's horse would be gone, the groom would be fired, and the gardeners would be gone. She believes the other servants could do those other jobs as well as their own. Father will not let her do any of that because he says the servants might be able to do the jobs as well but only at a loss of quality to all the jobs. It has been an ongoing argument for many years."

"Your father is right. Servants are human too and they make human mistakes."

"I think he restarts the argument just to get Mother angry at him. It is one of many things that work. And there used to be some days where I am sure he was out to make her as angry as possible with him."

"Maybe that is why she is poisoning him."

"But he has been doing it for as long as I can remember, the sickness which I think has to do with Mother poisoning him, has only been around for the last several months. If she wanted to do something about all his taunting I do not see any reason for her to wait this long. I think she is poisoning him for a different reason. I am just not sure what the reason is. She has the same control over the household she always had. As far as I can tell she does not gain anything from this."

"What about control over you?"

"Control over me?"

"With your father sick she can make decisions for you that your father might not approve of. By the time he is in any condition to do anything about the situation it would be too late."

"There is only one thing Mother is making me do and I told Father about it. And he did not say anything about it. It is definitely not at the point of being irreversible. I do not see any reason for Mother's behaviour."

"Perhaps it is something she does not want you to see."

"I do not know," Leah voice was tired, "I just wish it was not happening."

"Everything will work out," Caleb put a comforting arm around Leah.

"I hope so," Leah said letting Caleb's closeness be a comfort to her. Caleb did not say anything else and Leah left the quiet alone.

Sitting there in the clearing with Caleb, Leah felt like everything would be all right. She did not let her thoughts destroy the feeling as she usually would, because she was tired of the feelings of dread and fear. Here in this clearing Leah would let herself believe. She closed her eyes to hold on to this moment for as long as possible. It was so nice just to sit there.

Caleb watched Leah as she rested her head against his shoulder. Slowly her breathing even out and the muscles in her face relaxed. Caleb thought she looked angelic with the halo of hair and the serene look on her face. He wrapped his arms around Leah and she snuggled closer to him in her sleep. Caleb wanted to pull her fully into her arms and protect her from the world. But he knew it was not possible so he checked the impulse. It was better if she did not wake up in a compromising position though if someone did see them it would be compromising enough. Caleb was not worried about anyone else riding in the woods since he knew them so well.

Though a small voice in Caleb's head told him that if his father had promised him to someone else he should not be here let alone holding Leah in his arms. He should wait until his father was ready to talk about what he had planned. But Caleb could not leave Leah alone when she needed him. With her father sick and her mother against her, she was looking for someone she could turn to; even if she did not want to admit it to herself. After things settled down then maybe Caleb would talk to Leah about the facts of their relationship. Caleb nodded to himself. The voice was silenced, but Caleb doubted that it would last long.

Melissa lifted her head from Haines's chest and looked at his face. He lifted his head enough to meet her eyes.

"It seems Leah and Caleb are seeing each other," Melissa said, "And they are keeping silent about it."

"He said something about seeing a lady this morning," Haines said, "Now I know which one."

"Think it will last?" Melissa asked.

"As long as Caleb doesn't let his father get in the way," Haines answered, "Unless you know of something else that would stop it."

"Lady Winsand," Melissa said.

"Things will work out," Haines said. He sounded so confident Melissa had no choice but to believe him.

"When do you have to get back?" Haines asked.

"I need to be there when Leah needs my help to get her ready for supper," Melissa answered.

"Good," Haines smiled. Melissa smiled back.

CHAPTER NINE

Leah felt warm and comfortable, but the smell of horses told her she was not home in bed. She slowly opened her eyes. Leah realized she was in the clearing where she and Caleb had stopped. The horses were still standing by the pool of water. Her head was resting on Caleb shoulder and his arms were wrapped around her. Leah felt comfortable and did not feel like moving, but she knew she had. The afternoon had gone by fast after all.

"Have a good nap?" Caleb asked.

"I am sorry," Leah said, "I did not mean to fall asleep." Leah sat up so she was no longer leaning on Caleb. His arms fell to his sides.

"It is fine," Caleb said, "You obviously needed the sleep."

"I should get home," Leah said, "Not that I do not appreciate the loan of Jewel and the ride, but Mother will be furious if I am not ready for supper at the right time."

"Then we should get going," Caleb said. He got to his feet before helping Leah to hers and then they went over to where the horses were. Caleb helped Leah up on to Jewel before getting up on his horse. They rode back through the trees to the field. When they reached the field they headed straight for the door in the hedge.

Arriving at the door Leah handed the reins to Caleb and got down off Jewel. Leah went to the door and pulled on the knob. The door would not open. It felt like it was locked.

"It is locked," Leah turned to Caleb, "And I do not have a key."

"We can go around to the front," Caleb suggested.

"We have to hurry," Leah replied. Caleb got down and helped Leah back up on to Jewel. Leah got Jewel started as Caleb got back on his horse. Once Caleb had caught up to Leah they both pushed their horses into a run. Leah set the pace and Caleb followed without difficulty.

They went around several properties and finally came to the road. They went along the road until they came to the right drive. Leah and Caleb slowed the horses down once the manor came into sight. They stopped at the bottom of the steps to the manor. Leah got down from Jewel as Caleb got down from his horse.

"I was wondering if I could speak with your father," Caleb said as he took the reins from Leah.

"Certainly," Leah said. She stopped and waited long enough for Caleb to tie the reins around a post. Then she headed inside with him following her. Inside the manor Roger was not in sight and Leah could not hear anyone else. She figured her mother was probably still upstairs getting dressed and everyone else was in the kitchen. Leah started up the stairs but paused when she heard her mother's voice. Quickly Leah realized it was coming from up the stairs and it sounded like her mother was yelling at her maid. Continuing on Leah stopped again at the second floor and turned to Caleb.

"Father's room is the one with the door open at the end of this hallway," Leah pointed down the hallway.

"Thank you," Caleb said then he kissed Leah on the lips

before heading down the hallway. Leah stared after him in wonder for a moment before turning and heading up to her room. Melissa was waiting for Leah when she got there with the dress already laid out on the bed.

"Where were you?" Melissa asked.

"I went for a walk," Leah answered as she stepped behind the screen to start undressing.

"Next time you need to be back sooner," Melissa said, "You almost did not have time to get ready."

"I know," Leah said. She tossed the dress she had just taken off on the screen and took down the one Melissa had put on the screen. Melissa took down the other dress.

"Where did you go for a walk?" Melissa's voice was also shrill, "It is going to very difficult to get these stains out of your skirt." Leah tuned out as Melissa went on about the stain. Leah's mind went back to Caleb's kiss and how it felt. Her mind continued replaying the kiss over and over concentrating on the memory of how soft and wonderful his lips had been against hers.

This is not a good thing, Leah told herself. Tonight I am supposed to accept Randall's proposal if he gets around to asking. The Morleys are people Mother would not want me to associate with and she certainly would be angry if she knew about her ride with Caleb. And I do not want to get married right now, not while Father is sick. And...and...why do I feel like I am falling with only Caleb's arms at the bottom to catch me?

Caleb walked down the hallway. He came to a door on his right which was open but it was only half way down the hallway. He looked in to the room. It was the library. Caleb continued. The second door which was open was on the left side of the hallway near the end of it. Caleb looked in. The only light in this room was what came through the space between the heavy curtains over the window. Caleb stopped in the doorway to give his eyes a minute to adjust.

"Caleb Morley?" James's voice came out of the darkness. Caleb was starting to make out the bed. "What are you doing here?"

"I was wondering if I could speak with you," Caleb said.

"Of course, come in," James said. Caleb stepped into the room. He could now see James sitting up in the bed. Caleb went over and sat down in the chair. He looked at James. The man he remembered was now half the size he used to be with wrinkled, pale skin. If compared to his own father Caleb would have said James was at least ten years older, even though he knew they were the same age.

"Roger did not let you in," James said but it was not a question.

"No, your daughter did," Caleb said, "But she had to go get ready for supper. It sounded like there were guests coming."

"Probably the Lamberts," James muttered under his breath before turning back to Caleb, "How are your parents doing?"

"Well," Caleb answered, "They keep busy and entertain regularly, though they have missed your visits."

"I miss being able to go and visit friends," James said, "But every time I think I am strong enough I get another bout of whatever this is. When those happen it is like any healing is gone."

"I think you are being poisoned," Caleb said.

"What makes you think that?" James gave Caleb his full attention.

"I was talking to Leah," Caleb answered, "She told me what was going on."

"You mean like my wife using this illness to get her way?" James asked.

"Six months ago there was a rumour that Lady Winsand was looking for a man to marry Leah," Caleb said, "Suitability would be judged on how much money they were willing to pay to court her. My parents thought the rumour was foolishness you would put a stop to anything she was doing. If I am not mistaken that was about the time you started to get sick."

James took on a thoughtful expression. He did not say anything for several minutes and Caleb did not interrupt his thoughts. There were footsteps out on the stairs. They hesitated on the landing before continuing down the stairs. Then the footsteps were quiet and several voices were louder. The voices lasted for only about two minutes before they went farther away and were harder to hear. Caleb could not tell who was who because he did not recognize most of the voices, but he could tell Leah never spoke.

"Yes, it was about six months ago that I started to get sick," James's voice was quiet, "And she was always trying to increase our fortune even though we have more than enough to buy anything she needs or wants and still maintain the proper lifestyle. It is like an incurable disease. What happened with the rumour?"

"Three months ago someone told me Lady Lambert's bid was highest," Caleb answered, "And she paid double if Randall did not have to worry about courting Leah. Instead they were supposed to go straight to being engaged."

"Lady Winsand could not agree to terms like that," James said, "Unless I did not survive to see the wedding I would demand to know my daughter made the choice of her own free will."

"Which is probably why there has not been a wedding yet," Caleb said, "Randall is supposed to propose to Leah and thus make it her choice to marry him."

"Except Leah told me Lady Winsand was making her say yes and not giving her a choice," James said, "That destroys the illusion."

"I am willing to place money that someone else had to talk Leah into telling you," Caleb said, "Leah is so worried about your health she does not want to say anything to cause you to worry or get worse. She would quietly marry

Randall if she thought doing anything else would cause you any harm."

"She has been looking too old for her years," James said, "I thought it was just worry over me until she told me Lady Winsand was going to make her marry the idiot. Though why would it take three months for all this to happen."

"Because Randall Lambert has his head stuck in a book big enough to crush it," Caleb answered, "His mother has probably been waiting for her baby to do things on his own. Now I suspect she has given him a direct order to propose to Leah."

"That is why the Lamberts have been over so often," James said, "I thought she was just having them over to annoy me. So, Lady Winsand poisons me, auctions off my daughter for ill purposes, the winner is Lady Lambert and her baby son, who wishes to skip courting Leah and move right on to marrying her, and now it is very likely Randall will propose tonight."

"That would be the sum of things," Caleb said.

"You think she keeps the bottle of poison on her?" James asked.

"Probably," Caleb answered, "She has to have near enough so she can use it when an opportunity presents itself."

"Then if she does not I am going look like a fool and probably be dead if this does not work," James said as he moved the blanket, "Can you get me a pair of pants? They are in the wardrobe."

Caleb got up and went over to the wardrobe. He found a pair of pants as well as a shirt. Picking them out he brought them back to James, who had put his feet over the side of the bed. James accepted the pants and pulled them up under the nightshirt. He got to his feet to finish getting them on. Caleb grabbed James's arm to keep him on his feet.

"Too much time in bed," James said, "Not enough

exercise."

"Are you going to be strong enough to do this?" Caleb asked.

"For my daughter, I am strong enough to move the world," James answered as he straightened up. It took him another moment to steady himself. James pulled the nightshirt over his head before accepting the shirt that Caleb was holding.

"Do you need my help?" Caleb asked.

"Only to get down the stairs," James answered, "After that it would be much better if I do it on my own."

"Okay," Caleb said. James pulled the shirt on and tucked it in to his pants. Taking careful steps he went over to the wardrobe and found his comb on the top shelf. He used it on his hair before putting it back.

"Let's go face Lady Winsand and her accomplices," James said. He started for the door and Caleb followed him. James's steps got stronger as he went, but he would need to rest in a short amount of time. Caleb did help him down the stairs. At the bottom James headed to the dining room on his own while Caleb slipped out the front door.

Colleen Price

## CHAPTER TEN

"There you are," Melissa broke into Leah's thoughts, "You are ready for supper. Just in time too."

"Thank you," Leah said. Melissa nodded to herself before leaving the room. Leah looked in the mirror. The face that looked back had an air of resignation to it. This was most likely the night Randall would propose and with her mother there she could not say no.

Leah took a deep breath and let it out slowly. She stood up and went to the door. Leah hesitated briefly before opening the door and stepping into the hallway. Leah could see her mother going down the stairs. Leah went to the stairwell and started down. Reaching the landing for the second floor she paused. But as much as she wanted to Leah could not stop at the second floor to visit her father. He might be able to give her the strength to get through the evening, but Leah was scared Caleb would still be there. And then she would be fighting with herself about wanting to be in his arms rather than dealing with the Lamberts.

There was a knock on the front door as Lady Winsand reached the bottom of the stairs. With regret Leah started down the final flight of stairs. Her mother opened the door and Lady Lambert stepped inside. Lord Lambert and Randall followed her.

"Good evening," Lady Winsand said.

"Good evening," Lady Lambert said. Roger appeared and took the Lamberts' coats.

"How was your day?" Lady Winsand asked Lady Lambert as she led the party into the drawing room. Having reached the bottom of the stairs Leah followed behind Randall. In the drawing room, Leah managed to sit down in one of the chairs before anyone could suggest she sit with Randall on the settee, so Lord Lambert ended up on the settee instead. Lady Winsand and Lady Lambert once again dominated the discussion. Lord Lambert sat there and listened, though Leah was not sure how he could do so without getting bored. Randall seemed to be in his own world as he stared at a painting hanging on the wall opposite him. Leah sat there and pretended to listen to the conversation while she waited for supper to be ready, but her mind kept wandering off to other things.

What was Caleb saying to her father? Would it make a difference to anything? Was it just wishful thinking that anything would change the current outcome of things? Was her time with Caleb flights of fancy before her forceful confinement as Randall's wife? There were worst things in the world than being married to Randall, or she was pretty sure there had to be worse things worse. Not that Randall would even really notice he was married so much as Leah would be under Lady Lambert's thumb instead of her mother's. Being under control of neither was good, but at least her father could protect her from some of the plan which came to her mother's mind. The thought of Lady Winsand and Lady Lambert dressed in black witches costumes came to Leah's mind. This time Randall was not the honour bound knight without the ability to interrupt conversations. Instead he took on a more gruesome quality, almost like what her father had described a zombie would be. Her imagination could see him with body pieces falling off, no original thoughts and controlled by someone else.

"Supper is ready," Roger's voice interrupted Leah's day dreaming. Lady Winsand and Lady Lambert stood up and headed for the dining room without stopping their conversation. Leah got to her feet and followed them.

Once again Randall helped Leah with her chair before taking the one beside her. He did not seem to have any fears of having something spilled on him. Mother must have really convinced them the whole thing had been an accident, Leah thought, either that or Randall's memory was very short.

The salad course was already set out. Lady Winsand and Lady Lambert talked all the way through it. When they were finished Roger took the salad plates away and brought out the soup tureen. He set it on the sideboard along with the bowls. After dishing up a serving he set the bowl in front of the person, starting with Lord Lambert and ending with Leah. Then he took the soup tureen back to the kitchen.

Everyone was just starting their soup when Leah's father stepped into the doorway. James was dressed and looked thin, but was steady on his feet. He also looked angry.

"James, what are you doing up?" Lady Winsand asked, "You should be in bed."

"Silence," James's voice boomed without him yelling. Lady Winsand looked like there was more she wanted to say, but she did not speak.

"I want these people out of my house," James said pointing to the Lamberts, "Now."

"He must be having hallucinations," Lady Winsand said to Lord and Lady Lambert before standing to face James, "These are my guests."

"This is my house," James raised his voice, "And I want them to get the hell out. Roger!"

"Yes, sir," Roger said coming into the dining room.

"Get these people's coats for them," James instructed.

"Roger, James should be in bed," Lady Winsand said.

"Right away, sir," was Roger's response before he left the room.

"You cannot come down here and kick my guests out," Lady Winsand was trying to keep her rage under control. Lord and Lady Lambert looked stunned at this whole scene; even Randall was paying attention.

"I can and I have," James yelled back, "And if you do not like it you can go with them. I will not tolerate this kind of behaviour in my house."

"What kind of behaviour?" Lady Winsand demanded.

"Selling my child to the highest bidder," Father answered. Roger appeared with the Lamberts coats just as they were standing up. They barely took the time to put the coats on before following Roger out of the dining room.

"I am doing no such thing," Lady Winsand said. Her voice rose to a yell now that there was no audience to rein in her temper for.

"Then why are the Lamberts even here?" James asked, "You know how much I despise them and their idiot child. Leah is not interested in marrying the boy. I know because she told me you were making her do it."

Roger came back into the room but only stood there. Leah felt frozen to the spot.

"You are suffering from a mental break down," Lady Winsand said, "I have done nothing you claim. Lady Lambert is one of my friends. Because you despise her and her family, I can only have them over when you are sick."

"A sickness you caused," James said. He was starting to shake from tiredness.

"That is nonsense," Lady Winsand said, "I have not done anything you claim."

"Roger," James said.

"Yes, sir," Roger said.

"Take away Vivian's little bottle of poison and escort

her to her room," James said, "Make sure she is locked in and cannot get out."

"Yes, sir," Roger said. He went over and searched Lady Winsand. Lady Winsand did nothing to stop him. She just glared at James. Roger found and placed the bottle Leah had seen the other night on the table as well as her set of keys. Then he escorted her from the room. Once she was out of the room James made it to a chair before collapsing. Leah still sat there frozen unsure of what to do.

"I am sorry you had to see all that," James turned to Leah, "I did not think your mother would move so fast on some things."

"It is okay, Father," Leah said.

"Though now I understand your concern with getting married," Father said, "You will not marry Randall. I cannot believe Vivian would even think about doing any such thing. But it is over now."

Roger came back into the room. He set a bowl of soup in front of James before clearing the rest of the table. He left Leah's food as well the bottle of poison. Leah went back to eating. James still mumbled between bites of soup, but Leah was happy to see him back at the table.

When they were finished the soup Roger took away the bowls and brought out a plate of the main course for each of them. It was roast beef and boiled potatoes covered in gravy. James and Leah started to talk about his writing, which put James in a better mood. When Roger brought them dessert they were both laughing as if the last months had not happened.

After supper James said he had some things to do so Leah kissed him on the cheek and went upstairs. She stopped in the library for the book she had been reading before going to her room. Inside her room, Leah changed into her nightgown and prepared for bed before sitting on the window seat with the book. She opened the book and tried to read, but found her gaze going to the window.

Searching Leah found the lights she thought might belong to the Morley Estate. They looked so far away. Leah wondered what Caleb was doing. Was he wondering what happened over here? Did he just put it out of his mind after he left? Did he understand how her life had changed in just a few minutes and she now knew everything would be all right? Would he be there if she went out to the field tomorrow?

After a while Leah got tired. She left the book on the window seat and crawled into bed. As she closed her eyes Leah remembered how it felt to be in Caleb's arms. With that feeling she fell asleep.

Melissa slipped into the kitchen. No one was in there and everything had been put away for the night. It sounded like everyone was asleep already. That was fine with Melissa. She went through the kitchen and into the hallway. Melissa did not run into anyone so she continued up the stairs. The sound of voices coming from the library made her stop. It sounded like Lord Winsand and Roger. Melissa drifted closer to the doorway.

"I need you to keep an eye out for any actions the Lamberts might take," Lord Winsand said, "Lady Lambert is unlikely to just give up considering the money that must have already changed hands."

"I will," Roger said, "And I will tell the rest of the servants to do the same."

"Probably need more servants," Lord Winsand said, "Since Lady Winsand miserly nature has allowed the number of servants to drop so low."

"Would you like me to ask around the village to see if there is anyone who could be hired?" Roger asked.

"No," Lord Winsand answered, "We will have to do without more servants for a while. I cannot afford to hire someone whose loyalty is uncertain. I will not put my daughter at greater risk. But when you are in the village see who is looking for work. When this is all over we might hire some of them."

"Yes, sir," Roger said, "What is going to happen with Lady Winsand?"

"I do not know," Lord Winsand answered, "Right now her room is the best place to keep her. I will figure out what to do with her."

"Yes, sir," Roger said.

"Make sure to check on her hourly," Lord Winsand said.

"Yes, sir," Roger said. Melissa turned and went down the hallway to her room. She slipped inside and closed the door only a moment before she heard Roger in the hallway.

If Lady Winsand was locked in her room then something must have happened while Melissa was out in the garden with Haines. Whatever happened it sounded like changes would be made in the way the estate was managed. Melissa did not mind as long as it did not interfere with her visits in the garden with Haines.

Melissa felt exhausted as she slipped off her dress and climbed into her bed. Usually about this time she was sneaking off to the garden to meet Haines. Tonight they had been able to meet up while the Lamberts were over for supper. She was not sure where the people Haines worked for thought he was. Since he probably slept with the maids and possibly the housekeeper there, they probably thought he was off chasing one of their servants. Melissa did not care if Haines had other lovers as long as he was there for her.

Melissa let the memories of the afternoon and evening sweep through her mind as she drifted off to sleep.

CHAPTER ELEVEN



*August 4, 1865*

The next morning Leah dressed and was going downstairs for breakfast when there was a knock at the door. Leah stopped out of sight of the door. Roger came from the kitchen and opened the door but held it only partially open signalling that he would not admit the caller.

"Yes?" Roger asked.

"I am looking for Lady Winsand," Lady Lambert's voice responded. James came out of the drawing room. Roger turned to him.

"My wife is indisposed today," James said.

"And how long will she be indisposed?" Lady Lambert asked.

"That remains unknown," James answered, "I will mention that you stopped by looking for her once she is available."

"Please do," Lady Lambert's voice was cold. Roger closed the door. Leah went down the rest of the stairs.

"Good morning," James said.

"Good morning," Leah replied. A bubble of happiness filled her. Her father looked well, even if he was still thin and fragile.

"How did you sleep last night?" James asked as they went into the dining room.

"Well," Leah answered, "How are you feeling?"

"Much better than yesterday," James answered, "Now that I am not ingesting the poison I should be back to normal in the next week or two."

"That is good," Leah said. They sat down at the table. James's place had a plate of half eaten breakfast and there was a full plate of breakfast where Leah sat.

"What are your plans for today?" James asked.

"I am not quite sure yet," Leah answered, "I thought I might take a walk in the garden."

"I plan to sit and write, since I have enough ideas rolling around in my head for two books," James said. Leah smiled then started to eat breakfast.

After breakfast Leah went up to her room to get her hat and coat. Then she went down and waited for the carriage. She waited ten minutes before it pulled up to the steps. The door opened and Leah climbed inside. She sat down beside Hilary. The Kenley twins were on the other seat giggling over some piece of gossip they had just shared with Hilary. Hilary was looking at them like there were four heads instead of two.

"Good morning," Leah said.

"Finally a sane person," Hilary said, "These two keep finding stranger and stranger gossip." She waves at the two girls who giggle even louder.

"What is it this time?" Leah asked.

"Curt Erland," Margaret giggled with excitement.

"Has broken off his engagement," Meghan interrupted with the same breathless excitement.

"To Edwina," Margaret added.

"Because he says that he loves his horse more than he loves her," Hilary finished for them.

"Did the wedding invitation not arrive a few days ago?"

Leah asked.

"Apparently something happened," Hilary said, "Or people are making up gossip just to gossip." The giggling stopped.

"We do not do that," Margaret's voice had a wounded quality to it.

"We are just telling you what we heard," Meghan sounded insulted.

"What other gossip is there?" Leah asked.

"Well, there is still the rumour going that you are getting engaged to Randall," Margaret said.

"The Putnams are moving to town permanently," Meghan said, "Even selling their estate."

"Lady Julia is out one husband and one housekeeper," Margaret said, "Because the two of them ran off together."

"Her father is supposedly going to gather a hunting party and go after him," Meghan said.

"And then, of course, Curt Erland and his love for his horse," Margaret said.

"Is that it?" Leah asked.

"It is a slow gossip day," Hilary said. The carriage stopped in front of Mrs. Travers' house. Leah opened the door and the four girls got out. They went inside for lessons.


Caleb came down the stairs and went into the dining room. Breakfast was set out, but his parents were not there. Instead Percy was seated at the table eating from a full plate. Percy's light brown hair was in need of a comb and his cravat was in a knot that Caleb did not recognize. Percy's grey eyes had the usual laughter in them and the jam on his lips made his mouth look bigger than it was. Caleb sat down in his own seat.

"No breakfast at your house?" Caleb asked as he picked up his fork.

"Cook ran off with her lover," Percy answered, "Jack

has not been able to find a fitting replacement yet and his cooking is only edible to the pigs. After two days of it I figured I had to find someplace to eat with a real cook."

"That explains the plateful," Caleb said.

"I came around late yesterday afternoon, but I was told that you were not here," Percy said, "You were off riding. I know you like to go riding in the afternoons but that seemed late for even you."

"I stopped in to visit Lord Winsand," Caleb said, "He is a family friend and he has been ill."

"I heard he was sick," Percy said, "Does the doctor know what the cause is?"

"His wife," Caleb answered.

"I met Lady Winsand once, at a party Lord and Lady Whitelaw threw," Percy said, "And I would fully believe that she would make her husband ill. If I remember the party correctly she spent most of it on the arm of Lord Eglantine. I thought they might be lovers."

"They might have been," Caleb said, "He has enough money for her to be attracted to him."

"What happened to him?" Percy asked, "I have not seen or heard about him in a while and he was never one to stay out of the gossip this long."

"He moved to London to be closer to his bride," Caleb answered, "He had arranged himself a marriage to a sixteen-year-old girl with close ties to the throne and a more elegant title."

"To each his own," Percy said as he bit down on a sausage.

"Why were you looking for me?" Caleb asked, "I thought you were spending the day with Hilary."

"Her sister and brother-in-law showed up for supper and I had to make my excuses," Percy answered, "Jeffery is fine and I can stand him, but Alicia likes asking nosy questions about things that are none of her business. I came over here thinking I could get an invitation to supper, but you were not here. So, I had to go home and eat what Jack had boiled beyond recognition."

"Sorry, I barely made it home in time for supper," Caleb said.

"This breakfast more than makes up for it," Percy said before taking a large bite of egg. Caleb did not say anything as he ate his own meal.

"When I showed up John was not sure about letting me in since no one was awake," Percy said, "But in the end I talked him into letting me wait for you."

"Unless you eat all the food Father and Mother will not have a problem with you showing up," Caleb said, "Especially since they know that Hilary has lessons in the mornings."

"I do not spend all my time with Hilary," Percy said.

"Just every afternoon and evening since her parents left for London," Caleb said.

"You will understand someday," Percy said, "When love hits you and you find yourself craving the woman's company. It's hard to be away from her."

"Or not," Caleb replied.

"Why would you not fall in love?" Percy asked, "Or is it more that you do not think you would act like a fool?"

"My father informed me yesterday that he has an arrangement for my marriage, but this was not the right time to discuss it," Caleb answered.

"No wonder you were gone most of the afternoon," Percy said, "I would be angry too if my father dropped that kind of news on me, especially if he will not explain. Did he give a reason why he does not want to talk about it?"

"There are too many ifs," Caleb answered.

"Then I would not worry about it," Percy said, "That usually means if you find someone your father's deal is off."

"With my father it is more likely the deal would be off if she finds someone else than if I do," Caleb said, "But until

I know more it is all in limbo."

"You will get passed it," Percy said.

Lord and Lady Morley entered the dining room. They sat down. Lord Morley opened the book he had brought with him and started to read.

"Good morning, Percy," Lady Morley said.

"Good morning, Lady Morley," Percy said.

"What are you doing here so early in the morning?" Lady Morley asked.

"Visiting," Percy answered.

"Well, it is good to see you," Lady Morley said, "Especially since you have not been around much."

"I think what my mother is going to start hinting at is whether you are going to ask for Hilary's hand and when," Caleb said.

"Caleb, I was not going to ask," Lady Morley said.

"I cannot ask her father anything," Percy said, "Lord Whitelaw will not be back until Sunday. Then he will be busy."

"Why have you not asked before this?" Lady Morley asked.

"Because he was always busy when I tried to make time to talk to him," Percy answered, "Hilary figures he will make time next week."

"I hope so," Lady Morley said, "You and Hilary look wonderful together."

There was a knock on the door. After a moment they heard John answer the door, but could not hear who it was. Then the door closed and John came into the dining room. He was carrying an envelope. He set it down beside Caleb's plate before leaving the room to go back to his duties. Lady Morley watched Caleb, but he just left the envelope where it was. The conversation continued, but Lady Morley glanced occasionally at the envelope. Caleb ignored it.

When everyone was finished eating Lord and Lady Morley left. John came in and cleared away the dishes.

Caleb and Percy remained seated.

"You did not tell her," Percy said.

"I do not tell her much," Caleb replied, "Especially if she is digging for it."

"What is that?" Percy asked pointing to the envelope.

"I do not know," Caleb answered as he picked it up. He opened it and read the letter inside before putting it back.

"Well?" Percy asked.

"A thank you note from Lord Winsand for visiting yesterday," Caleb answered, "I guess he does not get many people visiting him these days."

"Let us go," Percy said as he got to his feet.

"Where do you want to go?" Caleb asked.

"Out of here," Percy answered. Caleb got to his feet. He followed Percy out of the dining room after putting the letter in his pocket. They headed out to the stables.

When they arrived they found Haines already mucking out stalls.

"Already at work?" Percy asked Haines.

"I've got to work some time," Haines stopped to look at Percy and Caleb, "Don't get paid to lollygag."

"Mother gave him an ultimatum last night," Caleb said, "She wants the stable as clean as possible before the end of today. And if he does not get it done he is not allowed in the manor for a month."

"I don't want to be begging at the kitchen door for scraps," Haines said, "Done it enough in my life to want to start doing that again." Haines started working again.

"Anything we could do to help?" Percy asked.

"Take the horses outside to the paddock," Haines said, "Let them run out there and not mess up everything I've just cleaned."

"Okay," Percy said. He and Caleb started taking the horses out of their stalls. The paddock was right next to the stable so it did not take much time before all the horses, with the exception of Warrior, were running around the paddock enjoying the morning. Percy had tried to open Warrior's stall but quickly backed off when it looked like Warrior was going to attack him.

"What is with your horse?" Percy asked Caleb.

"I am not sure," Caleb answered. He went over to the stall. Warrior did not do anything.

"He didn't get his treat this morning," Haines said, "He's been impatient for it all morning. I wouldn't recommend trying to get him to go anywhere until he's had it."

"I forgot," Caleb said, "Too many things for one morning." Warrior snorted in disbelief.

"You are not the only important thing in my day," Caleb told Warrior. Warrior gave another snort to go along with the shake of his head.

"Fine, I will go find you a treat," Caleb said, "You better behave while I am gone." Warrior stood there as if he was waiting for Caleb to leave.

"That horse is spoiled," Haines said, "If I could have his life I would be set."

"There are some days we all would not mind having a horse's life," Caleb said.

"Haven't figured out your woman trouble?" Haines asked.

"No," Caleb answered.

"Well, there is always the third option I suggested," Haines said.

"I do not think even that one would work at the moment," Caleb said, "Due to other things."

"I tried," Haines shrugged and went back to mucking out stables. Caleb headed for the kitchen door with Percy following him.

"You were taking advice from Haines?" Percy asked, "I am almost insulted that you did not come to me first."

"I was angry and went to the stable to cool off," Caleb said, "I was telling Warrior my problem and Haines overheard. I did not ask him for advice he gave it to me.

And you were busy getting ready to go to Hilary's house for the afternoon."

"Well, I gave you advice today so I guess that will have to do," Percy said. Caleb stopped at the half door that led to the kitchen.

"What can I do for you?" the cook asked from where she was standing at the table working with dough.

"I need a carrot or apple for Warrior," Caleb answered.

"Annie, get Master Caleb an apple from the breakfast basket," the cook told her assistant. Her assistant wiped off her hands and left the kitchen. She came back a moment later with an apple. She handed to Caleb.

"Thank you," Caleb said. Annie went back to her sink full of water and dishes.

"You are welcome," the cook said. Caleb and Percy headed back to the stable. Haines was not there when they arrived.

"I thought he needed to finish cleaning the stable," Percy said looking around as Caleb went to Warrior's stall.

"He is out in the rose patch," Caleb answered, "That is where he keeps his bottle. He will be back in a moment." Caleb held out the apple to Warrior. Warrior accepted the treat without biting Caleb's fingers. Caleb patted Warrior's neck. Warrior was busy chewing. Caleb led him out of the stall and out to the paddock. Warrior went quietly, but stood by the gate once it was closed as if he was waiting for Caleb to let him out.

Haines was coming back as Caleb turned from the paddock.

"He's nice and calm down now," Haines said as he passed Caleb.

"He will be better after we go riding this afternoon," Caleb said.

"Usually is," Haines replied. He went inside.

"Anything else we can do to help?" Percy asked as he and Caleb followed Haines into the stable.

"Having a problem at home or something?" Haines asked, "You two are usually helpful, but never this bored."

"We are looking for something to do," Percy answered, "And I cannot go see my fiancée until after her lessons end at noon."

"Only jobs I've got are dirty ones," Haines said, "But if you want them I can give them to you."

"We can do dirty jobs," Caleb answered, "As long as we get cleaned up before lunch."

"If Lady Morley comes out it and catches you looking it the help it ain't my fault," Haines said.

"She is busy with Father trying to figure out money stuff," Caleb replied.

Haines nodded before giving them the jobs.

# CHAPTER TWELVE

After lessons the girls head outside. Hilary's carriage was waiting behind the one which had brought Leah and Hilary. Hilary leads her towards it.

"Would you like to come for lunch?" Hilary asked Leah.

"Certainly," Leah answered. They went over and the driver opened the door for them. Leah and Hilary climbed in. Once inside the driver closed the door. They did not talk for the carriage ride to the Whitelaw's residence. When the carriage stopped they got out and went inside. Leah followed Hilary to the dining room, where lunch was set out. They sat down. Leah and Hilary ate without speaking for a few minutes.

"So, what happened with Randall?" Hilary asked breaking the silence between them.

"Father said I will not marry Randall," Leah answered.

"And?" Hilary asked.

"I told him it was Randall who Mother wanted me to marry," Leah answered, "He did not say anything at that time. Then the Lamberts came for supper. In the middle of the soup course father came downstairs and ordered the Lamberts to leave. And when they lingered he had Roger escort them out. After that Father told me I would not marry Randall."

"And your mother?" Hilary asked.

"Is locked in her room," Leah answered.

"She kept threatening to do that to you," Hilary said, "Now she gets to know how it feels. What is going to happen now?"

"I do not know," Leah answered, "But it is wonderful to have Father back in charge."

"So, that is it?" Hilary asked.

"Is what it?' Leah asked.

"Everything that is going on," Hilary said, "Your eyes suggest there is something else."

"I am just extremely happy that Father has taken back control over everything and I do not have to accept Randall's proposal," Leah answered.

"There is something else," Hilary said.

"I am not sure what you are seeing but I have told you everything that has been happening," Leah said.

"Okay," Hilary said. She did not seem to believe Leah, but she would leave it alone until Leah was ready to talk about it.

"How is Percival?" Leah asked.

"He has been over every day after lunch," Hilary answered, "And we talk over plans for the wedding."

"You two must be close to having it all planned out," Leah said.

"There is a lot to do when you are planning a wedding," Hilary said, "Besides if my parents were here he would not be allowed to come around so often. Since we sit in the drawing room and talk there is nothing my servants will do and Alicia and her husband are off with friends."

They talked about other subjects for the rest of lunch. After lunch Leah was taken home in the Whitelaw's carriage.

When Leah arrived back home it was quiet. There was

no one in the sitting room, so she went up the stairs. In the library Leah found her father was still working on his writing. She chose not to disturb him. Leah started toward her room, but saw Melissa waiting for her. Melissa had not seen Leah, but seemed to assume Leah would come up. Leah went back downstairs as quietly as she could. She went through the house and out the French doors. Since everyone was busy with other things Leah did not meet anyone on the way. Outside she walked across the lawn without worrying if anyone saw her. Leah headed into the hedge maze. She walked in and through it. The thought that Caleb might not be there kept her from running. If she was going to be disappointed Leah did not want to rush it. She walked passed each of the landmarks until she finally reached the door.

James put down his pen and stretched. He had been writing all morning and his muscles were screaming. They were not used to putting in that much work. He probably should be back in bed, but now that he had ideas for the story he might as well write them down while they were still fresh in his brain. James stood up and wandered over to the window. It looked like a beautiful day and maybe he should go out and sit in the sun for a while. James looked down on the lawn in time to see Leah go into the hedge maze. She is going for another walk in the garden, James thought with a smile. They have been good for her. I have not gone for a walk in the garden in years, James thought, it was so nice out there then. He remembered the flowers, the birds, and of course, the getting away. But back then he used to go through the door in the hedge maze and going walking in someone else's garden. Walking with Leanne had been the highlight of his day, something he would look forward to every time.

James wondered if Leah had found the centre of the hedge maze, or whether she was still searching for it. It was difficult to find unless you knew approximately where to look. James would not be surprised if she had found the door to the field, but doubted that she would have gone through it. There was not much out there but a fish pond anyway.

Leah stopped to listen, but she did not hear anything that sounded like a person was out there. Leah pushed the door open. Caleb was sitting there on his horse. Leah's heart pounded harder at the sight of him. She felt herself smile with relief and happiness to see him there. Caleb got down off his horse as Leah came towards him.

"I was hoping you would come out here," Caleb said, "Even though life is better for you."

"I had to come," Leah said as she stopped in front of him.

"Why?" Caleb asked.

"To thank you," Leah said, "For whatever you said to my father."

"You are welcome," Caleb's brown eyes met Leah's blue eyes. Something Leah could not identify passed between them. Leah pressed her lips to Caleb's lips. Instinct, not thought, brought Leah's arms around Caleb's neck. Caleb's arms wrapped around Leah's waist and pulled her close. She could feel her heart racing as her body molded into his. He smelled of horses and trees. It caused the butterflies in her stomach to speed up.

Nothing else existed in the world, except Caleb, to Leah. He was everything. He was the air she was breathing. He was the only solid object around and yet he was causing her to float. Her feet were no longer on the ground and her head was spinning off into space. Caleb deepened the kiss and Leah felt shockwaves go through her body as if explosions were going off in her head.

The sound of footsteps on gravel made Leah and Caleb jump apart. The ground was suddenly a solid force and the day was too bright. Leah turned to look through the doorway. One of the gardeners came into view. He picked up something from the path before looking up at them.

"Good day, Miss," the gardener said with a nod before disappearing around the corner again.

"I did not bring Jewel with me," Caleb said, "But would you like to go riding."

"Certainly," Leah answered. Caleb helped Leah up on his horse before climbing up behind her. Leah was very aware of how close they were as Caleb directed his horse towards the trees. Her mind battled between wanting him closer and knowing it was not appropriate.

"Did you stay for the argument?" Leah asked.

"No," Caleb answered, "I saw how angry your father was and thought it best to remove myself before the fireworks started. He thought it best as well."

"He kicked the Lamberts out and yelled at Mother before locking her in her room. He also took away her bottle of poison, so she cannot use it again," Leah said, "It is nice to see Father back on his feet and doing things. And Mother deserved it."

"It sounds like it," Caleb said.

"This was the worst I have ever seen her," Leah said, "And I hope I never have to see it again."

They reached the trees and Caleb picked a different path from the one they had taken yesterday.

"What is happening now?" Caleb asked, "With your father doing better and your mother locked away."

"I do not know," Leah answered, "I am just glad it is over."

Caleb was quiet and they rode without talking for a while.

"How do you know all these paths?" Leah asked as they came to a place where the path forked. Caleb directed his horse down the left one.

"I have been exploring these paths since my mother let

me ride alone," Caleb answered.

"How long has that been?" Leah asked.

"Since I was eight," Caleb answered, "So about eleven years. Being into horses my mother wanted me to ride and I took to it better than she thought I would."

"How does your father feel about that?" Leah asked.

"It means I am not underfoot," Caleb answered, "But it annoys him if I am not there when he wants me to be. But he only rides occasionally with my mother and when he goes hunting. Otherwise horses are just a way to get from one place to another for him."

"Someday I would like to have a horse of my own," Leah said.

"Why not ask your father for one?" Caleb asked.

"Because of the yelling match he had with Mother over getting me riding lessons," Leah answered, "Even then he only won the argument because someone else told Mother that it was proper for me to go to riding lessons. I did not want to cause them to have that kind of argument again."

"And now?" Caleb asked.

"I want to wait until Father is not as weak," Leah answered, "He has been known to do foolish things like going riding before his body is ready for it. And if I had a horse he would insist on accompanying me on his horse which is hard to handle."

"That would be a problem," Caleb said.

"Someday I will have my own horse," Leah said, "Just not right now."

Caleb did not respond and they continued without talking. They came to a place where the stream crossed the path. Caleb directed the horse off the path and down the stream. They went along it for a while. Another path crossed the stream and Caleb directed the horse out of the stream and along this path. Leah leaned against Caleb and just watched the trees go by. Leah was not sure how long it took for them to get out of the trees, but they came out into the field at the far end past where the path was to go to the Morley Estate.

Caleb directed the horse back down the field; finally stopping at the door in the hedge. Caleb got down and helped Leah down.

"Will you come riding with me tomorrow?" Caleb asked.

"Yes," Leah smiled at him.

"Then I will see you tomorrow," Caleb said. He leaned down and their lips touched. Leah felt the urge to wrap herself in Caleb's arms, but she refrained from doing any such thing as she was sure if she did she would never be able to let go. Leah went to the door and stepped on to the path before turning back. Caleb was still standing there. Leah waved before closing the door behind her and stood there. Leah's heart felt like it was singing and she wanted to dance all the way back to the manor. She stayed there for a minute trying to slow her racing pulse. It did not work so Leah just started back towards the manor.

Leah's father was sitting at the table on the patio. He had his writing materials in front of him as well as a glass of juice. There was another glass of juice sitting at the empty chair. Father looked up and smiled as Leah came towards him.

"Good afternoon," James said.

"Good afternoon," Leah replied.

"I thought I would spend some time enjoying the sunshine," James said, "Would you join me?"

"Certainly," Leah sat down in the empty chair.

"Excellent," James said.

"How far have you gotten in the story?" Leah asked.

"I have gotten a lot of writing done," James answered, "The princess has now met the prince."

"And will soon be living happily ever after?" Leah asked.

"There are still some bumps in the road before they will

get there," James said, "After all the witch is still out there, she can still cause trouble. The happily ever after does not happen until after the prince and the witch battle for the princess; which I should get to in the next few days.

"I cannot wait to read it," Leah said.

"There was something I wanted to talk to you about," James said putting his writing materials to one side. His tone did not sound too serious, but Leah felt dread grip her heart.

"Your eighteenth birthday is coming up soon," James said.

"Next month," Leah replied.

"Since your mother is indisposed, I think you should plan the party," James said.

"How big of a party?" Leah asked as she takes a sip of juice.

"Huge," James answered, "A party that people will be talking about for a long time."

"I will have to get the invitations out by next week," Leah said.

"Then you better hurry up and make a guest list," James said. Leah smiled before getting up and kissing her father on the cheek. She went inside and up to the library. Sitting down at the desk Leah found some blank pages and started planning the party.

"Supper is ready, Miss Winsand," Roger's voice surprised Leah. She looked up to see him in the doorway.

"Thank you," Leah said. She stood up and followed him downstairs. She went down to the dining room. Her father was already seated, though this time he did not have his writing with him.

"How is the party planning going?" James asked once Leah was seated.

"Well," Leah answered, "I have decided is should be a ball rather than just a party where people come and talk or come and eat.”

Roger brought in supper and set a dish in front of each of them before leaving the room.

“You want something fancy,” James said, “A masquerade ball?”

“No,” Leah answered, “Colourful dresses, music, dancing and lots of decorations.”

“That sounds like fun,” James said, “What colour are the decorations going to be?”

“I was thinking red and gold,” Leah said, “They would match the colours the ballroom is already. And I do not think the ballroom should be repainted just for this.”

“How about a guest list?” James asked.

“Every family who have a child about my age,” Leah answered, “With the exception being the Lamberts. That should fill the ballroom and everyone should have someone they can talk to and dance with.”

“I do not think the ballroom has seen that many people within my life time,” James said, “I cannot wait to see it. What shall my beautiful daughter be wearing?”

“I am not quite sure,” Leah answered, “I have written up a request for the groom to deliver to the dress shop the next time he goes to the village. Hopeful they will have some material that is suitable. I have also written up a rough draft of the invitation, but I will have to go over it again to make sure everything is correct. Then I will write those out.”

“Will there be a cake?” James asked.

“I had not thought about a cake,” Leah answered.

“Perhaps you can discuss what a cake could look like with the cook and then send a request to the bakery in the village,” James suggested. “It must be big enough for all the guests so it is best to have it done professionally.”

“I shall do that,” Leah said, “Then I will try to send that the same day as the message about the dress.”

They had finished eating and Roger came in to collect the dishes. Leah got up and went over to her father.

"Thank you," she kissed him on the cheek.

"You are welcome," James said.

Leah headed upstairs. She went into the library and wrote down a few notes on the papers. But rather than stay and continue to work on it she went to her room. Leah picked up the book she left on the window seat and started to read it.

When she was starting to feel tired Leah got ready for bed. Then she got into bed. But sleep was not immediate. Instead she ended up staring out the window at the full moon. I feel so light, Leah thought, like if I wanted to I could fly. The moon seems an easy reach from here. She could go there with Caleb and they could dance among the stars. Leah closed her eyes as she imagined them up there and contentment lulled her to sleep.

# CHAPTER THIRTEEN

*August 5, 1865*

"Miss Winsand," Melissa's voice called.

"Yes?" Leah's sleepy voice answered.

"Breakfast is served," Melissa said, "And if you do not hurry you will be late for your lessons."

Leah opened her eyes. The room was still dark. Clouds had come in overnight and the sky was grey. Leah got out of bed. Melissa helped her dress and then Leah went downstairs for breakfast. James was seated at the table, but he was already finished eating and instead was writing. The moment Leah sat down Roger brought her breakfast to her.

After she finished Leah went into the hallway to find Melissa was already waiting with her coat and hat. Leah put them on before opening the door. It was raining.

The carriage was coming down the drive. Leah waited inside until it stopped at the bottom of the steps then she made a dash for it. The carriage door opened as she reached it. Leah pulled it closed behind her as she got in. Hilary was the only one on the carriage today.

"The twins are off somewhere with their mother," Hilary said as the carriage started moving.

"So we will have to wait for more news," Leah said.

"I heard something," Hilary said.

"What?" Leah asked.

"Curt Erland and Edwina Lavern are still getting married," Hilary answered.

"Was the rumour wrong?" Leah asked.

"Apparently not," Hilary answered, "They had a big fight in front of all her parent's guests. Now their parents are demanding they get married anyway. Edwina is not happy about it, but Lord and Lady Lavern claim they have spent too much money on this wedding to call it off."

"I wonder what Edwina is going to do now," Leah said.

"If I were her parents I would have someone guarding her to make sure she does not run away," Hilary said, "Though with her parents it is likely they have hired someone to do that."

"Then any more developments in the story will be interesting," Leah said.

"I agree," Hilary said as the carriage stopped.

Hilary opened the door and Leah followed her down from the carriage. They made a dash through the rain to the door where the butler was holding open. The butler took their hats and coats before they headed for the room where Mrs. Tavers taught lessons.

The rain hit the window and streamed down the glass like tears. The dark clouds made it look like nature was mourning with Caleb, because he was not able to go riding. For the first time in his life Caleb found himself cursing the weather.

"I know you are an outdoors person, but your mood is gloomier than usual for a rainy day," Percy commented as he shuffled the deck of cards. Caleb turned from the library window and sat down in the chair across the table from his friend.

"I have never seen you this annoyed at rain," Percy dealt

out the cards.

"I have been feeling caged," Caleb said.

"Does this have something to do with your father telling you about the match he planned for you?" Percy asked.

"Probably," Caleb answered.

"Probably?" Percy asked, "You can barely concentrate on the game and you cannot sit still. What is the problem if not that?"

Caleb was quiet as they played a hand of gin. Percy won without Caleb answering him. Percy shuffles the cards while Caleb got up and wandered back over to the window. He stared out at the rain as if trying to make it stop and dry up.

"According to the rumours there is a girl in need of rescuing," Percy said, "We could help save someone else."

"Who needs help?" Caleb asked without turning around.

"Hilary's friend Leah Winsand," Percy answered, "Hilary has been telling me about Leah's problems. She could use our help."

"We cannot help there," Caleb said.

"Why not?" Percy asked.

"Because," Caleb answered, "We just cannot help the situation."

Percy was quiet for several minutes, but Caleb did not turn from the window. After a while, Caleb heard Percy deal out the hands for the next game. Only then did Caleb go back to the chair and sit down.

"If this match is causing you this many problems I am glad I got to pick who I am to marry," Percy said as he picked up his cards.

"I question whether you picked Hilary or whether Hilary picked you," Caleb said.

"Either way," Percy shrugged, "You should not waste energy worrying about it."

"That is only half the problem," Caleb said, "I would have rather my father had either told me about his deal before this or waited until he had absolutes."

"Okay," Percy collected the cards, "What are you not telling me?"

"I was supposed to go riding this afternoon," Caleb answered.

"You go riding every afternoon," Percy said, "What is different about today?"

"I was supposed to go riding this afternoon with Leah Winsand," Caleb answered. Percy was quiet as he looked over the cards in his hand.

"Your parents do not know," Percy said, "Lord Winsand probably does not know. Hilary certainly does not know, or she would have told me."

"No one knows," Caleb said, "Because my father has plans for me. We met and she needed some support with everything that was going on in her life. I thought I would listen and provide a shoulder to cry upon."

Percy nodded without comment.

"Then my father told me his plans," Caleb continued, "I did not want to add to her troubles by telling her that it was not a good idea to see each other, so I left things alone. Now her life is better and I cannot explain the situation to her."

"This is what I meant when I made that comment the other day about acting like a fool when you are in love," Percy said.

"I would not call this love," Caleb said.

"What would you call it?" Percy asked.

"Conflicted," Caleb answered.

"With the added fun of rain to spoil your plans, tortured might work as well," Percy said.

"And what would you suggest I do? Since you seem to think you have all the answers," Caleb asked.

"Ignore what your father said," Percy answered, "Love does not come around every day and you have never had an interest in any woman you have met so far. Now, you have an interest in a woman and you want to ignore it in favour of honouring your father's agreement, which may or may not ever happen. Of all the stupid things you could be torturing yourself with this seems the easiest to solve. You told me that if I truly loved Hilary I should not let anyone stand in the way of being with her. You need to eat some of your own words and apply them to this situation."

"An interest in a woman is not love," Caleb said, "I am not sure my feelings stretch all the way to love."

"Yet," Percy said, "Spend time with Leah. Maybe things will change again and she will need you. If you break it off now you will not be there when she needs you."

"You are appealing to that honour you just told me to ignore in favour of following your other advice," Caleb said.

"Is it working?" Percy asked.

"A little bit," Caleb said.

"Lady Winsand is still out there," Percy said, "Granted, she is not walking the streets, but that has never stopped people before. Lady Lambert is walking the streets and she likes to get what she paid for. Randall is out there too, which I count more of a threat because his mother is out there. Any of these people could change things for Leah."

"You make it sound like I should be hoping one of those people go after her," Caleb said.

"That is not necessary," Percy said, "But beware of the possibilities. And if something goes wrong you can go back to being the shoulder Leah can cry on."

"I will have to think on this further," Caleb said.

"As long as you can sit still for the afternoon," Percy said, "I spent the morning bored. I came over here to play cards with you."

"Why not go to the Whitelaw's Estate?" Caleb asked.

"Because Hilary is having a dress fitting," Percy answered, "And she told me I was not invited to see her dress before the party. That left me with coming over here."

"Fine," Caleb said. He gathered up the cards and shuffled them. They played several hands without talking.

"Do not tell anyone what I just told you," Caleb said after he won a hand.

"I will not tell anyone," Percy said.

"Not even Hilary," Caleb said.

"If Leah has not told Hilary then Hilary does not know," Percy answered.

"Thank you," Caleb said. They went back to the game as the rain continued to make noise as it hit the window.


Melissa pulled on her coat before leaving her room. She went down the stairs being careful to not meet anyone. She knew the cook would be in the kitchen at this time of the morning so she slipped out the front door. Then Melissa started around the house to the garden.

This rain was not good weather to be out in, but Haines said something about being out there just before noon. She was not sure whether he would come with the rain, but she was going to check anyway. It would not be the first time she made love in the rain.

The grass was wet and the soil underneath was soft, making things slippery. In the few spots where there was no grass it was muddy. Melissa tried to stay to where the grass was as much as possible. Only once she got to the back of the house did she reach the gravel path. Melissa went along this until it reached the lawn. She went across the grass to the gravel path that went into the hedge maze. The wind died down a bit in the hedges, but the rain continued. Melissa followed the twists and turns to the grass clearing.

Melissa reached the grass clearing to find that Haines was not there. She was not surprised by this since most people do not like to be out in the rain. However she was surprised to find a wax envelope on the ground in the middle of the clearing. She picked it up. The wax prevented the rain from getting inside. Melissa tucked the envelope into her coat pocket and left the clearing. She headed back to the manor.

Traveling back through the maze was easy. Across the lawn was not too bad. The path was good. But the grass and mud on the way back around the manor seemed to have gotten worse in such a short time. Melissa was trying to be careful about her footing. It was not like anyone was going to be looking for her any time soon, so there was no rush. Melissa was just about to the front of the manor when she slipped on something in the grass. She could not recover her balance causing her to fall on her backside into some mud.

Melissa slowly got to her feet. It was difficult with all the mud, but she managed without ending up back in it. Once she was on her feet, Melissa looked at the place where her foot slipped. There was something lying in the grass. Melissa reached down and picked it up. It looked like a broach. Melissa cleaned it off with her hand and let the rain falling clean off some of the rest of the dirt. Then Melissa studied the broach. It looked like the one Lady Lambert had been wearing the last time she had been at the manor. Melissa was sure Lady Lambert had not been around this side of the manor that night. She put the broach into her pocket and picked her footing around to the manor door. Before stepping on to the paving stones, Melissa tried to wipe off some of the mud. Some of it came off, but trying to get the rest was getting her dirtier than cleaner. Giving up Melissa stepped off the grass and headed for the door. She slipped inside. There was no one in sight. Melissa slipped off her shoes and was about to start up the stairs when Roger came out of the sitting room.

"Went for a walk?" Roger asked.

"A short one," Melissa answered. Roger shook his head before starting down the hallway.

"I found something," Melissa said. Roger turned back.

Melissa pulled the broach out of her pocket and offered it to Roger. Roger came back and accepted it. He looked it over.

"Lady Lambert's broach," Roger said.

"I found it in the grass around the side of the manor," Melissa said.

"Perhaps Lady Lambert is desperate enough to peak in windows," Roger said, "She was wearing it when she stopped by yesterday."

"How is Lady Winsand?" Melissa asked.

"The same as she has been since Lord Winsand had me lock her in her room," Roger said. Roger looked at the broach again. He shrugged and then turned to go back down the hallway. The broach slipped out of his hand and fell. It hit the table that was in the hallway before landing on the floor. Something clicked when it hit the table and when it hit the floor the front of the broach opened like a locket. Roger stopped and picked it up. There was enough space to hide something small in the broach, but it was empty.

"Perhaps I should check on Lady Winsand again," Roger said as he closed the broach and put it in his pocket. He went passed Melissa and up the stairs. Melissa followed him at a slower pace. When she reached the floor her room was on she headed there while Roger continued on up the stairs. In her room Melissa changed her clothes and redid her hair. When she was finished she took the wax envelope out of her coat. Opening it she pulled out the piece of paper that was inside. Melissa unfolded the piece of paper. On it were several pictures. Haines could not write, but he could draw. As she studied the pictures Melissa wondered why he had never tried to sell his drawings. From the drawings Melissa figured Haines was telling her that he would meet up with her again when the rain stopped, but he hoped she would send him a message in return.

Melissa was not sure what to write for a message so she

set the letter on the trunk with envelope. She left her room. Roger was coming down as she reached the stairs.

"Is she still there?" Melissa asked.

"Yes," Roger answered, "But I found this." Roger held up a vial that was small enough to fit into the broach. "Based on the smell I would say that it is poison. I just do not know how Lady Lambert got the broach to Lady Winsand."

"Maybe she threw it up to the window," Melissa suggested, "That is the side of the manor with Lady Winsand's window."

"Either way we will all need to be watchful for trouble from Lady Winsand and the Lamberts," Roger said. Melissa nodded before following Roger down the stairs.

# CHAPTER FOURTEEN

When lessons were over Leah followed the rest of the girls back to the door, where the butler was handing back coats and hats. Outside there were two carriages waiting and a third coming up the drive. Before Leah could start towards the first carriage, Hilary tugged on her sleeve and directed Leah to the second carriage.

It was only lightly raining so they did not have to rush from the shelter of the house to the carriage. The driver got down and opened the door for them. Hilary and Leah climbed in. The driver closed the door and a moment later the carriage started to move.

The carriage had not reached the road when the rain started coming down heavier. Leah wondered if Caleb would still want to ride in this weather. Would he wait outside the garden door for her or would he understand that she could not be there? With the weather people would notice if she disappeared and she could not claim that she wanted a walk in the garden. And if Melissa was upset about grass stains she would be even more upset about a rain soaked dress.

Hilary tapped Leah on the knee. Leah looked up at her.

"Where are your thoughts going?" Hilary asked.

"My father told me I had to plan the party for my eighteenth birthday since Mother is not available to do it," Leah answered, "I started yesterday and got a lot done, but there are a few things I still need to work out."

Hilary did not immediately respond, instead she studied Leah's face. Leah was not sure Hilary believed her thoughts had been on party planning, however Leah did not say anything more.

"Do you have a guest list yet?" Hilary asked after a few moments.

"Yes," Leah answered, "And the first draft of the invitation."

"Sounds like a very good start," Hilary said, "I remember when Alicia was planning her eighteenth birthday party. It took her two weeks to come up with a guest list and that was before she started making decisions on decorations or food."

"I have to get the invitations out next week if I want anyone to show up," Leah said, "And I have some ideas as to what I want, though I have never had to plan a whole party by myself."

"I know you will figure it all out," Hilary said, "Alicia's problem is that she is best at making decisions when she is only given one option."

"She planned her own wedding," Leah said.

"She asked to and Father and Mother let her. They had wanted three months between the announcement and the wedding," Hilary said, "It took six months. And the only reason it did not take her longer was Father told her that if it took any longer he would not pay for it. Alicia did not like that, but it succeeded at getting the wedding planned."

"Did he put a restriction on how long you can take to plan your wedding?" Leah asked.

"Not that he has told me," Hilary answered, "But for my birthday party Mother and I discussed it one afternoon.

Now the only thing I am waiting for is the party itself."

"Are you going to wait until after the party to start planning your wedding?" Leah asked.

"No, I have already started," Hilary answered, "Percival has been coming over in the afternoons for the last couple days to help me. His friend Caleb has been busy with other things or something. So he comes over and we go through what we want for a wedding. We should have most of the plans written out by the time Father and Mother return."

"I thought your mother wanted to help you plan it," Leah said.

"Not really," Hilary said, "She keeps saying that, but when it comes to the actual planning she is not helpful. That is why I have been planning it. When she gets back she will think it is wonderful and make a few suggestions. However, once I have the plans and am ready to start into the preparations she will be the person I need helping. If I wanted she would have the wedding done and running smoothly a week after the announcement of my engagement to Percival."

"That is fast," Leah said.

"But I do not want it to be that soon," Hilary said, "It feels wrong to rush a day as important as my wedding. So, Mother will have a couple months to do it all."

The carriage stopped. Leah looked out at the manor before turning back to Hilary.

"Would you like to come in for lunch or is Percival expecting you?" Leah asked.

"Percival is spending the day with Caleb," Hilary answered, "I can stay for lunch."

The driver had gotten down and opened the carriage door. Leah climbed down before dashing up the steps to where Roger was holding open the door. Hilary followed. Once they were inside Roger closed the door before taking hats and coats.

"Lunch will be served shortly," Roger said.

"Thank you," Leah replied. Then she and Hilary went into the drawing room. They each sat down in a chair.

"Your mother has redone this room since I was last here," Hilary commented as she looked at the paintings.

"She decided it did not fit with the current fashion trends," Leah said, "And that she would be embarrassed to have friends over with how it used to look. I liked how it was before she changed everything."

"As did I," Hilary said, "Maybe you can replace the paintings with the portraits that used to be there, unless your mother got rid of them."

"I believe they were just put into storage," Leah said, "I will have to ask Roger."

Leah's father came into the drawing room. He was dressed for a day of writing and Leah could see a few new ink spots on his shirt that matched the old ones. But his hair had been combed and he had put on shoes, so Leah was not worried about his shirt.

"If I had known that we had a guest I would have found better clothes," James said, "How are you today, Miss Whitelaw?"

"I am well," Hilary answered, "And I had not been planning on staying for lunch until Leah invited me."

"I have seen so few people lately that any guest is wonderful," James said.

Roger entered the room.

"Lunch is ready," Roger announced before leaving the room. Leah and Hilary stood up and followed James into the dining room.

They sat down at the three places that had been set. Once they were seated Roger brought the plates out.

"So, what is the news of the world?" James asked when Roger had left the room.

"Curt and Edwina had a fight at her parent's party," Hilary said, "He said he loved his horse more than he loved her. They decided they were not going get married, but

Edwina's parents will not allow them to do that. So the wedding is still on."

"Perhaps this fight will make their relationship stronger," James said, "Since I do not believe it was an arranged marriage."

"Maybe if they start talking to each other again," Hilary said, "At the moment they are keeping their distance from each other."

"The wedding is in a month, right?" James asked.

"Yes," Leah answered.

"Then there is plenty of time for them to work things out," James said, "What else is happening?"

"The Putnams sold their Estate and have permanently moved to London," Hilary said, "Though no one seems to know why."

"He invested in a bad enterprise last winter," James said, "He was hoping it would bring in the money necessary to support his wife's extravagant lifestyle. I am just surprised it has taken this long before they have had to move to London, unless he was selling off some of her jewelry to have money."

"I knew they threw some lavish parties, but I did not think they were having money problems," Hilary said.

"It is all about appearances," James said.

"Lady Julia knows about appearances," Hilary said, "She is keeping them up the best she can with her husband's attempt to destroy them."

"Lady Julia?" James asked.

"Julia Norward," Leah answered, "She used to be Julia Hadden. She married Lord Norward back in March."

"What did Dean Norward do?" James asked.

"He ran off with the housekeeper," Hilary answered, "Her father took a party of men and went after him. Apparently they found him because they returned and brought her jewelry back with them. But her husband did not return."

"Does anyone know what happened?" James asked.

"It sounds like Julia will remain Lady Norward," Hilary said, "But should Lord Norward return to claim anything she will become a widow."

"I am surprised Dean Norward would run off," James said, "His parents are both dead so it is his house. Why not just continue with the housekeeper on the side? Or has Julia moved back to her parent's house."

"Julia is pregnant," Hilary answered, "And is has to be Dean Norward's child; which means according to Norward tradition Julia has every right to keep the house not matter what he does."

"It is not a good thing when family tradition dictates the preservation of the line over the interests of its current members," James said, "Any other news that is interesting?"

"Not much else," Hilary answered.

"How are you and Percival doing?" James asked.

"Well," Hilary answered, "He finally asked Father for my hand, but Father and Mother want to wait to make the announcement. And all the arrangements for my party are on schedule."

"That sounds like things are going well," James said, "I am sure Leah has been keeping you informed on what is going on around here."

"Yes," Hilary said, "And it is good to see you as healthy as you are."

"Given time I will be back to my old self again," James said, "Until then I will take things a day at a time."

Roger came in and took away their empty plates.

"Thank you for lunch," Hilary said, "I have things at home I need to do."

"I hope we see you soon," James said. Hilary and Leah stood up and went out to the hallway. Roger retrieved Hilary's hat and coat for her.

"Good luck with your planning," Hilary said, "And see

you tomorrow."

"See you tomorrow," Leah said. Hilary stepped out the door and made a dash for the carriage that was still waiting by the front steps. The driver was waiting and opened the door for Hilary to climb inside. Then he closed the door and climbed up on to the driver's seat. The carriage started moving. Leah stood there and watched it go down the drive.

After it disappeared from sight Leah closed the door. She went back into the dining room where her father was still seated at the table.

"How was your morning?" James asked as Leah sat back down.

"Good," Leah answered, "How is your writing going?"

"The witch has kidnapped the princess and the prince has to find them," James answered, "I should be finished soon."

"Then I shall be able to read it," Leah said. Leah's father smiled at her.

"How is the party planning?" James asked.

"I have not gotten back to it since we talk about it last night," Leah answered.

"Today is the perfect day for party planning and writing," James said.

"It is," Leah looked out the window. The rain is still streaking down the glass.

"And I should get back to writing," James said as he stood up. He left the room. Leah remained where she was for several more minutes.

She seemed to snap out of her day dreaming and look around. She was alone. Leah got up and went up to the library. She sat down at the desk and pulled out her party planning notes. But rather than read them and read them over, Leah stared out the window. Is Caleb out there waiting for me? Leah wondered, or is he inside with Percival? The memory of yesterday's kiss warmed Leah's cheeks.

Leah got up and walked to the library window. Leah looked out, but she could not see anything on the field. Leah went back to the desk and picked up her notes. She took them into her room and set them down on the bed. Leah went over to the window. Looking out this window she could see the field, but could not tell if anyone was out there. She stepped up on the window seat and leaned against the window. The field appeared to be without people, but it was hard to tell through the rain. With a sigh, Leah stepped down off the window seat, but kept staring out the window.

"Sir," Roger's voice floated up the stairs.

"Yes, Roger," James's voice responded. It sounded like they were standing on the stairs.

"Lady Winsand declined lunch," Roger said, "She said she will not eat until you let her out."

"Then do not bother her at all for the next three days," James said, "Except to make sure she is not trying to escape."

"Yes, sir," Roger said. Then the only sounds were footsteps and the rain outside.

Leah picked up her notes and sat down at the window seat. Eventually her eyes focused on the pages and she made a couple notes. Then her eyes would drift back to the window and watch the rain for a few minutes. Very little planning was done for Leah sitting there all afternoon.

"Supper is ready," Roger's voice made Leah jump. She put down her notes and went downstairs. Her father was already seated at the table. He was busy writing. Roger brought in the plates and set them in front of Leah and James. Leah started to eat, but James continued to write.

Leah finished eating and sat there for several minutes, but her father was too deep in his story to notice her or the food.

"Father," Leah said. James looked up. He looked around

in surprise at his food and her empty plate.

"I got lost in the story," James said, "I am sorry."

"It is okay," Leah said, "And I would have left you alone, but you should eat something." James smiled at her before turning his attention to his plate. He ate a few bites then looked up at her.

"You did not have to stay here and watch me eat," James said, "I will get through this plateful before going back to writing."

"If you promise to eat I will not nag," Leah got up.

She went to the kitchen and talked about types of cakes with the cook. When she had enough idea of what she wanted Leah left the kitchen. On her way back upstairs to write in all down she stopped in the doorway to the dining room. Her father was back to writing, but his empty plate sat beside him. Leah headed upstairs. In her room she wrote down the cake information. Then she took her notes back to the library. There she sat down at the desk and started to write out the invitations to her party.

When Leah was through the list of names and everything was addressed she stopped for the night. She left everything where it was and went to her room. In her room Melissa helped Leah get ready for bed. Leah climbed into bed and Melissa blew out the lamp on her way out of the room. Leah stared out the window. Even through the dark Leah could tell that it was still raining. I am happy with my party planning, Leah thought, but I wish I had been able to go riding with Caleb.

# CHAPTER FIFTEEN

*August 6, 1865*

Leah woke up to the sound of someone opening her door. She opened her eyes and looked over. It was just Melissa coming in. She left a moment later closing the door behind her. Leah sat up and stretched. It was still dark outside. Leah got out of bed and went over to the window. It was morning, but rain clouds were covering the sun and making the world look dreary. I guess I will not be going out to see if Caleb is there to go riding, Leah thought. I do not really know why but I really want to go out and see him this afternoon. Everything is going fine here and yet I still want to run to the field to spend time with Caleb. It does not make sense.

Sighing, Leah turned away from the window. She went over and lit the lamp for some light. Using that light Leah started getting into the dress Melissa had put out for her. As she finished getting dressed Melissa came back into the room to help Leah put her hair up.

When Melissa was finished she left the room. Leah sat there on the stool in front of the mirror and stared at her reflection. She had never really studied the face in the mirror, just used it to make sure she looked fine before going off. But she could tell that there were some differences. Her face was a little more tanned than it had been a week ago. Probably more than what was fashionable, but she did not mind the way she got it. Her brown hair looked the same as it always had. She was on the skinny side of her usual weight, which was why Roger had been getting on her case for the last couple weeks to eat regular meals.

But the main difference Leah could really see was her eyes. They were holding back a smile she had never noticed before. Perhaps it had not been there before. It looked like they knew something the rest of Leah had not figured out yet. But they were not sharing the reasons for it.

Leah heard someone coming up the stairs. They went passed the floor where Leah's room was and continued up the stairs. Leah figured it was just Roger checking on her mother.

Leah stood up and left her room. She glanced up the stairs and saw it was Roger headed for her mother's room. Leah went downstairs to the dining room. Two places were set, but Leah's father was not there. Leah sat down in her place and waited.

Several minutes later Roger came into the dining room carrying a pitcher of juice.

"Where is my father?" Leah asked Roger as he filled her glass.

"He is in the library writing. He said he would be down in a few minutes," Roger answered as he filled James's glass. Leah nodded. Roger left the room. Leah took a sip of juice as she waited for her father.

Ten minutes later James came into the dining room. He was walking slowly and his face was white. Leah could tell he was sick again. With her mother locked away and none of the servants likely to hurt her father, Leah was trying to figure out if he had been poisoned again. Fear wrapped around Leah's chest and held her down.

"Father, are you all right?" Leah asked.

"I did not sleep well," James answered, "I will be fine. Do not fret about me." James pulled out his chair and lowered himself down to sit on it. He missed the chair and collapsed on the floor.

"Father!" Leah knocked over her own chair as she stood up. She shoved the chair out of the way as she hurried around the table to him. James was sitting on the floor. His skin had gone a greyish colour.

"Father?" Leah asked as she knelt down beside him.

"I am fine," James tried to wave her away, but he had trouble lifting his hand. He was sweating from the effort of sitting up.

"Lie down," Leah said, "I will get Roger to help you back to your room."

"I will be fine," James's words sounded weak as he obeyed his daughter's instructions. Once he was lying down and did not look like he was going to try to get up, Leah got to her feet and left the dining room. She ran once she was in the hallway. In the kitchen Roger was standing and waiting while the cook was putting the plates together. Roger looked up when he saw Leah in the doorway.

"Miss Winsand?" Roger asked.

"Father collapsed," Leah said, "He needs to be taken up to bed."

"I will get some help," Roger said as he started toward the kitchen door.

"And send for the doctor," Leah said.

"Yes, Miss Winsand," Roger said when he had stopped at the door and looked back at her. Then he opened the door and stepped outside. The cook had stopped what she was doing and rinsed off her hands, but Leah did not wait around to see what she was going to do. Leah ran back to the dining room.

Her father was still lying on the floor, but his eyes were

closed. Leah knelt down beside him. She took his hand in hers. He did not open his eyes so Leah figured he must have been unconscious. Leah griped his hand hoping to somehow keep him from leaving her even though he did not grip hers in return.

A moment later the cook came into the dining room. She saw where Leah was and went over. She had a blanket with her. Leah let go of her father's hand to help the cook wrap him in the blanket. When they were finished Leah took his hand again.

"Roger sent the groom for the doctor,' the cook said, "And he is getting one of the gardeners to help him move Lord Winsand."

Leah nodded, but did not say anything.

"He will be all right," the cook patted Leah's shoulder.

"Thank you," Leah said. She held the tears back as she studied her father's face. If she could not hear a slight rattle when he breathed, Leah might have thought he was dead. She sent silent prayers that he would live.

Leah did not know what she would do without him. She did not know what would happen if he died. The thought came that her mother would be let out to run the household again, which would mean Leah would have to marry Randall. Leah pushed the thought aside. Whatever happens, Leah would not let her mother take over her life again. She would figure something out. Though she did not know what she would do, Leah hoped she would not have to do anything at all.

Melissa had spent half the night on the picture she had drawn for Haines. She was not a very good artist, but she managed to draw one picture where you could tell what the picture was supposed to be. Then she had put it in the wax envelope and left it while she tended to Leah. When she was finished Melissa had taken the envelope and her coat and gone to the kitchen. The cook and the cook's helper were busy. They barely noticed Melissa as she put on the coat and went out the kitchen door. Now she was on her way down the path in the hedge maze. It was only lightly raining down so it made things easier for walking.

Melissa had seen one of the gardeners already and figured the other was around somewhere. But she was not worried about them. They had not bothered to speak to her about her presence in the hedge. Melissa found the clearing. It looked like the gardeners had already done their work in this part of the garden, which was good for Melissa as she did not want one of the gardeners taking the envelope. She took out the envelope and placed it in the exact spot she had found it.

Melissa left the clearing and was starting back to the house when she heard a yell. It was coming from the part of the path going back to the manor. Melissa sped up to see what was happening. She reached a corner just before where she had seen the gardener. Roger's voice came from the other side of the hedge.

"I need your help," Roger sounded out of breath.

"What happened?" the gardener asked. There was a clink. Melissa figured he must have set down his pruners.

"Lord Winsand collapsed and I need help getting him back to his bed," Roger answered.

"What are we waiting for then?" the gardener asked. Melissa heard two pairs of feet head toward the manor. She followed at a distance.

"I thought Lord Winsand was getting better," the gardener said.

"He was," Roger replied, "And hopefully he will again."

The men did not speak again as Melissa followed them the rest of the way to the manor. Once they were out of the maze she waited for them to get to the kitchen door before heading across the lawn. Inside Melissa found the kitchen empty. She slipped out into the hallway and up to her room to get rid of her coat. It was going to be a long day.

# CHAPTER SIXTEEN

To Leah it took a long time for Roger to come back with one of the gardeners. When they arrived, Leah and the cook moved out of the way for them to get to James. They carefully lifted James and carried him out of the room. Leah followed as they carried James to his room.

Once James was set on the bed the gardener left while Roger tucked James into the bed. Leah sat down in the chair and took her father's hand again.

When Roger was done he left the room.

"Do not leave me," Leah whispered, "I still need you. Please, Father." There was no response, but Leah could tell her father was still breathing. Leah sat there holding his hand and watching him breathe.

Melissa stopped in the doorway of James's room and knocked on the door.

"Yes?" Leah tried to keep the unshed tears out of her voice.

"The carriage to take you to lessons will be here soon," Melissa said.

"I will not be going today," Leah answered.

"Miss Winsand," Melissa said, "Your father would want

you to go."

"I will not go anywhere until I have spoken with the doctor," Leah said, "So I will not be going to lessons today."

"Yes, Miss. Winsand," Melissa said before leaving.

A while later Roger came into the room carrying a tray, which had a mug and a plate of bread and cheese on it. He set the tray on the table beside the bed. Roger handed Leah the plate. She let go of her father's hand to accept it. While Leah ate Roger tried to get James to drink some broth from the mug.

When Leah was finished and Roger had given up Leah stepped out of the room and into the hallway so Roger could clean her father up. She went and sat on the bottom steps which went to the next floor. Leah wrapped her arms around her knees and tried not to cry.

Why was this happening? Leah wondered, he has been poisoned again, but Mother is locked away so who would have done it. Father never hurt anyone, why would anyone want to hurt him? It made no sense.

Roger came out of James's room and headed down the stairs carrying the tray and the clothes James had been wearing. Leah did not move. She thought she had heard horses outside.

Roger reached the bottom of the stairs when there was a knock at the door. Leah heard him put the tray down before opening the door.

"Yes?" Roger asked.

"I need to speak with Lady Winsand," Lady Lambert's voice was firm and demanding.

"Lady Winsand is indisposed," Roger answered, "I can pass the message along that you stopped by looking for her."

"It is extremely important I speak with her," Lady Lambert said.

"I shall pass that along," Roger replied in a tone that

sounded as if it was the end of the conversation as far as he was concerned.

"May I speak with Leah?" Lady Lambert's voice was still firm, but had sped up as if she was trying to stop Roger from closing the door in her face.

"She is at lessons," Roger answered, "And will not be home until just before lunch. But I will pass along the message that you wanted to talk to her." The door closed firmly, but it was not slammed. Leah held her breath, scared Lady Lambert might knock again. It was quiet for several minutes before Leah heard Roger pick up the tray and head towards the kitchen.

Leah stood up and went down the hall to her father's room. James lay on the bed. Nothing had changed with his condition. Leah sat down in the chair and took his hand again. While she sat there she watched him and prayed he would survive this.

Leah heard the front door open and close then footsteps coming up the stairs. The footsteps sounded like Roger and the doctor. They came down the hallway until Leah saw them enter the room.

"Hello," the doctor nodded to Leah as he set his bag down on the table beside the bed.

"Hello," Leah replied. She stood up and left the room so the doctor could do his examination. She went back to sitting on the stairs.

Ten minutes went by before the doctor stepped out of the room with Roger following him.

"It was another attack," the doctor told Leah, "Each one is getting progressively worse. At this rate the next one could kill him. There is nothing I can do for him."

"Thank you for coming, Dr. Radburne," Leah said. The doctor nodded before putting his hat on and following Roger down to the door. Leah did not move.

After letting the doctor out, Roger came back upstairs.

"What happened to Mother's bottle of poison?" Leah asked.

"Your father threw it into the fire place," Roger answered.

"Did Father eat or drink anything that no one else did?" Leah asked.

"He got up and wrote some more on his book this morning," Roger said, "And he asked for a cup of cider. The cook's helper prepared it for him and I delivered it. However, both the cook and her helper had to leave the kitchen for a few minutes this morning when a delivery arrived. I was out there as well."

"What happened to the rest of the cider?" Leah asked.

"The cook poured it out after your father collapsed," Roger answered, "She told me no one else drank any of it."

"Good," Leah stood up. Roger went down the stairs while Leah headed down the hallway. In her father's room she sat down in the chair beside the bed. She watched him sleep.

Leah remembered the time when she had been very sick. Her father had sat by her bedside and told her a story. The story had ended up as his second book. Leah smiled at the memory. The story had made her feel better.

Leah watched her father for several more minutes. She felt nervous about telling her father a story, but she decided to give it a try. Maybe it would help him come back to her.

"Once upon a time there was a girl," Leah told her father, "The girl had a father and a mother and lived in a large home. She was surrounded by love all of her live and her father called her his greatest joy. And the girl was happy for many, many years. One day when the girl was at the edge of womanhood, her father, who was healthy man, collapsed. Her father was placed in bed and the doctor was called. The doctor could not figure out what was wrong with the father. Her father started to get better as he was left to rest, but then he had another attack which once again caused him to become sick. This cycle continued for months. And the girl sat and watched her father waste away.

"Now this girl's mother was a horrible witch and unknown to everyone else in the household had brewed the poison in her room. After so many years of being married, she had decided to get rid of her husband, but believed it would look suspicious if he collapsed one day and died. So, she bided her time and only used a small amount of poison in the cups of cider the servants gave him to help him feel better knowing eventually he would die from it. And then she would be rid of him. She could have the title and the wealth to do with as she pleased. To keep the girl from figuring out what was going on the witch promised the girl in marriage to a troll."

Leah stopped. She thought she saw her father's lips twitch into a smile, but there was no further movement.

"This troll was large and ugly with breath that smelled of onions," Leah continued to tell the story, "The girl was horrified but could not find any way out of the marriage. However, the witch would not allow the troll to marry the girl until he paid the agreed upon price. The troll had the gold, but he could only get at it on the night of the full moon. Since that was weeks away the girl was kept busy by the witch with manual labour.

"One day, while the girl was bathing in the stream, a prince stumbled upon her. The girl ran from the prince in embarrassment. But the next day when the girl went to get water he was there. She tried to run away again, but he convinced her he meant no harm. So they sat by the stream and talked. And as they talked the girl found herself falling in love with the prince. The girl had to get back before the witch noticed she was gone. The next day the girl made up an excuse to go down to the stream. The prince was there waiting for her. Again they talked until she had to go back to the house. The girl returned to the river every day in hope he would be there. The prince must have felt something as well because when the girl went to the river he was there.

"One day the girl was late, so the prince went in search of her. Going through the trees he reached a large house. He was about to enter the house when two white tigers came around the corner and attacked him. The prince subdued them before going into the house. He had closed the door behind him so if the tigers got free they could not come after him. The door closed with a click. The noise woke something that was sleeping in the shadows of the room. Whatever it was moved from a prone position and stretched. Only when it yawned and a bit of flame came out of its mouth did the prince see that it was a young red dragon. Red dragons were known to be dangerous and not very intelligent. The dragon realized the prince was there and that he was an intruder. The prince pulled out his sword and battled the dragon. The prince received a few scratches and scrapes before managing to run his sword through the dragon. He found his way out of the room and into a torch lit hallway. Since the girl's father had been sick the witch had made herself a more comfortable home. The hallway twisted and turned with doors going off at regular intervals, leaving the prince with the feeling that the house was bigger inside than outside. The Prince headed down the hallway stopping to check each room. He fought a variety of monsters the witch had taken in as pets. Each time did not seem to bring him closer to finding the girl.

"There was lots of hallway left to go but the prince was getting tired. He decided to just try one more door before giving up. The prince opened the door and found the girl in the drawing room being forced to sit by the smelly troll while the witch talked and cackled. Without thinking about it the prince rushed in and slayed the troll before going after the witch. She was too fast for him and ran from the drawing room. With the girl's help the prince managed to lock the witch in the tower.

"Then the prince was going to take the girl back to his castle to marry her, but she refused to go because she would not leave her father to die."

"Miss Winsand," Roger knocked lightly on the door. Leah looked up at him. "Supper is ready."

Leah looked back at her father. His breathing was better and his colour was returning, but she still did not want to leave his side.

"His colour is coming back," Roger said, "He has lived through it. You will not help him in any way by not coming for supper. Come down stairs and eat."

"Very well," Leah said. She stood up and left the room. She felt exhausted as she followed Roger down the stairs. She went into the dining room while he continued on to the kitchen. The emotions of the day were taking their toll as she sat down in the only chair with a plate in front of it. The food was already there, but none of it looked appetizing to Leah. After several moments of looking at it she started to eat.

Leah ate half of the food on the plate, knowing if she did not at least eat that much Roger would start to stand over her to make sure she ate more. Afterward Leah left the dining room and headed back upstairs. She stopped in the library and picked out one of the books of fairy tales her father used to read to her. Then she went back to the chair at her father's bedside. She sat there and read the stories out loud to her father. If Roger had not come in and told her to go to bed Leah probably would have sat there all night.

# CHAPTER SEVENTEEN



*August 7, 1865*

Melissa rolled on to her side. Despite feeling exhausted she could not fall back asleep. She closed her eyes again and tried to relax. It probably was not even dawn. Leah would not need her for a couple hours. And Melissa could not get on with her chores until Leah was finished getting dressed and had moved on to other things for the day, which was probably going to be sitting by Lord Winsand's bedside. Melissa could not blame Leah for doing that.

Finding sleep was not coming Melissa opened her eyes again. The room was dark. She reached over and lit the candle in the holder in the wall. The light showed the bare and small room around her. Melissa sat up. A wave of nausea hit her forcing her to lie back down. After a few minutes of breathing through her nose, Melissa sat up again. The queasiness was still there, but if she focused on other things it did not feel so bad. Without getting up she picked up her dress off the trunk and started to get dressed. She stood up only when she needed to as she dressed. When she was finished Melissa was not sure whether her stomach was doing better, getting worse, or had not changed.

Concentrating on breathing through her nose Melissa stood up and went to the door. She opened it and stepped out into the hallway. It was only slightly brighter out in the hallway than it was in her room. Melissa was not sure that it was not still the middle of the night. She looked around. There was no one in sight and she could not hear anyone moving around. Melissa went down the hallway to the stairs and then down them. Melissa went down it until she arrived at main floor before turning in the direction of the kitchen. From the sounds and smells coming from the kitchen Melissa guessed the cook was already busy. The smells were close to causing Melissa to lose what little was in her stomach.

Melissa entered the kitchen. The cook was busy stirring something, but looked up at Melissa.

"Good morning," the cook said.

"Good morning," Melissa answered, her voice lacked any enthusiasm at the idea of a good morning. The cook looked at her as Melissa sat down at the table.

"You look a little pale," the cook said, "You are not sick, are you?"

"I do not know," Melissa answered, "Aside from being a little tired, I was fine yesterday."

"Did you have any of Lord Winsand's cider yesterday?" the cook asked.

"No," Melissa answered.

"Well, try some bread and water," the cook said as she set both down in front of Melissa, "If they do not stay down then you will head back up to bed and I will explain where you are to Roger."

"I have not gotten sick in years," Melissa said, "Even when everyone else does."

"Then you are about due," the cook replied as she went back to whatever she was stirring. Melissa did not respond, instead she ate a little bit of the bread.

After several minutes Melissa was feeling better. The smell of what was cooking was still bothering her, but her stomach did not seem to as interested in giving up its contents.

"Doing better?" the cook asked.

"Yes, actually," Melissa answered, "Though I am not sure why that helped."

"I have a good guess," the cook said. Melissa looked up at the cook. The cook was busy pulling the bread out of the oven. The cook brought the fresh bread and put it on the table. When she was finished she stopped and looked back at Melissa.

"Tiredness and morning nausea sound like you going to have a baby," the cook said, "That and the fact you are feeling better now." Melissa was silent for a few minutes.

"I can't be," Melissa said as she shook her head.

"Why not?" The cook interrupted Melissa before she could finish the sentence. "You have been sneaking out to see someone. And you are not with what's his name." The cook gestured to the area of the kitchen her helper usually worked in.

"I just can't be," Melissa said.

"If you say so," the cook said. She turned and went back to the pot she had been stirring.

Melissa sat there as if she was a statue. The word baby rang through her head. It was like an endless echo. She wanted to deny it again, but there was doubt. Could she really be expecting? If she was, what was she going to do now?

The door to the kitchen opened. Melissa and the cook turned to see the cook's helper stagger inside.

"Where have you been?" the cook demanded, putting her hands on her hips. Her helper looked up at her, opened his mouth to say something and then collapsed. His body shuttered once and then was still. Melissa and the cook were frozen for a second before the cook moved to kneel down beside her helper. She tried to wake him by shaking his shoulder, but it did not seem to be working. Without thinking first Melissa got up and left the kitchen. She ran up to the room across the hall from Lady Winsand's room. She hammered on the door. It was a minute before the door opened. Roger was standing there. He was dressed, but had not finished doing his hair.

"The cook's helper collapsed and he stopped breathing," Melissa gasped out. Roger closed the door behind him before they both headed back to the kitchen.

Leah opened her eyes to another grey morning. She got out of bed and went to the window. It was drizzling but not raining as hard as it had been yesterday. It still did not look like a day to go out riding. With a sigh, Leah turned from the window. Melissa had not gotten up and set out Leah's clothes, so Leah found them for herself.

After getting dressed Leah left her room and went down the stairs to the second floor. She went down the hallway to her father's room. The door was open and she could see him lying in bed. There was slightly more colour in his face, but he still looked ill.

Before Leah could step into the room she heard loud voices coming from downstairs. She followed the sounds to the kitchen. In the kitchen, Leah found Roger, the cook, Melissa and the doctor all standing around something on the floor that was covered with a blanket. They were so busy talking they had not noticed her. Leah took the time to analyze the situation. Based on the size and shape of the thing under the blanket, Leah guessed it was the body of the cook's helper. Leah stepped into the kitchen.

"What happened?" Leah made sure she was heard over everyone else without yelling. Everyone stopped to look at her in surprise.

"I am sorry if we disturbed your sleep, Miss Winsand," Melissa said as she went over to where Leah was standing.

She seemed as though she was going to direct Leah out of the kitchen.

"The cook's helper became sick last night," Roger said causing Melissa to stop where she was, "He came in to start his chores for the day when he collapsed. The cook sent the groom for the doctor."

"The man is dead," the doctor said, "Hard to tell what killed him." Leah looked Roger in the eyes and figured he was thinking it was poison.

"I will take the body back with me," the doctor said, "See to it that he gets a proper burial."

"Did he have any family?" Leah asked.

"Yes, Miss Winsand, he did," Roger answered, "His parents live in the village."

"Let them know what happened." Leah said, "And tell them that his burial expenses will be paid for by my father."

"Yes, Miss Winsand," Roger said.

"Melissa, you can help the cook until another helper can be hired," Leah said, "In the meantime, I will be upstairs with my father."

"How is he doing this morning?" the doctor asked.

"He appears to be doing better, but I do not know if he has woken up yet," Leah said. The doctor nodded. The cook went over to the pot simmering and ladled some of its contents into a mug. She brought it to Leah.

"If he does wake up he should have something to drink," the cook said.

"Thank you," Leah accepted the mug. She took it and left the kitchen.

When Leah reached her father's room she found him sitting up in bed.

"Good morning," Leah smiled as she entered the room.

"Good morning," James smiled back. He looked tired and weak. Leah offered him the mug and he took it. As he took a sip she sat down in the chair.

"Perhaps the prince finds the antidote to the poison," James said as he placed the mug on the table beside the bed, "Then the girl can leave him."

"I have not figured out what happened next," Leah said, "But that sounds like a good next piece. How would the prince discover what poison it is to figure out the antidote?"

"Perhaps there is something in the witch's work room," James suggested.

"I will think about it," Leah said.

"I would love to hear the end of it," James said. He smiled at his daughter, she smiled back. They were quiet while he took another sip from the mug.

They talked about James's story until Roger brought breakfast. Then Leah sat there and watched her father sleep.

Leah spent the morning at her father's bedside. At noon Roger came into the room carrying a tray. There was a mug of broth and some bread on it. He set it on the table.

"Lunch is ready," Roger said, "A plate is waiting in the dining room for you."

"Thank you," Leah said. She got up and went down the stairs to the dining room A little bit of sunlight was coming through the windows. Ignoring the food that set on the table, Leah went to the window. The rain had stopped and the dark clouds were moving away. Everything was still wet, but the sun was starting to dry things off. Maybe Caleb would be out waiting to go riding, Leah thought. She sat down in her spot at the table and started to eat. She wanted to get outside before it started to rain again.

When Leah was finished eating she went up to her room and changed into an outfit that she could go riding in. Once dressed, Leah left her room and headed down the stairs. Leah stopped at the second floor landing. Roger was coming down the hallway carrying the lunch tray.

"How is my father doing?" Leah asked.

"He had some lunch and is resting," Roger answered,

"Since his colour is coming back, I think he will be fine."

"Good," Leah said before starting down the last set of stairs.

"Going out this afternoon?" Roger asked as he followed her down the stairs.

"I am going for a walk in the garden," Leah answered.

"Have a good time," Roger said. At the bottom of the stairs Roger headed for the kitchen while Leah headed out back to the garden.

Outside the air was moist, but everything looked refreshed. Leah walked into the hedge maze. The minute she was out of sight of the house she broke into a run. It felt good to run. Leah felt that her pain and fear were being left at the manor and safety would come when she reached the door.

When the door came into to sight Leah stopped running and walked the rest of the way so she could catch her breath. Once she had her breathing under control Leah opened the door. Caleb was sitting on his horse with another horse standing beside his. Leah found herself in need of catching her breath again.

"Good afternoon, Miss Winsand," Caleb said as he got down from his horse.

"Good afternoon," Leah stepped off the path and on to the field.

"I had to bring Blackie for you to ride because Mother was exercising Jewel," Caleb said. Leah went over and held out her hand to Blackie. He sniffed it before moving to nuzzle Leah's hair.

"He likes you," Caleb said.

"Hello to you too, Blackie," Leah said. She patted Blackie's neck before Caleb helped her up into the saddle. Then Caleb climbed onto his own horse. They headed across the field towards the trees. Leah let Blackie pick his own pace and he chose to walk beside Caleb's horse.

"What happened?" Caleb asked.

"Someone poisoned my father," Leah answered, "I know it was not Mother, because she is locked up. Whoever did it snuck into the kitchen and put the poison into a batch of cider."

"You could have been poisoned as well," Caleb said.

"Father was the only family member to have a cup," Leah replied, "The cook got rid of the rest of it when Father collapsed. Unfortunately, the cook's helper, who mixed it up, died this morning and the fear is that he tasted it. But Roger and the cook are going to be extra vigilant now."

"Is your father going to be all right?" Caleb asked.

"He is already starting to look better," Leah answered.

"I know your father has not been doing well," Caleb said, "But is he going to write another book?"

"He is currently working on one," Leah answered, "Being sick has given him time to work on it. Have you read his others?"

"I have read two of them, but I had trouble trying to read the first one that he wrote," Caleb answered.

"I tried reading that one as well, but I could not get through the first chapter," Leah said, "When I asked Father he told me the book was on the meaning of life and I would understand it when I was older."

"The meaning of life?" Caleb asked.

"I do not think Father understands it himself," Leah answered, "It is based on a journal Father found. He claimed the book demanded to be written. I find Father's other two books much easier to read."

"What is his next book going to be about?" Caleb asked.

"It will be similar to the other two," Leah answered, "But I do not think Father would like it if I told the story before he is finished."

"Then I will not ask anymore," Caleb said, "Have you read the new book by Lewis Carroll?"

"No, I have not heard about it," Leah answered, "What is it about?"

"A girl falls down a rabbit hole and meets some very strange creatures," Caleb answered, "It is peculiar in places, but a good read."

"It sounds interesting," Leah said, "I will have to see if I can find a copy to read."

They reached the trees and went single file along the path. Caleb and Leah continued to discuss books. They had read many of the same books and were recommending ones to each other the ones that the other had not read.

When Caleb and Leah arrived back at the door in the hedge they were laughing over a story. Caleb got down and helped Leah off Blackie. They looked into each other's eyes. There was an emotion in Caleb's eyes Leah could not quite identify, but could feel her body responding to it. It was a strange and wonderful sensation. Their lips met and held on. Leah let the feelings take her away as Caleb's arms wrapped around her pulling her to him. Leah felt like every nerve ending in her body was suddenly extra sensitive. Without thinking Leah reached up and put her hand through Caleb's hair. It was perfectly soft and finely textured so her finger felt good as it slipped through it. Time seemed to stand still for Leah.

Finally the kiss ended, but they continued to hold on to each other.

"I should get back," Leah's voice was quiet.

"Then I will see you another time," Caleb said.

"See you," Leah said. Caleb's lips captured hers one more time before he let her go. Despite the ground being solid under her feet Leah was sure she was floating. She walked back to the door as Caleb climbed up on his horse. Leah stopped once she was on the path and turned around. When Caleb looked back Leah waved. Caleb waved back before gathering the reins from Blackie as well as from his own horse. Leah closed the door most of the way before watching Caleb ride off.

She closed the door the rest of the way before walking back to the manor. Inside the manor, Leah went up to the library. She found the book she had been reading and sat down in a chair. Before she opened the book Leah noticed all three of her father's books were sitting on the edge of the desk. The bottom was red with silver lettering that read, Observations of a Lost Man by Lord James Winsand. She would try reading it again someday, Leah decided before opening her book and starting to read.

"Miss Winsand," Roger's voice broke the spell of the story. Leah looked up at him.

"Yes?" Leah asked.

"There is a delivery for you," Roger answered, "And when you are ready supper is served."

"Thank you," Leah said. She stood up and set the book down on the chair before leaving the library. Roger was already on his way downstairs. Leah followed him down and found a bouquet of flowers sitting on the table in the hallway.

"There was no note with them," Roger said as Leah opened her mouth to ask. Then he headed for the kitchen. Leah looked at the flowers. It was a bouquet of bellflowers with a single light pink rose in the centre of it. The mixture of bellflowers and the rose meant the sender was a humble admirer. Leah put her nose near them and inhaled the sweet scent. She smiled to herself before going into the dining room.

After Leah was finished eating she went upstairs to her father's room. James was sitting up and drinking out of a mug. He smiled at Leah as she came into the room.

"How are you?" Leah asked.

"Better," James answered, "And hoping to be up and about again tomorrow. How was your afternoon?"

"It was good," Leah answered, "I went for a walk in the garden after the rain stopped. It was a pleasant walk."

"I am glad to hear it," James said, "I think I am well enough to write. Can you get my writing supplies from the library?"

"Certainly, Father," Leah said before leaving the room. Going into the library she gathered up his writing and writing supplies. Then she took them all back to her father's room. Leah handed the pile to her father before sitting down in the chair. James sorted through it all and set up his writing. Then he started telling Leah the story as he wrote it down.

# CHAPTER EIGHTEEN

*August 8, 1865*

This day being Sunday, Leah prepared for church. She dressed, ate breakfast and went back upstairs for her coat and hat. When she came down she found her father sitting on a chair by the door waiting for her. Leah was surprised to see him.

"I decided to come to church," James said as he got to his feet, "The person who poisoned me is likely to be there and I want them to see that I am fine. I hope they will realize poisoning me will not help them in any way."

"Are you sure you are up to this?" Leah asked.

"I will be fine," James smiled at his daughter, "Are you ready to go?"

"Yes," Leah said.

"Then let us go," James said. He opened the door for Leah and then followed her out. The carriage was waiting for them.

At church many people greeted James and were glad to see him. Leah saw the Lamberts were there, but they did not come near Leah or her father. After the service Leah and James went home despite the many invitations for lunch. James immediately went upstairs to his bed while Leah ate lunch alone. And the rest of the day was quiet while James rested and Leah read.

Caleb stepped out of the kitchen door and into the moonlight. He closed the door without making a sound before starting toward the stable. Inside the stable Caleb picked up his saddle. Warrior snorted impatiently as Caleb opened the door to his stall.

"Be quiet," Caleb whispered, "If you wake Haines there will be no more nighttime rides." Warrior went quiet and still as Caleb put the bridle and saddle on him.

When Caleb was finished he led Warrior out of the stall. Caleb walked Warrior out of the stable before mounting. Then he held Warrior to a slow and quiet pace until they were out of sight of the manor. The moment Caleb let him Warrior started to run.

They went along the path in the woods, into the field, passed the fish pond and the door in the hedge. Something caught Caleb's attention and he pulled the reins to halt Warrior. Caleb looked over and saw the door to the hedge leading to the Winsand Estate was partially open. Caleb directed Warrior closer to the door. Warrior did not like it, but sensed that making noise about his dislike was a bad idea.

When Caleb felt they were close enough he got off Warrior and went the rest of the way on foot. He stopped just outside the door and listened. There was a sound might have been the rustling of clothing coming from behind the door.

"There is always something else wrong," a female voice said, "If it wasn't for the time I spend with you I would never be in a good mood."

"I'm glad I can help," Haines's voice replied.

"Of course, there are probably others who could lift my mood," the female said, "Especially ones who are closer."

"You wouldn't do that?" Haines said.

"Why not?" the female voice asked, "You do."

"It's true I do," Haines answered, "But you're different and wouldn't do everything I do."

"Do any of the others find partners besides you or are they like me and only want to be with you?" the female voice asked.

"As far as I know you are the only one," Haines answered.

"Good," the female voice said. Then there was more rustling of clothing. Caleb quietly went back to Warrior. He was glad it was not someone trying to break in to the Winsand Manor, but he was not sure he wanted to know that much about Haines's activities. Caleb mounted Warrior again. He got Warrior going in the right direction and let Warrior pick his own speed.

Down the field, into the woods on the far side, down the path, out of the woods, across the road, into some more woods, along that path, and out of those trees to where Percy was sitting on his horse, waiting. Warrior stopped beside Percy's horse.

"Where is Curt?" Caleb asked.

"I do not know," Percy answered, "I only got here a few minutes ago. And I have not seen him. I also have not received any messages from him since we talked after the church service."

"Then I guess we wait for him," Caleb said, "Hopefully he gets here soon."

"Anything new with you and your situation?" Percy asked.

"No," Caleb answered, "How are you and Hilary doing?"

"We just about have all the plans for the wedding written out," Percy answered, "Her parents came back yesterday so I expect to not be over there as much as I was. Do not worry though I will not be taking up your afternoons."

"I am not worried about you taking up my afternoons," Caleb said.

"I am sorry I am late," Curt said. Caleb and Percy turned to see him coming out of the trees on horseback. "But it took longer than I thought it would to sneak out."

"I am still not sure why you and Edwina want our help to elope," Percy said as the three of them started along the line of properties, "You said you were coming back here and you are supposed to get married soon."

"Concern for her safety," Curt answered, "Due to current conditions at the Lavern Estate and the people around it I think it would be safer if we marry now. Then hopefully she can move in with me and be away from it all."

"Are these safety concerns going to prevent us from getting to Edwina?" Caleb asked.

"I do not think so," Curt answered.

"Good," Caleb said.

They continued to ride until they reached the back of the Lavern Estate. They stopped and took stock of the situation. The other properties they had passed had beautifully done gardens and dark windows. The garden of the Lavern Estate looked like a herd of wild horses had gone through it recently. The building itself looked like it was being redone. There were lights on in two of the windows on the main floor, but it was impossible to tell what was happening in the room from where they were sitting on their horses. The windows above the main floor were dark, except one with a candle placed in the window.

"That one is her room," Curt pointed to the one with the candle.

"Okay," Caleb said as he got down off Warrior, "Percy and I will go get her. You wait here with the horses."

Curt nodded. Percy got down from his horse and put the coil of rope he had with him over one shoulder. Caleb and

Percy started across the garden. As they went they had to be careful of debris that was scattered every which way. Finally they made it to the manor.

There was no alarm raised and in the lit windows the two people were busy with other things. Under the window with the candle Percy started his climb. There were a lot more things to use as hand and foot holds than usual. The window opened as he approached it. Then he went inside. Caleb watched for any signs of an alarm as he waited. A moment later one end of the rope was tossed out of the window and came down the side of the manor until it hung a foot off the ground. Then Edwina came out climbing down the side of the manor using the rope. Caleb watched and when she was near enough he helped her descend to the ground. When she started to say something he signalled for her to remain quiet.

Once she was on the ground the other end of the rope came down the side of the manor. Caleb picked it up and coiled it while Percy climbed back down.

When he was back on the ground they started back across the garden. They were half way across the garden when Edwina cried out as she tripped over a root. She fell forward. Caleb helped her to her feet and they started forward again. There was noise from the house. None of them looked back, instead they went faster.

When they reached the horses Caleb helped Edwina up behind Curt while Percy climbed up on his own horse. There was shouting coming from the manor as Caleb climbed up on Warrior. The alarm was raised even if they did not know what people were doing on the property.

Percy continued along the property line speeding up as he went. Curt followed and Caleb was behind him. They rode their horses as fast as they could for as long as they could. Once there did not seem to be anyone following them horses could be slowed down to a walk. They still travelled as silently as they could. When they reached the cross roads they needed, Caleb and Percy sent Curt and Edwina down the one road while they went down the one that would take them home.

"Think they will make it?" Percy asked.

"Yes," Caleb answered, "As far as the church, yes, after that I have a few doubts."

"Well, good luck to them," Percy said, "And I hope we do not get into trouble over it all."

"Curt and Edwina are not going say anything," Caleb said, "No one else knows or is likely to know. Those that might suspect are people we helped in similar situations. Although this rescuing people will have to end once you get married. I doubt Hilary would like the idea of you climbing into other women's rooms."

"We helped enough people I do not feel bad about stopping to concentrate on my own happiness," Percy said.

"Not to mention Hilary's happiness," Caleb said.

"What can I say," Percy said, "I am in love."

*August 9, 1865*

Monday morning Melissa woke Leah up in time to eat breakfast before the carriage would arrive to take her to lessons. At the dining room table Leah's father was busy writing and did not even let breakfast disturb him. She ate quietly so as not to disturb him.

When the carriage arrived Leah was standing outside waiting for it. Getting in Leah found the Kenley twins were there, but Hilary was not.

"Good morning," Leah said as she closed the door behind her.

"Have you heard?" Margaret started.

"About Curt and Edwina?" Meghan finished.

"No, what happened?" Leah asked.

"They eloped last night," Margaret said.

"But their parents found them shortly after they had done it," Meghan said.

"Lord and Lady Lavern are very angry," Margaret said, "Especially since the wedding was supposed to be next month and everything is already paid."

"Apparently Curt and Edwina eloped because she was pregnant," Meghan said, "And they did not want to embarrass their parents and cause a scandal."

"However, Lord and Lady Lavern are currently denying anything of the sort happened," Margaret said.

"So, the wedding will probably go ahead as planned," Meghan said.

"Where is Hilary today?" Margaret asked.

"She did not say anything about missing lessons," Meghan said.

"She is getting ready for the party this afternoon," Leah answered.

"Oh yes, the party is today," Margaret said.

"Is it her eighteenth birthday already?" Meghan asked.

"Yes," Leah answered.

"Does that mean she does not have to go to lessons anymore?" Margaret asked, "Because her sister, Alicia, did not have to go after she turned eighteen."

"Mother says we have to go to lessons until we are married," Meghan said.

"Hilary has not told me whether she is continuing with lessons or not," Leah said.

The twins found several more pieces of gossip to share during the rest of the ride.


Caleb was out in the stable sitting on the gate to Warrior's stall when Percy came looking for him.

"Are you not supposed to getting ready for Hilary's party?" Percy asked

"I am ready for Hilary's party," Caleb answered, "Right now I am hiding until my parents are ready to leave. Otherwise my mother starts to question my choice in attire. Should you not be on your way to the party?"

"Hilary told me to arrive when all the rest of the guests were arriving," Percy said, "Which means I have some time before I have to be there."

Haines came into the stable.

"Good afternoon," Haines said.

"How are you this afternoon?" Percy asked.

"Terrific," Haines answered, "Lady Morley exercised the horses this morning and all my chores are done. Once I've hitched up the carriage I'll have no responsibilities for the afternoon."

"I would recommend staying out of trouble," Caleb said.

"Me? Get into trouble?" Haines asked.

"Being found passed out in the rose patch by the gardeners is going to get you in trouble this time," Caleb said.

"You know me," Haines said, "With this gimped leg I don't get into trouble anymore." Haines headed down to where the carriage horses were stabled. Percy climbed up to sit beside Caleb.

"Lord Winsand was at church yesterday," Percy said.

"I saw that," Caleb said, "He must be doing better."

"He looked old and worn thin," Percy said, "I know he has been sick, but he looked just short of dead, especially after the service."

"Probably should have been home resting," Caleb said, "But too stubborn to do so."

"Ever figured out what you are going to do about your father and Leah Winsand?" Percy asked, "Or are you still conflicted on the matter?"

"Right now I am taking your advice and ignoring my father," Caleb said, "Because when I last talked to Leah she still needed me. That does not mean I am going with anything else you said."

"You will not concede defeat?" Percy asked.

"Why did it take two years to finally ask Hilary to marry you?" Caleb asked.

"This conversation is about your love life, not mine," Percy answered.

"Fear," Haines called, "She was too good for him and she would dump him when she found someone who was."

"I do not recall asking your advice," Percy said.

"Master Caleb told you she'd picked you out of everyone who was interested in her," Haines continued, "That's why you got the nerve up to ask for her hand. But Master Caleb's problem is a little more complicated than that. He's got two sides to fight with over his choice of bride not just personal voices."

"Actually it is more complicated than just two sides telling him what to do," Percy said, "If I am not mistaken Miss. Winsand's mother sold her to the Lamberts. That is the rumour anyways."

"The Lamberts? Those people are crazy, especially the lady," Haines said.

"That would be part of the problem," Caleb said.

"Not if you took my advice," Haines said.

"What advice did Haines give you?" Percy asked.

"That he should elope with the girl," Haines answered.

"That is a good suggestion," Percy said, "Then she cannot be married off to Randall Lambert."

"There is a problem with that," Caleb said.

"What is the problem?" Percy asked.

"Leah would never agree to it," Caleb answered, "She is not going to leave her father to marry me, especially while he is sick."

"That is not really a problem," Percy said, "You two disappear to Greenwich for a day or two and come back married. Miss Winsand does not have to leave her father alone for long. And I doubt Lord Winsand would be upset about you marrying his daughter."

"Except maybe for the part of not asking for his permission first," Caleb said, "He is still standing between Leah and her having to marry Randall Lambert. You think he would just let his daughter disappear for a couple days and then not have a lot more than lecture for me when she turned up married?"

"This would also solve the problem with your father," Percy said, "If you get married then his plans fall though and you are not waiting for the moment he considers the right time."

"No, I would have two fathers angry at me," Caleb said, "And the only thing stopping them from ripping me apart is the fact that then Leah would be a widow and able to marry Randall. It is not a good suggestion or good advice and I would rather the family groom and the man who calls himself my best friend did not push me on this subject."

"Okay," Percy said, "I am sure you will figure it out by yourself. But you have been moping a lot lately and we were just trying to help."

"And I have listened," Caleb said, "It has not helped at all."

Haines had the horses ready and walked them passed Caleb and Percy.

"Just have to hook these two up to the carriage and Jack can take all of you away," Haines announced.

"I have my own horse," Percy said, "So, I do not have to worry about a carriage."

"There is a stall you can use for your horse and ride in the carriage," Haines said.

"Why?" Percy asked.

"Because it is going to rain soon," Haines said.

"It is beautiful and sunny out there," Percy said.

"Think what you want," Haines said, "But it is going to rain. I can feel it in my leg." Haines walked the horses out.

"He can feel it in his leg?" Percy asked.

"If you do ride with us," Caleb said as he climbed down, "Make sure you get your horse to Haines before he disappears into the rose patch." Caleb went in the direction of Haines. Percy stared after them for a moment in puzzlement. Then he got down and followed them.

When Leah arrived home from lessons she immediately went to the dining room. Her father was not there, but there was a plate of food for her. She ate lunch before hurrying up the stairs to get ready for Hilary's birthday party. Melissa was waiting with the party dress all laid out. Leah changed before letting Melissa put up her hair.

Once Melissa was done, Leah looked at herself in the mirror. The cream coloured dress with light pink trim looked perfect for an outdoor party. Satisfied with how she looked, Leah headed downstairs. She found her father was waiting for her by the door. He looked up at her.

"You look beautiful," James smiled at her.

"Thank you," Leah smiled back.

"Shall we go?" James asked.

"I am ready," Leah answered. James opened the door and they stepped outside. James closed the door behind them. Going down the steps they got into the waiting carriage. They did not say much on the carriage ride. Leah watched the world through the window. It was a beautiful day, but there were some dark clouds on the horizon. They were far enough away Leah doubted they would affect the party.

# CHAPTER NINETEEN

Finally the carriage pulled up to the path leading to the garden at the Whitelaw's Estate. It looked like most of the other guests were already there. James got down and offered his hand to Leah. Leah accepted his hand, but did not let him take her full weight as she descended from the carriage. James closed the carriage door before they followed the path around the house to the garden.

The garden had been decorated in blue and silver. A table full of food was set up near the doors to the manor and a dance floor was set up on the lawn. Leah and her father appeared to be late. The other guests were in small groups scattered all over the lawn, those who were not over by the dance floor. There was a large group on and beside the dance floor. The brightness of the colours the guests were wearing reminded Leah of a flower bed, especially with the sun overhead.

"I see a chair I wish to claim," James said, "Here is the birthday girl to greet you." James stepped away as Hilary came through the crowd. Hilary was wearing a beautiful red dress which looked perfect for her. Her hair was done up properly and her green eyes were shining

"I am so glad to see you," Hilary said as she grabbed Leah's arm and steered her towards the hedge separating the lawn from the other parts of the garden, "I have been surrounded by people all morning."

They went through the opening in the hedge and sat down on the bench.

"How is the party going?" Leah asked.

"Good," Hilary answered, "Except for a couple of things. The first one being Randall showed up even though I did not invite him."

"Why did he come?" Leah asked.

"I do not know," Hilary answered, "But Mother and Father would not let me turn him away. So unless he causes trouble I cannot do anything about him. But he is pretending to be social and has not yet brought up his favourite topic."

"What else is there?" Leah asked.

"There you are," Alicia stepped through the opening in the hedge, "You cannot hide during your birthday party. Mother and Father are going to do a waltz and want you and Percival to join them."

"I am talking to Leah," Hilary said.

"And you can talk to her again after the dance," Alicia said as she took Hilary's wrist and pulled her to her feet. They headed back through the opening in the hedge. Leah stood up and followed them. Once on the lawn Alicia dragged Hilary to where the dancers were. Leah looked around. Her father was still sitting down, but he had found companionship for the moment. Most of the people Leah usually talked to were either dancing or watching the dancers. Even the Kenley twins had found dance partners. Leah headed for the table where she could see the punch. She was several feet away when she could see Randall coming toward her.

"Miss Winsand," Randall said when he reached her, "It is nice to see you here."

"What do you want?" Leah asked as she picked up one of the cups. Randall was taken aback by her abruptness. Leah filled the cup with punch.

"I was hoping for some pleasant conversation," Randall answered.

"I have never had a pleasant conversation with you and I doubt that will ever change," Leah replied. She turned away from Randall and ran, punch cup first, into someone else. The punch ended up all over his clothes with only a few drops splashing on Leah's dress. Leah looked up and saw it was Caleb who she had soaked with punch.

"I am very sorry," Leah said. The joy of seeing Caleb was second to the horror she felt for having just dumped punch on him.

"It is all right," Caleb replied as he accepted a towel from a very quick servant, "I have been told I should shuffle my feet when I walk so people can hear me coming." He used the towel to brush off his clothes. Leah's cheeks flushed with embarrassment but there was nowhere to run. Caleb was still in front of her and Randall had not moved. Fortunately, most of the people at the party were still focused on the dancers and missed the accident.

"You need to be more careful, Miss Winsand," Randall chided her.

"She did not do it on purpose," Caleb told Randall, "And we both know she was trying to get away from you." Caleb handed the towel back to the servant. Randall looked like he was going to make an angry retort, but he swallowed his words and stalked off a few steps but only to the other side of the punch table.

"Thank you," Leah kept her voice soft, "And I am sorry."

"It is okay," Caleb said, "Would you like some more punch?" Caleb picked up a cup from the table. The servant had already taken the one Leah had emptied away.

"Yes," Leah answered as she took a step back from the

table. Caleb poured a cup and offered it to her. Leah accepted it and then Caleb got himself a cup. Randall moved away from the table but not so far as to be of sight.

"I am surprised to see Randall here," Caleb said, "I did not think he came to social events."

"Hilary said she had not invited him," Leah said.

"Very few people do," Caleb said, "He does not show up if he is invited, unless his mother is with him. I have not seen Lady Lambert at all today."

"Perhaps she is trying to get her baby to grow up," Percival said coming up beside Caleb. The waltz had obviously finished and people were starting to drift away from the dance floor, those who were not continuing to dance.

"It does not seem to be working," Caleb said.

"What does not seem to be working?" Hilary asked as she joined them.

"Randall," Percival answered. Hilary made a face to show her thoughts on the matter. Percival stepped passed Caleb and poured cups of punch for himself and Hilary.

"Mother and Father have taken over the dance floor," Hilary said, "If you get close they will find you a partner."

"I did not think they were going to let us leave," Percival said as he handed Hilary the cup of punch.

"We will have to extract them later," Hilary said, "Right now they can have their fun."

They continued to talk. They moved away from the table as more people came to get some punch.

"Mother said I should not just talk to one or two people," Hilary said after a little while, "So, I have to go around and then I shall be back." Hilary drifted off with Percival going with her.

"How are you today?" Caleb asked.

"Good," Leah answered, "Father was well enough to come to the party."

"So soon after the latest attack?" Caleb asked.

"This is Hilary's birthday party," Leah answered, "He would not miss it unless there had been another attack this morning and he had been too weak to get out of bed. That and he wishes me to be go out and visit with people."

"He seems to have found someone to talk to as well," Caleb said glancing over to where her father sat talking to his own.

"Yes," Leah said.

"Good afternoon," Edwina said as she and Curt joined Leah and Caleb.

"Good afternoon," Leah replied.

"It is good to see you and your father here," Edwina said, "He must be doing better."

"He is doing much better," Leah said.

"What is Randall doing here?" Curt asked apparently noticing Randall for the first time.

"No one has figured that out yet," Caleb answered, "And no one really wants to ask him directly. Hilary says he was not invited."

"He does not come when he is invited to a party," Curt said, "Why come when he is not invited?"

"Who is Randall?" Edwina asked.

"Randall Lambert," Curt answered, "is the man standing there on the other side of the food table from us."

"The man with the bright red hair?" Edwina asked.

"That is him," Curt answered.

"Is it a bad thing he is here?" Edwina asked, "You make it sound like he is an eel."

"More like a leech," Curt answered, "As in he will latch on and not let go. Any friendly overtures tend to result in discussing his favourite book. This book is thick, boring, outdated, and has nothing to do with the current views on anything. Randall has managed to memorize that book."

"Perhaps if more people talked to him then he would not need to read the book so much," Edwina said.

"Nothing seems to help," Caleb said, "People have tried

and all of them have found it easier to ignore or stay out of the way of Randall."

"It still does not seem right," Edwina said.

"Would anyone like more punch?" Caleb asked.

"Sure," Leah gave him her cup.

"Thank you," Edwina gave him her cup.

"No, thank you," Curt's cup was still mostly full. Caleb took the cups and went back over to the table.

Caleb went over to the punch bowl and refilled the cups. Randall tried to appear to be ignoring him, but Caleb could tell Randall was watching him. Caleb did not remember exchanging more than two or three words with Randall, so it could not have been a problem Randall was having with him. More likely Randall was watching Leah, which did not bother Caleb as long as Randall was content with watching Leah from the other side of the table. However it was more the reason behind it that troubled Caleb. If James Winsand had locked Lady Winsand up and promised Leah she would not have to marry Randall, then why had the Lamberts not gotten the message? Or perhaps they had and that was why Lady Lambert sent her son alone to the party; to try and get Leah through charm and wit. Unfortunately for them Leah had not wanted to marry Randall before and she definitely did not want to marry him now. If Randall wanted to stand there looking creepy then Caleb would leave him alone, just as long as Randall did not try to do anything to Leah. Caleb picked up the punch cups and turned back to the group.

"Your birthday is coming up too, is it not?" Edwina asked.

"It is," Leah answered, "The invitations will be out this week."

"I cannot wait," Edwina said, "Did you hear who bought the Putnam Estate?"

"No, I have not," Leah said.

"A marquess has bought it to use as his summer home," Edwina said.

"A marquess?" Leah asked.

"No one seems to know what his name is," Edwina said, "Or much about it. The servants who have been sent to the place are certainly closed mouthed. Father only learned it was a marquess because the man who was managing the sale told him."

"The marquess will probably not move in until next year then," Curt said, "Because the summer is just about over." Caleb came back and handed the cups back.

"Maybe he will move in for the last few weeks," Edwina said.

"Edwina," Lady Lavern showed up, "There are some people I would like you to meet." She wrapped her arm around Edwina and pulled her away.

"Sorry about her," Curt said, "She has been doing this for the past couple weeks." Then he followed them.

Before Leah or Caleb could say anything Lord Whitelaw stood on the top step and waved to get everyone's attention. Slowly people quieted down and turned to him. Those who were too far away moved in closer.

"I am glad so many people could make it," Lord Whitelaw said, "Today is the day my baby girl becomes a woman. It is a great celebration. However, I have another announcement that adds to my joy." Lord Whitelaw paused for a moment. Everyone was quiet, but people were glancing at each other. They were trying to figure out what he was about to say. Leah noticed Caleb was smiling at this. Like her he must have known what was coming.

"I am happy to announce the engagement of our daughter, Hilary, to Percival Spencer," Lord Whitelaw said. Applause broke out as Hilary and Percival went up the steps to stand beside her father. They acknowledged the applause.

"Now that has been dealt with," Lord Whitelaw said when it had quieted down, "We can go back to the celebration." There was a brief round of applause then people went back to their conversations. Many of them were more animated now. Lord and Lady Whitelaw headed back to the dance floor with Hilary and Percival following.

Melissa went around the last corner of the hedge and into the clearing. Haines was sitting there in the middle of the clearing waiting for her. The whole speech Melissa had been practicing all morning was gone. A small voice in her head told her if she did not say anything now she would not, but the words were gone from her lips. Haines looked at Melissa and smiled. Melissa smiled back. After that there was not room for talking. The voice in Melissa's head told her she just missed her opportunity to tell Haines about the baby, but it was quickly shut out with other thoughts and emotions. Nothing mattered but Haines.

# CHAPTER TWENTY

"Would you like to dance?" Caleb asked.

"I am a horrible dancer," Leah answered with a blush of embarrassment, "I tend to trip over my own feet as well as my partner's."

"Sometimes the best thing is practice," Caleb said as he put his punch cup on the table, "Would you like to dance?" Caleb offered her his hand. Leah looked at him and saw his smile.

"I can try," Leah answered as she put her cup down before taking Caleb's hand. Caleb led her away from the table, but did not head towards the dance floor. Instead he headed to the opening in the hedge. They went through and followed the path. It went passed the bench and twisted around flower beds until it brought them to the steps of a gazebo. From here Leah and Caleb could clearly hear the music from the party.

"Is this okay for a place to practice?" Caleb asked as he escorted her up the steps in the gazebo.

"Yes," Leah answered. She found herself relaxing a little bit at the idea of dancing here, rather than is a space crowded by everyone else.

"Good," Caleb said as they got into position. They started into the dance that went along with the music. The nervousness crept up on Leah again. She tried to ignore it and just concentrate on the dance steps.

Leah found herself tripping over her own feet as she usually did when trying to dance. Caleb caught her and kept her on her feet multiple times. He also kept her in time with the music. Unlike many others Leah had danced with, she found he did not get frustrated and give up, but seemed to have an infinite amount of patience. If fact he seemed to be having a good time dancing with her.

Leah was starting to relax when she did not pick up her right foot fast enough for the music and managed to catch Caleb's ankle with her ankle, causing them both to fall. He landed on his backside and she landed on his lap. Leah flushed with embarrassment, but Caleb laughed. She was starting to get to her feet when he stopped her. Caleb lifted her chin so she was looking into his eyes. There was seriousness in those eyes.

"It is okay to fall down," Caleb's voice was soft, "Life is about getting up and trying again." The heat Leah could feel welling up inside her had nothing to do with embarrassment. She leaned forward and pressed her lips to his. His mouth opened under hers and she found hers opening in response. The world spun as they continued to kiss.

They stayed that way until a much more lively tune started and the change brought caught their attention.

"Shall we try again?" Caleb asked Leah with a smile.

"I would like that," Leah smiled back. She got to her feet letting Caleb get to his. They took up their positions as the music started again. This time Leah felt herself relax. This improved her dancing.

She had spilled punch on him and had tripped him up while dancing and Caleb had not mocked her or said something rude to her. Instead he encouraged her to try again. He was the first man she had even known, aside from her father, who had done that. Although she freely admitted her father's encouragement took a much different form.

Right there, dancing with Caleb in the Whitelaw's garden, Leah was happy. And this man was the cause of it. Was this love? Leah wondered.

"See you do get better with practice," Caleb said.

"I guess it has been too long since I have danced," Leah replied.

"Then it is passed time to get back to it," Caleb said. Leah smiled.

They danced through several more songs when the music stopped in the middle of the song. Both Leah and Caleb stopped dancing and listened to figure out what happened. All that they could hear was the soft sound of raindrops hitting the roof of the gazebo. Leah looked out. The dark clouds she had seen on the way over had arrived to blot out the sun and brought the storm. As she and Caleb stood there the rain fell at a faster rate and with bigger drops. In the distance they could hear the rumble of thunder.

"They must have taken the party inside," Caleb said.

"Or this is the end of the party," Leah said.

"According to Percy, Hilary was not going to end the party until after the birthday cake," Caleb said, "Which was going to be served this evening and it is still just late afternoon for all this sudden darkness."

"If we head back we will get soaked," Leah said, "But it does not look like it will lighten up."

"As much as my clothes are in need of cleaning, I do not feel like getting wet right this moment," Caleb said, "Perhaps if we gave it sometime it will slacken off enough so we can get to the house."

"We can do that," Leah said. Caleb took her hand and led her back to the centre of the gazebo. Leah smiled as they started into another dance, this time to the music of the rain.

When they got tired of dancing Leah and Caleb sat together and watched the rain.

"It does not seem to be slacking off," Leah commented.

"We can wait a little longer," Caleb said, "Unless you are getting cold."

"I am fine," Leah replied, "I am just worried about my father. He gets tired easily and I was going to stay close in case he needed to go home. But out here that really is not an option."

"If he gets tired he can ask the Whitelaws for a place to lie down," Caleb said.

"You know my father, do you think he would admit to being tired?" Leah asked.

"No," Caleb answered, "But maybe someone else will notice and he will be offered a chance to lie down."

"Maybe," Leah said. Her voice suggested she did not believe it would happen.

Caleb let the rain take over the conversation. Leah rested her head on his shoulder as if she was tired. Physically she probably was not tired, but he had seen tiredness in her eyes when she arrived. Her spirits had lifted a little as they had danced, but the tiredness was starting to come back as they sat there and she did not have anything distracting her from the worries coming into her head. He wished he could take those away permanently, but it did not seem possible.

She was right about her father not wanting help and not willing to accept it. They were both stubborn in that way except it was starting to take a toll on Leah. Even James had noticed his daughter's malaise and he did everything he could if she was right about him wanting her to get out to visit people. Caleb seemed to be able to distract her for a couple minutes, but it did not last. Hopefully something would happen soon to cheer her up.

"I have not heard any thunder or seen any lightening for a while," Leah broke the quiet.

"Maybe the storm will stop soon," Caleb said, "It would be nice. I am starting to feel hungry."

"I am starting to get cold," Leah said, "Food would be nice as well."

"We will give it five more minutes before running for it," Caleb said.

"Okay," Leah said. They sat there for several more minutes.

"I guess it is not going to slacken off," Caleb said, "Ready?"

Leah nodded. They stood up and left the gazebo. Within seconds of stepping out of the shelter they were soaked. Leah started to run and Caleb followed her example.

At the manor someone opened the door for them and they were immediately wrapped in towels once inside. From the noise the party was in full swing, but only a few people were standing around the door. Hilary and Percival were there. Hilary took Leah by the arm and led her out of the room. Caleb was getting a similar treatment from Lord Whitelaw. Hilary took Leah upstairs to her room.

"I was wondering where you had gone, your father was asking if anyone had seen you," Hilary said as she went through her wardrobe, "Even with Caleb also missing I did not think you would be together although Percy had suggested that you might. I thought it more likely you had gone for a walk by yourself."

"Caleb asked me to dance," Leah said, "And rather than trip up the dancers we went to the gazebo to dance." Leah used the towel to dry off as much as she could.

"How long have you been seeing Caleb?" Hilary asked.

"We met on Tuesday," Leah answered, "I went for a walk to calm down after my fight with my mother. And he was riding in the field beyond the hedge maze."

"Why did you not tell me?" Hilary asked.

"Because I did not think there was a reason to think it all that important," Leah answered, "We would just sit and talk."

"That would explain the spacing out," Hilary said, "Do you now, you admit there is something going on?"

"I think I have fallen in love," Leah kept her eyes on the towel she was twisting in her hands. Hilary looked up at Leah and then went over to her.

"What is wrong with that?" Hilary asked.

"There are too many things in my life that make it difficult for me to be able to be social, with father and mother and everything that's happened," Leah said.

"When you are around Caleb did not worry about those," Hilary said, "And just enjoy his company. Love works out in the end." Hilary went back to the wardrobe and pulled out a light blue dress. She offered it to Leah.

"Try this on," Hilary said.

"This does not look like your colour," Leah said as she took the dress and stepped behind the screen.

"It was made for Alicia, but she never wore it," Hilary said, "So it got passed to me. I never fit into it. Maybe it will fit on you."

"Thank you," Leah said.

"You are welcome," Hilary replied, "It is better than you having to go home because you got caught out in the rain."

They were quiet for a few more minutes while Leah changed. Then Leah came out from behind the screen. The blue dress fit her in all ways except one. The bust had been made for someone of a smaller chest size.

"It does not quite fit," Leah said.

"Considering a few of the other dresses I have seen at the party, you look fine," Hilary said, "Unlike Lady Mander you are not falling out of the dress, it just shows more than your usual dresses. Just do not keep trying to pull it up, that will cause people to look."

"Okay," Leah dropped her hands to her sides.

Leah and Hilary left the room and went downstairs. After visiting the food table they went over to where Caleb and Percival were standing. Caleb has also found some clothes to change into. Leah noticed they fit him well, though they were not made of the high quality fabric his others had been.

"What are you two talking about so seriously?" Hilary asked.

"We noticed Randall has disappeared," Percival answered.

"He must have left before the rain started," Hilary said, "I do not remember seeing him talking to anyone for more than a minute and is not be fun at a party where you do not have friends."

"Unlike the fun Meghan Kenley and Oliver Borden were having," Caleb said.

"What happened?" Hilary asked.

"They were caught kissing in the library," Percival answered, "Oliver now cannot get within ten feet of Megan without her mother glaring at him."

"If they are caught together again he may find the glare to be replaced by a wedding ring on his finger," Leah said, "Lady Kenley has been looking for ways to marry those two off."

"Is that why she is sending them to London for several months?" Hilary asked.

"Yes," Leah answered.

"Well, there are worse reasons," Hilary said, "Though it will mean less gossip for those months."

"According to the twins they do not want to go to London," Leah said.

"Lady Kenley is going to have a problem then," Hilary said, "Because they will find an excuse to stay home."

"A wedding would do that," Percival said.

"More like weddings," Leah said, "If one gets married the other still has to go to London. Lady Kenley believes the twins are more likely to find men to marry in London, so she is set on sending them there. It would take her a lot to convince her otherwise."

"The twins will try," Hilary said, "They might even succeed."

Lady Whitelaw came into the room and went over to where the group was standing. She tapped Hilary on the shoulder.

"I need to talk to you for a moment," Lady Whitelaw said.

"Okay," Hilary said, she turned back to the others, "I will be back in a couple minutes." Percival nodded. Hilary followed her mother out of the room.

Percival opened his mouth to say something, but the three of them were distracted.

"Let go of me," Meghan's voice filled the room. Lady Kenley had Meghan by the elbow and was trying to lead her out of the room. Margaret was still sitting down. Lady Kenley looked very upset, but Meghan looked furious. Everyone turned to look. Meghan pulled away from her mother and Lady Kenley turned to grab her again.

"I already told you we are leaving," Lady Kenley snapped trying to grab Meghan's elbow again. Meghan moved so her mother's hand could not reach her.

"If you want to leave you can," Meghan said, "But I am not ready to leave yet."

"This is not a discussion," Lady Kenley said, "Or a debate. We are leaving now. Margaret."

"Yes, Mother," Margaret got to her feet. Lady Kenley caught Meghan's arm again, despite Meghan's attempt to avoid her grasp. Lady Kenley dragged Meghan out of the room with Margaret following at a safe distance.

"I did not think that was good," Percival said.

"Did not look good," Caleb said.

"I think it was Oliver and Meghan together that started it," Percival said.

"Why would Lady Kenley have a problem with that?' Leah asked.

Before Percival or Caleb could answer the butler entered the room.

"Cake will be served in the ballroom in two minutes," the butler announced.

Percival headed out of the room and Caleb and Leah followed. In the ballroom they found most of the party were either there or coming. Hilary was cutting the cake and servants were handing out the pieces. Leah saw that her father had found another chair and was sitting eating his cake. He did not look too tired or in need of help so Leah decided she could continue to talk with Percival and Caleb.

Once they had their cake the subject changed. Percival and Caleb started to talk about horses. Leah listened, but added very little. Hilary joined them once she was finished her official duties as birthday girl.

After the cake was finished and the servants collected the plates someone noticed that it had quit raining. Since it had quit but looked like it might start again any time people quickly started to make their way to the exit with the idea to get home before it started again.

# CHAPTER TWENTY-ONE

Leah and her father were the last ones to leave the party. James said he had had an enjoyable time, but looking at him Leah could tell he should have been home and in bed hours ago. He started to drift off to sleep as the carriage rolled down the road towards home. The rain started and stopped tapping on the carriage a number of times before they reached the turn off to the estate.

When they came in sight of the manor Leah could tell there was something wrong. There were too many windows with light in them, a horse was tied up next to the steps, and the door was open. Leah reached over and shook her father's knee. Slowly his eyes opened.

"Are we home?" James asked stretching a little.

"Yes," Leah answered, "But I think there is something wrong." James looked out the window of the carriage at the manor.

"Oh dear," James said.

The carriage had barely come to a stop in front of the steps when Roger came out of the manor followed by the cook and the village constable. James opened the carriage door and stepped down.

"What happened?" James asked.

"Lady Winsand escaped," Roger answered.

"How?" James asked.

"That was my second question," the constable said. Leah got down from the carriage.

"Let us go inside and discuss this," James said as he took Leah's arm. Everyone turned and went inside James tried to rush Leah, but she ended up supporting some of his weight. Once in the sitting room James sat down on the chair while Leah sat on one end of the settee. The constable took the other chair. Roger and the cook remained standing.

"How come Lady Winsand was locked up?" the constable asked.

"It was discovered that she was poisoning me," James answered, "I am still alive and I felt it was a private matter so I had Lady Winsand locked in her room. That was where she was supposed to stay until I figured out what to do next."

"How did she escape?" the constable asked.

"We were all in the kitchen," Roger said, "Supper was over and the clean-up was starting. I thought I heard a noise from upstairs. I had checked on Lady Winsand earlier and everything looked the same. I wondered if she might be trying to get out. Everything appeared to be normal as I went up the stairs. When I got to Lady Winsand's door something hit me on the back on the head and I did not remember anything until the cook woke me."

"Roger had not come back from investigating the noise," the cook said, "There also seemed to be a draft so Melissa and I went to investigate. We found the front door open and rushed up the stairs to find Roger lying on the floor. The door to Lady Winsand's room was open and she was gone."

"Was everyone in the kitchen when the first noises were heard?" the constable asked.

"Yes," Roger said.

"Who would want to help Lady Winsand escape?" the

constable asked.

"Lady Lambert," James answered, "They have been scheming together for months. And after I locked Lady Winsand in her room Lady Lambert was the only person who came looking for her."

"Do you think Lady Lambert is hiding her?" the constable asked.

"Very likely," James answered.

"What do you want me to do about it?" the constable asked.

"Keep them and their schemes as far away from me and my daughter as possible," James answered, "There is not much else anyone can do without causing a scandal."

"I will send two of my men here to keep an eye on things," the constable said, "How many men around here can help?"

"Roger, the groom," James answered, "The gardeners after they arrive for work tomorrow. And the cook's helper."

"The cook's helper cannot help," Roger said.

"Why not?" the constable asked.

"He died," Roger answered.

"From what?" James asked looking alarmed.

"We believe it was the last batch of poisoned cider," Roger answered.

"Poisoned by Lady Winsand?" the constable asked.

"No," Roger answered, "That was after Lady Winsand was locked in her room. We do not know who put the poison into the cider and the kitchen was empty for several minutes that morning while the cider was being made. We believe he drank the poison to make certain it tasted good and was ready. He died the next morning after becoming ill. Only he did not tell anyone he felt ill. Instead he simply went back to bed so no one knew it had happened until he tried to come back to work and died from the effort."

"Do you know who put the poison in the cider?" the

constable asked.

"No," Roger answered.

"I will go," the constable turned to James, "And I will send my men back here. But I can only promise protection for a month."

"That will be fine," James answered, "If we need protection for longer than that I will hire some."

"Very well," the constable stood up and left. Roger followed him.

A moment later Roger returned to the room in case Lord Winsand has more orders for him.

"Who is helping with the cooking?" James asked.

"Melissa," Roger answered.

"Hire a new helper tomorrow," James said, "Melissa needs to be spending more time with Leah. I do not want my daughter unchaperoned."

"Yes sir," Roger said. The cook left.

"Roger, explain the situation and tell everyone to be on their guard," James said.

"Yes sir," Roger said before leaving. James turned to Leah.

"I want someone with you at all times," James told her, "And I would prefer if you did not leave the manor."

"What about lessons?" Leah asked.

"As much as I would like you to go I am more worried about your safety," James answered. Leah nodded and sighed.

Melissa entered the room. Leah stood up and left the room with Melissa following her.

When Leah was ready she crawled into the bed. Melissa wrapped herself in a blanket and lay down on the floor. Leah was pretty sure Roger was sitting outside her door. She stared out the window. The rain had started again and the water was running down the glass. Leah wanted to go back to dancing with Caleb in the gazebo. She had been happy, Caleb was there, and her mother had been safely locked away. Now it was unlikely she would get to see Caleb until they figured out what her mother was up to. Not seeing Caleb was going to be the worst part and probably the hardest outcome of this change.

Lady Lambert was waiting by the front door and opened it as soon as she heard the carriage stop. Randall got down before helping Lady Winsand out. They came to the door.

"Welcome, Vivian," Lady Lambert said letting Lady Winsand and Randall inside.

"Thank you, Jennica," Lady Winsand replied, "It has been an absolutely horrible several days." Randall closed the door behind him.

"Come into the drawing room," Lady Lambert said leading the way. In the drawing room Lady Lambert made Lady Winsand comfortable before getting the butler to bring some food.

"What is the plan from here?" Lady Winsand asked as they waited for the food to arrive.

"Randall was supposed to get Leah and bring her when he brought you," Lady Lambert said, "And then they would marry." Lady Lambert turned to Randall, who was still standing near the door. He looked like he might be trying to sneak out before his mother noticed him.

"Where is Leah?" Lady Lambert asked.

"She was at the party," Randall answered, "But she always had someone around her. I tried to talk to her, but she refused. I could not just grab her and drag her off, someone would have stopped me."

"I explained this to you before," Lady Lambert's voice rose, "You have to be charming if you want Leah to trust you. You start out complementing her and then you talk with her about the weather or how the party is going. You have to take it in stages. Then you can suggest the walk alone in the gardens, where you knock her out and kidnap her. Without the charm and the stages it is not going to work."

"I tried," Randall said, "But I could not get near her and then she and the man she was talking to disappeared into the maze and I could not go after them because someone chose just that minute to speak to me."

"What man?" Lady Winsand asked.

"I did not know his name," Randall answered. "He seemed to be friends with Hilary's fiancé."

"Do you think your husband moved faster than we thought and Leah is engaged to someone else?" Lady Lambert asked.

"No," Lady Winsand answered, "He was not planning on telling her until her birthday. He will not move it up. She could have been talking to anyone."

"Well, unless he marries her before we can get to her it does not matter to us," Lady Lambert said.

"There was something else," Randall said, "Lord Winsand was at the party."

"He was at church the other day too," Lady Lambert said, "You did not put enough poison into his drink."

"I did exactly what the doctor instructed me to do," Randall frowns and crosses his arms over his chest.

"Which obviously was not enough if he is up and going to parties," Lady Lambert told him.

"I could try again," Randall said.

"You would not get near the kitchen," Lady Winsand said, "Especially now I am gone. Everyone there will be extra alert. Anyone who does not belong there will be noticed and escorted off the property."

"This is why it was important for you to get Leah at the party," Lady Lambert said, "So we would not have to try to get inside when they are watching for us. Now how can we get Leah before she is engaged?"

"I heard someone talking about Leah having a party for her birthday," Randall said.

"We are not likely to get her then," Lady Lambert said, "She will be the birthday girl and every one will be paying attention to her. And Lord Winsand will probably start off with the announcement of the engagement."

"But the preparations for the party will be the week before," Lady Winsand said, "James will spare no expense for Leah. There will be people coming and going from the manor all week and not all of them will be familiar to the staff."

"That would work," Lady Lambert said. She turned back to Randall. "You shall watch the house the week before while they are busy and you shall kidnap Leah when the opportunity presents itself. If you fail on this, we will not have another chance. And then I will be very upset with you."

"The food you requested," the butler said coming into the drawing room. He set it down on the table before leaving.

"Once we have her we will have to move quickly," Lady Lambert said.


Caleb closed the door to his room. It had been long, but good day. The lamp in his room had not been lit. He did not bother lighting it. Caleb smiled as he got ready for bed. He felt like whistling, but refrained from doing so because he did not want anyone else hearing it. When he was ready for bed Caleb opened the curtains so he could look out at the stars. He noticed there were still lights on at the Winsand Estate. Usually it was dark by this time and tonight there was a light on in just about every window.

The image of Randall standing by the punch table watching Leah came to Caleb's mind. Caleb was to the door to his room before any other thought entered his head. He stopped himself before he turned the knob. It would not do any good to ride over to the Winsand Estate. He could not do anything and it was unlikely they would need his help.

In fact he would probably end up answering uncomfortable questions from James Winsand as well as his parents. Then his meetings with Leah would come out and he would get interrogated on all of his activities. It would not be good for his and Percy's activities to be discovered now while Hilary might object.

Caleb dropped his hand from the knob and walked back to the window. The lights were still lit, but one window was dark that had not been before. As Caleb stood there and watched more windows went dark. Something had happened, but it was over now and everything was calming down. However there were some windows that did not go dark.

Caleb turned from the window and got into bed. Lying there Caleb tried to go to sleep, but his eyes kept drifting to the window. Thoughts and worries tumbled over themselves in his head. None of them would let Caleb sleep.

It was getting late into the night, but Caleb could not sleep and he could still see lights on. Caleb got out of bed and pulled on shirt and pants. He went to the door of his room and quietly opened it. No one else was in the manor was making noise. Being careful where he stepped Caleb left his room and headed down the hallway. When he reached the study he went inside. Caleb closed the door behind him before lighting a lamp. He went to the bookcase and pulled out the book he wanted. It had very little wear on the binding so the lettering on the cover seemed to shout out that this was the complete guide of tax laws of England. Caleb took it over to the chair and sat down. Opening it to the third page he started to read where he had left off from the last time. After three pages his eyes closed, his head bowed and he was asleep.

The hammer of rain on the window woke Melissa. She sat up and looked around the room. Leah was asleep in the bed and no one else was in the room. Melissa wrapped the blanket around herself again and lay back down. The floor was not the most comfortable place to sleep, but until Lady Winsand was found Melissa did not have a choice. She hoped that whatever Lady Winsand was planning she would put into action sooner than later. Then Melissa could go back to sleeping in her own bed. She had a hard enough time getting enough sleep to function during the day without the added interruptions and laying on the floor made various parts of her body hurt.

Melissa closed her eyes and tried to go back to sleep. But her mind would not let her relax. The little voice was back and it was telling her she should have told Haines about the baby. Melissa tried to ignore it. She was not sure what the voice wanted her to do about things now. She could not go out and meet Haines in the garden as she promised him. Roger was sitting outside the room and would stop her. He would have questions she did not want to answer. There was no way of getting a message to Haines. Melissa was not sure what the voice expected would happen if she told Haines she was pregnant. It was not like he was going to buy her a house and they would get married. She knew that when they became lovers. It was just an occasionally meeting, without any promises beyond tomorrow.

Maybe not being able to go out tonight was a good thing. If she did not see Haines again she did not have to put up with the voice lecturing her on not telling him. He also would not find out any other way and after a few times he would stop coming because he would realize the relationship was over. Then she would not have to face him. There would be no memories of the break up or the anger over her explanations, just the memories of the good times spent out in the hedge maze.

Having made the decision Melissa rolled over and closed her eyes. She relaxed and pushed all thoughts out of her head. For a few minutes it worked. She was starting to drift when a memory came back to Melissa of another servant who had gotten pregnant. She had been a friend of Melissa, but they worked for different people. The girl had been sent away without references or money. Just taken to the cross roads and dropped off. This starting bringing to her memory other worse stories that Melissa had heard about servants who had ended up pregnant.

Melissa felt the tears run down her face as this all went through her mind. She was going to have to figure out what to do before someone else realized she was with child. Not telling Haines was just the beginning of her problems.

CHAPTER TWENTY-TWO


*August 10, 1865*

Caleb said nothing about the lights at the Winsand Estate to his parents the next morning at breakfast. His father read through the meal and his mother talked about how great the party had been. When he could Caleb took an apple from the fruit bowl on the table and left. He went out to the stable. Haines was nowhere in sight when Caleb arrived. So he went over to Warrior's stall. Caleb offered Warrior the apple and Warrior took it. Then Caleb picked up the brush and let himself into the stall.

Caleb was done brushing Warrior when Haines entered the stable. Haines did not look like he had spent the night in the rose patch.

"Good morning, Master Caleb," Haines said.

"Good morning, Haines," Caleb said, "You look like there are no lingering effects from having a night off."

"That is because I didn't drink until I passed out in the rose patch," Haines said, "Not that I didn't drink. It was a good night."

"And you did not get into any trouble?" Caleb asked.

"No trouble at all," Haines replied, "Nothing that will

get me thrown out."

"I am told there is a marquess moving into the Putnam Estate if you need to find work," Caleb said.

"I don't know about him being a marquess," Haines said, "Unless he got the new title during his time in London, but the man moving into the Putnam Estate is Lord Eglantine. I've no interest in working for him. Especially since I'm told his wife isn't leaving London when he comes out to visit. It makes no sense to me as to why a man would have a summer home his wife doesn't visit."

"It makes perfect sense," Caleb said, "It is a place for him to spend time with his mistress. Whether he brings her with him or she is already living in the area."

"Did he have a lover before he left?" Haines asked.

"Someone said he might have been lovers with Lady Winsand, but I do not know for certain," Caleb answered, "If she was then he might get a surprise in finding out she is not available."

"She's available now," Haines said, "She escaped from wherever her husband was keeping her."

"Is that what happened last night?" Caleb asked.

"Yup," Haines answered, "She is gone and they didn't find her. Course, I'm not sure how much looking they were doing and how much was locking the doors behind her so she could not get back in. Anyway, no one is coming or going from the Winsand Estate today."

"And probably will not be until they figure out where Lady Winsand is and what she is planning," Caleb said.

"Don't know anything about that," Haines said, "But isn't her daughter the one you aren't sure you love?"

"I suppose you could put it that way," Caleb said.

"What's her mother want anyway?" Haines asked.

"To marry her off to Randall Lambert," Caleb answered.

"Elope with her," Haines said, "Save her from that horrible fate."

"It is not that easy," Caleb said.

"You keep saying that," Haines said, "Either you are repeating it so you believe it or you're over thinking it all. Eloping with her would save everyone some worry."

"Like all the advice I have been getting, I will consider that," Caleb said.

"Don't spend too much time thinking about it all," Haines said, "Otherwise she might not be there when you decide to act."

"I cannot speak with her on any matter at the moment," Caleb said. He headed out of the stable, while Haines started his chores for the morning.

Caleb went into the manor and upstairs to the study. His father was off doing something else when he entered. Caleb went over to the desk. He took out a piece of paper and carefully thought about it before putting pen to paper. He wrote out a note to Leah, though he was not sure how he could get it to her. When he was finished Caleb put the note in an envelope and wrote her name on it. Then he studied it for several minutes thinking of ways to get it to Leah. The idea came to him. Caleb got up and went to the bookshelf. Taking down the Lewis Carroll book, Caleb took it back to the desk. He carefully put the letter inside the book. Then he took both to his room and left them there until he could figure out some way of delivering it.

Leah sat in the library with a book in her land and Melissa doing mending nearby. It had been a long week and Leah was sure Melissa was starting to rip up clothes so she would have something to fix. Leah had finished reading one book and moved on to another book. She might have read more, but she was having trouble concentrating. Having spent most of her life being left alone to read, it was hard to focus on her book with another person sitting close by. Instead she had four people within the room. Melissa had sat and done mending or other quiet stuff. Roger had sat at the desk and done paperwork, which was noisy. James was the easiest to be in the same room with because he was fully engrossed in his writing.

Sometimes Leah and James would discuss his writing, or he would read some of what he had written. This helped the time pass quickly and also helped Leah's mind from wandering places it should not. However, when she could not concentrate on the book in her hand Leah found herself staring into space. All of her life, she had been allowed outside, but chose not to go. Now she wanted to go outside and they would not let her. Leah felt trapped and more than once she was sure that the walls were getting closer together and the air in the room was slowly leaking out.

Leah knew her father could not leave either, but he would disappear into his story and the situation would not bother him. She tried to lose herself in a book, but it did not work in quite the same way. For one thing, every time a romance element came up in the story, she wondered what Caleb was doing. Did he know why she could not see him? Had the news reached him, or was he at the door looking for her?

If Leah could have gone out to meet him she would not have been sitting here in the library slowly being driven mad. She wished for his arms to comfort her and she could forget about the worries over her mother's plans. Maybe they could even go riding again and she could feel carefree for an hour or two.

One day when just Melissa was with her she heard footsteps in the hallway outside the library. Leah looked up to see Roger go passed. He must have met James in the hallway, because Leah could hear them talk.

"The constable left a message for you," Roger said.

"And what did he have to say?" James asked.

"That he has found evidence of Lady Winsand at the Lambert place," Roger answered, "But he does not have enough evidence to demand her to come out to be arrested."

"Then we shall continue to sit and worry about her plans," James said.

"Have you thought about what to do about Lady Winsand?" Roger asked.

"No," James answered, "Did the constable say anything else?"

"That he was continuing to look into what he needed to arrest Lady Winsand," Roger answered, "And that his men would stay here until Lady Winsand is in jail, or something bigger comes up."

"Good," James said, "Hopefully she will act soon. After being locked away in this place for so long, I would really like to enjoy time outside."

"Yes, sir," Roger said. Both footfalls came toward the library. Leah went back to looking at her book. Roger continued passed, but James came into the library with his arms full of his writing supplies. He sat down at the desk and set out the materials before getting to work.

*August 11, 1865*

Jenny was just finishing with Hilary's hair when Charles knocked on the door.

"Yes?" Hilary asked.

"Your guests have arrived," Charles said, "They are waiting for you in the drawing room. Cook has everything prepared."

"Thank you," Hilary said. Charles left. Jenny stood back. Hilary checked in the mirror to make sure everything was perfect before standing up. She left the room and went downstairs to the drawing room. Percival was sitting on one chair and Caleb was sitting on the other. Both rose when Hilary entered the room.

"You look beautiful," Percival said as he stepped forward to kiss her on the cheek.

"Thank you," Hilary said, "Lunch is ready." Hilary led the way to the dining room. In the dining room Percival helped Hilary with her chair before he and Caleb sat down.

"Where are your parents?" Caleb asked noticing the table was only set for three.

"They received an invitation to have lunch somewhere else," Hilary said, "They wanted to stay if I was having guests over for lunch but I convinced them they should go."

"I thought you said something about inviting Leah Winsand," Percival said.

"I did, but she was not able to come," Hilary replied, "Her mother is out there somewhere with plans for Leah and no one wants her mother to get a chance to grab Leah."

"So, she is locked away until they figure out what her mother is planning?" Percival asked, "Sounds like a situation that would drive me crazy."

"That was part of why I was hoping she could come for lunch," Hilary said, "But

Her father refused to allow her to take that chance. I was thinking of sending a message to see if I could go and visit her. I do not think I will be turned down."

"When you go can I get you to deliver something for me?" Caleb asked.

"Sure," Hilary said. Caleb took the book out of his pocket and offered it to Hilary. Hilary accepted it and put it beside her plate.

"You ever figured out what to do about your problem?" Percy asked.

"Ignore people who want to talk about it," Caleb answered.

"Hardly a solution," Percival replied.

"Does the problem involve Leah?" Hilary asked, "She told me about seeing you."

"It has something to do with that," Caleb answered, "But that is not the whole problem. My family has made other plans for me."

"That sounds complicated," Hilary said.

"That is what I keep trying to tell your fiancé," Caleb

said, "But he will not leave it alone."

"I am just trying to help," Percival said.

"It is better if he figures it out for himself," Hilary said, "Did either of you hear about a marquess moving into the Putnam Estate?"

"No," Percival answered.

"A few times," Caleb said.

"Do you know anything about it?" Hilary asked.

"It is Lord Eglantine moving back," Caleb answered, "He wants a place where he can get away from London and his wife."

"I thought he arranged a marriage for himself," Percival said, "Why would there be problems already?"

"Maybe he missed his former lover," Caleb said.

"Who was that?" Hilary asked.

"Based on observation," Percival said, "Lady Winsand."

"I believe that," Hilary said, "Though it seems to me Leah's problems started about the time Lord Eglantine left for London."

"Lady Winsand needs to keep busy?" Percival asked.

"Could be," Caleb answered, "But since most of this is just speculation it might be best if we do not say anything to anyone else."

Charles came into the dining room to collect the plates. Hilary, Percival and Caleb return to the drawing room to continue their conversation.


On Thursday Leah received a message from Hilary asking if Leah was all right. Leah sent back an invitation for Hilary to come over for tea. Hilary sent the reply she could come for tea on Friday.

Friday morning and afternoon Leah had trouble sitting still while she waited for tea time to arrive. Hilary showed up a few minutes early, but Leah was already waiting near the door. They went into the drawing room and Melissa and Roger left them alone.

"What happened?" Hilary asked once Leah had poured them each a cup of tea.

"Someone came and broke Mother out," Leah answered, "Since then Father does not want me going too far. I have not been allowed to leave the house for a week."

"I would be going crazy by now," Hilary said, "What have you been doing?"

"Reading, mostly," Leah answered, "There is not much else to do; though I have been able to deal with some of the stuff for the party but only by writing notes to the tradesmen."

"I received the invitation," Hilary said, "And I brought something for you." Hilary took out a book and handed it to Leah. Leah looked at it. It was a copy of the Lewis Carroll book Caleb had told her about. Leah flipped through it and an envelope fell out. She picked it up. Her name was written on it in small, but careful handwriting on one side of it. Leah put it back into the book.

"Percival and Caleb were over yesterday for lunch," Hilary said, "And Caleb asked me to pass it on to you."

"Thank you," Leah said before setting it aside.

"How long will it be until you are able to go visiting again?" Hilary asked.

"No one knows," Leah answered, "It depends a lot on Mother and her plans."

"Even when she is not here she is controlling your life," Hilary said.

"That is just who my mother is," Leah said, "As much as I would prefer otherwise."

"You know this is all about who you are going to marry, right?" Hilary asked.

"It has more to do with the fact that my mother sold me," Leah said, "The Lamberts were not around as much until Mother started poisoning Father. The only time Mother had Lady Lambert over was when she had a group of ladies over. It was only after Father got sick they became best friends. I was sold to Lady Lambert so Randall could have an heir without having to worry about someone turning him down."

"Who does your father think you should marry?" Hilary asked.

"He has not said anything," Leah answered, "I think if I am happy he does not care who I marry."

"Tell him about your relationship with Caleb," Hilary said, "Maybe it will help."

"How would that help?" Leah asked.

"If you are engaged to Caleb your mother cannot marry you off to Randall," Hilary answered, "Once your engagement is announced you will be safe. Lady Lambert is not likely to hide your mother if there is no chance of Randall getting to marry you. Then she will have to figure something else out."

"Mother was willing to kill Father," Leah said, "If I married Caleb she would not give up. It might speed up her plan if it was announced I was engaged. I am just not sure I want to tell Father about Caleb right now."

"When will you, if not now?" Hilary asked.

"I told you before I was not sure where my relationship was going with Caleb," Leah said, "And I did not want to go there until after things with my mother settled down. However, if nothing has happened by my birthday I will tell him the day after."

"Very well," Hilary said.

"What is happening outside these walls? I would love some news." Leah asked.

"Nothing new with Edwina and Curt," Hilary answered, "But I think they have instructions to keep their mouths shut and stay out of trouble."

"They only have three weeks before the wedding," Leah said.

"A lot can happen in three weeks," Hilary said, "Remember at my party when Percival said Meghan was caught in the library with Oliver."

"Yes," Leah said.

"Oliver asked Lord Kenley for Meghan's hand in marriage," Hilary said.

"That was fast," Leah said.

"Lord Kenley told him no," Hilary said.

"Why?" Leah asked, "I thought Lady Kenley wanted the twins married off as fast as possible."

"Apparently Lord Kenley has a different view on the twins and marriage," Hilary said, "Nothing else has happened there, but Percival believes that Oliver will do something."

"Has Meghan said anything about it?" Leah asked.

"No," Hilary answered, "But those two are more like to gossip about others but they talk about themselves or each other."

Leah and Hilary continued to talk. Hilary did not leave until just about suppertime. Then Leah was back to having the servants watching her again. She spent the evening in the library reading her new book. She laughs at the strange antics and silently thanks Caleb for distracting her.

That night Leah lay awake with Caleb's letter under her pillow and waited until Melissa was snoring. Once she knew Melissa was asleep Leah quietly got out of bed with the letter. Stepping softly Leah went to the window. The moon was shining in, providing Leah with barely enough light to read by.

*Dear Leah,*

*I was hoping that we could go riding again, but I heard your mother escaped so you are not able to come out. Blackie was disappointed when I broke the news to him. I sympathize with him. I hope this problem solves itself quickly so we can go riding again soon.*

*It was wonderful dancing with you at Miss. Whitelaw's party. I received the invitation to your party and hope there will be dancing at it so I can hold you in my arms again.*

*Very lonely,*
*Caleb, (and Blackie)*

Leah smiled as she folded the letter up before creeping back to her bed. She put the letter back under her pillow and then got into the bed. She closed her eyes and had memories of Caleb replay in her mind. She drifted off to sleep with the smile still on her face.

Caleb watched as lights went out at the Winsand Estate. The evening slowly turned into night and the lights in the different windows blinked out. However, as with the rest of the week, some lights did not go out. Caleb figured it was for the people who were staying up to watch for danger. He had ridden past this afternoon and had noticed there was no one guarding the door in the hedge. Perhaps they had someone farther in to keep guard. Or James forgot it needed to be watched. When there was a lot on your mind sometimes things were forgotten. Caleb doubted Lady Winsand knew about the door. She was not the type to venture outside on her own and he would bet that she had ever explored the garden. He knew from waiting for Leah that it locked from the inside.

Percy had stopped by that morning to say Hilary was going to tea at the Winsand Estate this afternoon. Caleb hoped she remembered to take Leah the book. He wondered what Leah thought when she read the letter and how she reacted. Thinking back at what he had written in the letter Caleb thought about how much he did not put in the letter. But how do you express in words a longing to see someone that is so strong you end up thinking about them every minute of every hour? Things that had nothing to do with Leah had Caleb thinking about her and wanting to have her in his arms again. It was like a powerful drug and he was going through withdrawal.

Caleb sat down on the bed, still looking out at the lights in the distance. He wanted to sneak out and ride toward them. He would find Leah and wrap his arms around her and tell her she was everything he needed. Caleb stopped at that thought. It felt right to say Leah was everything he needed. The man that thought he would never meet the right woman found himself acting like a fool in love and the thought did not scare him like it was supposed to. Caleb was in love with Leah Winsand. And there was nothing he could do to change that. He did not want to change that.

Caleb now understood what Percival was talking about. Perhaps his father would understand if Caleb explained it to him about his feeling for Leah then maybe whatever arrangement his father had would not happen. Caleb shook his head. No, he did not care what his father's plans were any more. He was going to whatever it took to be with Leah. Perhaps he could convince her to elope with him, Caleb thought.

# CHAPTER TWENTY-THREE

Leah did not leave the manor the next week but she was not completely idle as the party approached. On Tuesday the seamstress from the village arrived for a fitting. Since Leah had sent her the measurements that the seamstress needed, the dress only required finishing touches. Leah tried it on and while the seamstress checked that it fit right Leah studied herself in the mirror. The dress was white with blue trim. The neckline was in between the dress Hilary had loaned her and what she usually wore. But rather than make Leah feel self-conscience it made her feel beautiful. Despite the measures to keep her safe Leah could feel the excitement for the party start to build up and she could not wait until it was here. Preparations for the party had started, so the household staff are kept busy. But there were also consultations with the florist for the final selection of flowers as well as visits from the cook to finalize the menu and with Roger over the choice of decorations to grace the food tables and walls in the ballroom. Melissa was helping to sew decorations for the party which meant Leah was not constantly being watched. However her father told Leah to stay upstairs and only select people were allowed upstairs to see her. So Leah found herself most days sitting on the window seat in her room and staring out. She looked wistfully at the hedge maze and the field beyond it thinking it would be nice to go riding.

Tuesday evening there was a knock on the door when Leah was headed back up to her room after visiting the library. She looked and saw her father come into the hallway. He opened the door.

"Yes?" James said.

"A message for Lady Winsand from Lord Eglantine," the boy that was standing there held out an envelope. James accepted it. The boy turned and left. James closed the door. He opened the envelope and read the first few lines of the letter inside before tearing both of them up and taking the pieces into the drawing room. Leah wondered about it as she went back to her room.

*August 18, 1865*

It was late evening when Caleb sat on Warrior with Percy sitting on his own horse nearby. They waited in the shadows of the trees of the garden as they waited for the lights in the upstairs rooms to go out.

"Have you conceded defeat over Leah Winsand?" Percy's voice drifted over to Caleb.

"I do not think this is a good time to discuss this," Caleb said.

"I know you believe in love," Percy said, "Otherwise you would not be out here. But do you believe you are in love with Leah Winsand?"

"She just needs support while she deals with her mother," Caleb said, "My father has plans for me."

"Why are you being so stubborn?" Percy asked.

"Why do you keep asking?" Caleb asked.

"Because I keep hoping you will come to your senses," Percy answered, "It does not do anyone any good if you bury your head in the sand and end up sacrificing your heart."

"What about Leah's feelings on the matter?" Caleb asked, "Or do they not matter?"

"She told Hilary about you two," Percy said.

"That does not tell me anything about her feelings," Caleb said, "She could be in need of someone to talk to without having any interest in me at all."

"Ask her how she feels," Percy suggested, "Then you will know."

"I cannot," Caleb said, "She is locked up to avoid her mother."

"Her party is coming up soon," Percy said, "Ask her then."

"Will you leave me alone if I tell you that I will ask her then?" Caleb asked, "If we do not get strung up for this little adventure."

"I will leave the subject alone until after the party," Percy said, "And they did not catch us when we helped Edwina and Curt. Oliver knows where to meet us, right?" The last light in the upstairs windows went dark.

"Yes. That is the signal," Caleb said as he nudged Warrior forward.

"Do you remember which window it is?" Percy asked as he followed.

"No," Caleb answered, "But Oliver arranged for that."

"How?" Percy asked. Then a candle appeared in one of the windows.

"That would be how," Caleb said. They went to the wall under that window. Caleb put the coil of rope across his torso before standing up in the saddle. He grabbed handholds on the wall and pulled himself up.

It took about ten minutes for Caleb to get up to the window, tie off the rope, help Meghan Kenley out the window, wrap the rope up again and climb back down the wall. Meghan was already mounted behind Percy. Caleb mounted Warrior. And they rode away from the Kenley

Estate as quietly as they could.

*August 20, 1865*

Friday Leah looked out the window just after lunch. She saw someone near the lake. It was impossible to tell who it was from that distance, but Leah wanted to believe it was Caleb. She wanted to run down there and see if she was right. Instead Leah picked up the book she had set down before lunch and opened to the place she had marked and she read the next sentence from the page. Her eyes would not focus on the second sentence. Leah looked back out the window. The person was still near the lake. Leah set down the book and stood up. She left the room. The house was quiet. Her father was in the library writing and everyone else was busy getting ready for the party. Leah went down the stairs. The ballroom took up one side of the house, as it was an addition by one of the previous owners of the manor and not part of the original construction as such if a person was in the ballroom they might as well be in a different building and that's where most of the servants worked.

Leah went through the dining room to the French doors. She did not see anyone, though she could hear that they were in other rooms. Leah stepped out the doors on to the patio and looked around. The constable's man was nowhere in sight, but based on what Melissa had said he spend most of his time at the kitchen door and only came this way once every half hour. Leah hoped she had timed it right as she started across the lawn. She made it across the open part of the lawn and into the hedge maze.

James watched Leah go into the hedge maze. For several minutes he thought he could see her moving, but he was not sure. James wanted to go back to a time when she would run to him to be held. She would wrap her arms around him and tell him she loved him. James knew she still loved him, but now that she was just about eighteen she was looking for a different type of love. The light in Leah's eyes had reminded him of a similar light in two of the most beautiful green eyes he had ever known. A girl he used to meet with in a garden.

James has also seen what the confinement had done to the light. It made the light come out as a fever, rather than just love. James wondered if his daughter knew she was in love. The light in Leah's eyes were the only thing stopping James from sending someone after her to make sure nothing happened to her. The light he had dreaded since the moment he held her in his arms for the first time. She was the only good thing that came out of his marriage and soon she would be married and gone, despite the story of the girl not going with the prince because she could not leave her father. It was not the father's job to get in the way of a marriage, just to make sure the girl was happy.

"Sir?" Roger's voice called from the doorway. James wiped the tears away before turning from the window.

"Yes?" James asked.

"Lord Morley is here to speak with you," Roger said.

"Show him up," James said.

"Yes, sir," Roger said before leaving. James sat down at the desk and a moment later Lord Ainsley Morley entered the library. He looked around briefly before taking the chair opposite from James.

"We need to talk about our agreement," Ainsley stated without introduction to the topic.

"I think they have taken things into their own hands," James said, "Or am I mistaken as to who Leah is hoping to meet out in the field."

"I doubt you are mistaken," Ainsley said, "But it changes the perspective on things. Like whether we should stick to the agreement or just let nature take its course. Taking into consideration you have an evil wife with her own plan for Leah."

"Those plans were the reason I made up the agreement

in the first place," James said.

"And so far it seems the agreement has just about killed you," Ainsley said.

"I think we should tell them about the agreement," James said, "We can give them a choice about announcing the engagement at the party or waiting for another time."

"What about Vivian?" Ainsley asked.

"I hope she does something which means I can shoot her," James answered, "But other than that I do not know what to do about her. Even if Leah got married, Vivian is not likely to stop. More likely Caleb would have to be cautious to stay alive."

"So, we tell them about the agreement and they can choose to tell the world or not be engaged," Ainsley said, "It might work."

James did not say anything and they were quiet for a few minutes.

"How are you doing health wise?" Ainsley asked.

"Good enough to go hunting with you when this mess is all sorted out," James answered.

"If you have it sorted out before the snow hits," Ainsley said.

"The minute the engagement is announced the mess will be dealt with," James replied.


Leah reached the door. She had no seen anyone at all in the maze, nor had she seen any signs of anyone coming or going through there. Since the door locked if closed Leah figured the gardeners were not worried about anyone coming in this way. She was not sure anyone else knew about the door.

Leah opened the door and looked around. There was no one, but she could see Caleb down by the lake. The field looked inviting and the lake shone in the sun. But Leah was not completely sure about going out there. Caleb saw her and climbed up on his horse. He rode over to the door, where he got down again.

"Hello," Leah said.

"Hello," Caleb said, "I thought you were stuck inside."

"I needed some air, so I snuck out," Leah said.

"What happens when they notice you are missing?" Caleb asked.

"I shall in trouble when they find me," Leah answered, "But I was not thinking about being gone too long. I saw you out here and found that I could not stay away. I got the book and your letter. And I miss you too."

Caleb leaned down and kissed Leah. Immediately she wrapped her arms around him. She felt like she had been dying of a thirst only Caleb could satisfy. With the way his arms went around her pulling her against him, she knew he felt it too.

Finally they both had to come up for air.

"I love you," The air from Caleb's breath tickled Leah's ear. His words filled her with unspeakable joy.

"I love you too," Leah felt tears of joy come to her eyes. She did not try to keep stop them from falling. Caleb kissed them away before finding her lips again. Leah kissed him back.

"How are you doing?" Caleb asked once the kiss had ended.

"Better now that you are holding me," Leah answered, "But it is hard to sit around waiting to see what Mother is going to do next. I feel trapped."

"There is a way you would not have to sit around and wait," Caleb said.

"What it that?" Leah asked.

"We could elope," Caleb said. Leah smiled.

"They would be out looking for me before we could get very far," Leah said, "And Father might head straight for the Lamberts' place. He is still recovering and I do not want to worry him. That and I cannot leave before my birthday party."

"What about after the party?" Caleb asked.

'Then it might be possible, we might even get father's blessing." Leah answered. Caleb kissed her again.

The sound of hoof beats could be heard startling both of them. A horse and rider was coming from somewhere.

"See you at the party," Caleb said before kissing Leah lightly. They separated and Leah went back to the garden path. As she closed the door Caleb was already getting back onto his horse.

Leah closed the door and walked back along the path. She stopped where she could see the manor and not be seen. The constable's man was walking passed the French doors, making sure there was no one lurking around. Leah waited until he had passed by the end of the building. Then she went back across the lawn to the manor. She slipped in the French doors. There was no one waiting there to catch her. Leah went up the stairs without meeting anyone. In her room Leah picked up the book again and went back to reading.


Melissa sat in the middle of the grass clearing. She had come out here an hour ago to sit and think. She had heard Leah come out and talk to Caleb before heading back to the manor. Their plan to elope meant nothing to her.

Sometimes she thought she could feel the baby growing inside of her. Feel it move, feel her stomach getting bigger. But she knew enough about babies to know it was too soon to expect those kinds of changes and all of these minutes wasted on sitting and worrying did not seem to be doing her any good.

Melissa got to her feet and left the clearing. She went back through the maze to the kitchen. The cook was sitting at the table watching the food cook. Her new helper was not in the kitchen.

"Have a seat," the cook invited when Melissa entered the kitchen. The cook signalled the seat across from her.

Melissa sat down on the seat.

"Still trying to figure out what to do?" the cook asked.

"The answer is not coming easily," Melissa answered.

"Why worry about it?" the cook said, "Lord Winsand will figure it out when you start showing. Everyone else who needs to know about it already does; unless you have not bothered to inform the father."

"There is no point in telling the father," Melissa said, "It is not like he is going to quit his job and take me away from all this. He works the same as I do. He cannot afford to support a child. I know he is not going to marry me just because there is a child on the way."

"Why do you not tell him and give him a choice in the matter?" the cook asked, "He might surprise you."

"And then what would he do?" Melissa asked, "Try to buy a house, afford a marriage license, and find another job he could do. None of those fit who he is and I do not want him trying to change who he is just because he feels honour bound. I will figure out something. I can take care of myself."

"Be careful," the cook said, "You go too far down some roads and it is harder for someone else to help you when you need it."

"I will figure it out for myself," Melissa said as she stood up. She left the kitchen.

# CHAPTER TWENTY-FOUR

*August 21,1865*

When Leah opened her eyes the sun was shining in her window. Rather than getting up Leah did not move and just watched the play of light across the floor. She could hear other people moving around the house. The preparations for the party were in full swing and there was likely to be people all over the place. Leah had been instructed by her father last night to stay within sight of Melissa. There were too many people around and many of them could not be recognized on sight, which made it possible for someone to be there uninvited. The worry about intruders meant being extra careful about where Leah went and what she did.

The longer Leah stayed in bed the less time she had to be followed everywhere she went. And Melissa was probably busy at the moment anyway. Leah pulled out the letter from Caleb that was still under her pillow. She read it again to herself before refolding it and putting it back. Despite the fear of what her mother had planned and the annoyance of too many people, Leah was looking forward to this birthday, or at least the party where she would be able to spend time with Caleb. The memories of their kisses came to Leah's mind as if they were just sitting and waiting for her to think about Caleb. Rather than just remembering it, Leah craved to be back in Caleb's arms. Fantasies were not a good as the real thing.

Sitting up Leah stretched before going looking for some clothes. After opening the wardrobe door she stopped. Maybe she should tell her father about Caleb and about how they felt about each other, father would understand, Leah knew he would. Though she would get a lecture on not telling her father what was going on, but she did deserve one. If she told her father perhaps he would give his permission for them to marry, then they would not have to elope. Although Leah was not sure about Lord and Lady Morley, their opinion might be the reason Caleb suggested they should elope. Leah took out a dress before closing the wardrobe doors. A knock came at the door before it opened and Melissa stepped into the room.

Caleb was saddling Warrior for their morning ride when he heard someone come into the stable. He looked towards the door to see his father standing there. His father stepped into the stable looking very uncomfortable

"We need to talk," Lord Morley said.

"About what?" Caleb asked.

"You remember when you were asking about the agreement I had for you to marry?" Lord Morley asked.

"Yes," Caleb answered.

"I think now is the right time to talk about it," Lord Morley said.

"Okay," Caleb turned from Warrior to his father. Warrior voiced his complaint about the delay in their exercise, but Caleb just patted his neck.

"You were about a year old when Lord Winsand showed up at our door," Lord Morley said, "He had a baby daughter and could see certain problems arising from that fact. So, he and I signed a legal agreement. It states that you will be engaged to Leah Winsand on her eighteenth birthday if you or she are not promised in marriage to some else."

"Which would be why Lady Winsand has been frantic to get Leah engaged to Randall before her birthday," Caleb said.

"Yes," Lord Morley said, "We decided not to tell you two because we did not want to stop you from finding someone else. But today is her birthday and I spoke to Lord Winsand and he agreed it was time to tell you two."

"So, you are going to announce Leah and I are engaged, as per your agreement, tonight at the party?" Caleb asked.

"Actually, I was supposed to talk to you and Lord Winsand would talk to Leah," Lord Morley said, "before we make the decision. As of this morning, the lawyer who witnessed the agreement considers you to be engaged."

"With this agreement," Caleb said, "What would have happened if we hate each other?"

"We did not discuss that at any point," Lord Morley said, "Nor did we discuss the possibility that you might not need our help in getting together, especially since it looked like you were not going to meet until the day of the party. We should have made the introduction but Lady Winsand would not allow it."

"If Leah is willing then the engagement can be announced," Caleb said, "But if she does not want it announced then respect that it is her party."

"Her father would never let me do otherwise," Lord Morley said before turning to leave. Caleb turned back to Warrior, who had been impatiently waiting.

"So, you didn't need the advice after all," Haines's voice came from somewhere in the back of the stable, "The one you love is the one your father planned for you to marry. Though that does make sense based on the friendship between Lord Winsand and your father." Haines came into sight swinging a bucket.

"Apparently," Caleb said.

"I wish my life worked out as smoothly," Haines said, "But I suppose it works out to I'm a groom and you're nobility."

"I am pretty sure even grooms can find love," Caleb said, "Or have their life work out." Caleb opened the stall door and Warrior walked out.

"Best deal I've ever had in my life was getting the job here," Haines said.

"Then things have not worked out too badly for you," Caleb said.

"True," Haines replied, "But that doesn't stop me from looking for something better." Caleb smiled as he shook his head. Haines took his buckets and left the stable.

After making sure the saddle was on right Caleb climbed up and headed out of the stable. He headed for the field. Once clear of the garden Caleb spurred Warrior to go faster. Warrior willing obliged. Caleb let the thoughts spin through his head for several minutes before letting any of them come to the forefront of his thoughts. But one came up anyway. It had nothing to do with his father not telling him anything, or the party, or which direction Warrior was going. The only thing that came out of the many thoughts was one that made him smile and want to cheer. He was going to marry Leah Winsand, the one girl in the world who he liked from the minute he had seen her and it had only a little bit to do with how much leg he could see at the time.

Leah stared into the mirror. The dress was beautiful. The seamstress had added gold strip to all the edges since the fitting. Melissa had spent extra time on Leah's hair to make sure it was just right. Standing there looking in the mirror Leah thought she looked like a birthday girl should. She could not wait for guests to start arriving so she could show off the dress.

The door opened and Melissa came in.

"Have the guests start arriving?" Leah asked.

"Not yet," Melissa answered, "But the first ones should be arriving soon."

Melissa stayed where she was by the door.

"Is there something else?" Leah asked.

"Your father wants to speak with you," Melissa said, "He is in the library."

"I will come," Leah said. She turned to the door and let Melissa go out ahead of her. Melissa led the way to the library before leaving. Leah went into the library. Her father was sitting behind his desk with a pen in hand. Leah sat down in the chair opposite him and waited for him to finish what he was writing.

Finally he looked up.

"You look incredible," James said.

"Thank you," Leah smiled, "What did you want to talk to me about?"

"Oh yes, that," James said. Leah waited patiently while her father gathered his thoughts.

"When you were born I was worried about the future," James said, "I knew your mother would have some scheme involving your marriage and dowries. She was always trying to figure out how to make extra money even when I married her. However, I did not want you to marry whoever your mother decided. I hoped you would make your own decision on that matter that you would find someone you loved." James paused but Leah just sat waiting for him to continue.

"So, I made up a legal agreement with a friend," James continued, "If you had not found someone to marry by your eighteenth birthday then you would marry his son. Your mother found out about this agreement, which was why she poisoned me and tried to sell you off to the Lamberts. The agreement is still legal and unless I write a letter to the lawyer saying otherwise he considers you to be engaged as of this morning."

"Who am I engaged to marry?" Leah asked.

"Caleb Morley," James answered, "The Morleys were the only ones I believed could protect you from your mother."

"Why are you telling me this now and not before my mother sold me to the Lamberts?" Leah asked.

"Because I did not want you to be influenced by my agreement when you looked for someone to marry," James answered, "And the agreement says the announcement about the engagement should be tonight at the party. But Lord Morley and I decided it might be better if we asked you before saying anything at the party." Leah was quiet while she thought about it. Yes, she wanted to marry Caleb and get away from her mother. Hilary had said it was a good match. And her father apparently had already decided for her. But she loved Caleb and this seemed like an answer to everything.

"Yes, you can make the announcement," Leah said, "But only near the end of the party."

"Very well," James said. He picked up his pen to start writing again.

"Melissa says the guests will start arriving anytime," Leah said, "And if I am supposed to make my grand entrance after everyone has arrived you should be down there to greet people."

"You are right," James said. He put down his pen and stood up. Going over he kissed Leah on the forehead before leaving the library.

After Leah went into the library Melissa went to her room. She stuffed everything she thought she would need into a bag. She made sure she only took what was hers and not anything that did not belong to her. She looked around the room one more time. It was the size of a closet, but it was her own space and something she was loath to give up.

Melissa blew out the candle. Stepping out of the room Melissa listened to see if anyone was around. Aside from voices coming from the library she did not hear anyone. Putting the strap over one shoulder Melissa went down the hallway and then down the stairs. There would be too many people out front for her to go that direction so Melissa went through the dining room and out the French doors. She went across the lawn and into the hedge maze. Once on the gravel path she stopped and looked back at the manor. The lights would have been a welcoming sight to her any other time, but this one. This time she knew she would not likely see them again.

As a pregnant servant she did not have any other choice. Leaving would prevent shame from spreading from her to everybody else around her. With Lord Winsand's plans to hire more staff Melissa was sure her position would be filled shortly. Even if she did try to stay her position would have to be filled by someone else within the year or eliminated when Leah married. And then there would be a baby to deal with. They tended to cost money without giving anything back to the household. Either that or the baby was sold to someone else with the means to look after it. Melissa had no intention of letting anyone else raise her child. Even if she ended up in the poor house she would be there for her child. She did have a few skills if she could find someone who was willing to hire her.

Melissa turned and headed into the maze. She walked to the door to the field. She opened it and stepped outside. Closing it behind her Melissa looked around again. There was no one around. That suited Melissa's purpose. She started long the hedge with the idea she would go all the way around the hedge to the road and then follow road to the village. From there she would find some way to get farther than that. And hopefully on what little money she saved since she had little other option.

The sound of hoof beats came down the field. Melissa

tried to hide in the shadows made by the hedge as she looked around. The horse was coming from the other direction. It came down the field. Melissa recognized the rider as Randall Lambert. She froze, but he was concentrating on the door and did not see her. At the door he dismounted and pulled out a key to open the door. It took several tries to get the lock to work with the key, but he finally managed it. Then he went into the hedge maze. Melissa started to move toward the door, but stopped herself before she went two steps.

Yes, Randall was there uninvited, but she would not get there before him no matter which direction she went. And by now someone else would be with Leah. As long as there was someone with Leah she would be fine. Melissa turned and continued toward the village. It was the only way things would work out.


Leah sat there twisting her hands as she waited. She wanted to scream for joy, but she also felt like crawling into a corner with nervousness. Was Caleb okay with this legal agreement between their fathers, or was he upset about it? He had told her he loved her, but that did mean he was ready to make it official? Leah stood up and paced to work off some energy. Her mind was going a mile a minute and like her feet when she danced it was tripping over itself. Finally she tiptoed out of the library and went across the hall to one of the rooms with a window facing to the front of the manor. Through the lace in the curtain she watched the guests arrive.

Hilary and her parents arrived with Percival. They looked so happy with Hilary and Percival talking while Lord and Lady Whitelaw followed them. Margaret Kenley arrived alone, without even her mother as an escort. Leah had heard Meghan was missing as well as Oliver Borden. Lady Kenley was likely at home waiting to see if anything turned up. It was thought the two had run off together, but no one had been able to find them and figure out whether it was true. The next carriage arrived and Caleb stepped out. He looked so handsome to Leah that she wanted to go down and wrap her arms around him. He turned and helped a woman, who Leah figured was his mother, out of the carriage. Then a man about the same age as her father got down. Lord and Lady Morley were talking with each other, but Caleb seemed a bit withdrawn. Was he upset over the agreement, or just that they had not been told until now? Leah wondered. Edwina and Curt arrived in the same carriage. Neither of them had their parents with them. With Edwina's glow Leah figured the rumours were true about her being expecting.

More people arrived until finally it looked like everyone was here. Leah noticed that Randall had not shown up, which to her was a relief. Leah heard footsteps on the stairs and she went out into the hallway. Roger reached the top of the staircase at the sight of her he nodded to her before turning around heading back down the stairs. Leah followed him down. This was going to be her grand entrance.

When they reached the door to the ballroom Roger went inside to tell her father that she was waiting. Leah took a deep breath quell the nervousness. Before she could let it out someone grabbed her from behind. Leah screamed and struggled with all her might. A sweet smelling cloth was put over her mouth and nose. Leah struggled for a few seconds longer before she went limp. Whoever it was threw her over his shoulder and she passed out.

# CHAPTER TWENTY-FIVE

"Where the hell is the butler this time?" Lord Eglantine muttered under his breath as he strode through the hallway. The knocking on the front door came again. Whoever this visitor was they were persistent. Since the butler disappeared it took him several knocks before he realized he had to answer the door himself. Lord Eglantine walked across the entranceway as he continued to mutter unpleasant things about the missing butler.

Lord Eglantine opened the door to find a woman standing on the front steps. She was wearing a navy cloak with the hood up so he could not see her face in what little light came through the door from the lamps inside. He could see the carriage that stood in front of the steps and could tell it belonged to the Lamberts. The woman standing on his doorstep was not Lady Lambert. He could tell because the woman was shorter than Lady Lambert.

Lord Eglantine took a step back out of the doorway so the lady could come inside. The lady stepped inside. Lord Eglantine closed the door before turning to the lady. The lady was studying the entrance with the two stairways go up to the second floor. The various doors off this area were closed. Lord Eglantine himself had been vastly impressed the first time he had seen it. Now he was just impatient as to whom this lady was who was interrupting his work.

The lady removed her hood as she turned back to face him. It was Vivian Winsand. Lord Eglantine stood there appraising her, but did not say anything. She looked exactly as she had when he left; though the dress looked like it had been altered to fit her rather than made for her. Perhaps it had something to do with the fact that he had not received a reply to the message he had sent to her residence.

"I need your help," Vivian said as she stepped closer to Lord Eglantine.

"With what?" Lord Eglantine asked.

"I arranged a marriage between Leah and Randall Lambert," Vivian answered, "James did not like it and locked me up for it. Jennica and Randall helped me get out, but for the marriage to take place we are going to have to get Leah away from James. There are three of us against the people he has gotten to help him. I need your help if we are going to arrange this wedding."

"What about Lord Lambert?" Lord Eglantine asked.

"He has decided he has done enough and refuses to help us any farther," Vivian answered, "He refuses even to have it discussed in his presence."

"And what do I get out of helping you?" Lord Eglantine asked.

"When this is all over I cannot go back to James," Vivian answered as she wrapped her arms around Lord Eglantine's neck and pressed her body to his.

"I have a wife," Lord Eglantine said.

"I hear she is in London, while you are living out here," Vivian said, "It gets lonely out here in the country." She moved so her lips were brushing his ear. "And no one has to know I am here."

Leah's scream echoed in the ballroom above the noise of

everyone talking. It was cut off in the middle. Silence descended like a weight around the room. Everyone seemed frozen in their place. James was the first one to start moving and Caleb was the second. People moved out of the way as the two men ran for the door. When they got there and went into the hallway it was empty. Roger was close behind them.

"I only left her for a second," Roger puffed out, "to find you."

"Where was Melissa?" James demanded.

"I do not know," Roger answered, "I could not find her when I went to get Leah and I have not seen her for a while."

"Get the constable," James said, "And tell him to meet me at the Lambert residence."

"Yes, sir," Roger answered and ran off. James turned and went into the ballroom.

"I thank you all for coming," James said, "But there is a problem. I hope it gets resolved quickly, but the celebration is over for tonight. It will be rescheduled."

No one asked any questions as James turned and left the ballroom. Caleb had waited in the hallway.

"This was what you were afraid of, was it not?" Caleb asked.

"Yes," James answered as he started for the door. Before he could get very far Lord Morley came out of the ballroom.

"What are we going to do about this problem?" Lord Morley asked. Percival and Lord Whitelaw also entered the hallway.

"We go to the Lambert residence and get my little girl back," James answered, "All help is appreciated." Then he went through the door with Lord Morley close on his heels. Caleb followed his father out the door with Percival and Lord Whitelaw behind them. They got out in time to see the groom ride off to get the constable.

"Did you see someone come out here a minute ago?" James demanded of the closest driver.

"No, sir," the driver answered.

"He must have gone out a different way," Lord Whitelaw said.

"Then we may get there before they do," Lord Morley said.

"Good," James said, "Then we do not have to worry about getting into the house."

Roger came out of the house. He was carrying two muskets and a flintlock. James took a musket. Roger handed the other two weapons to Lord Morley and Lord Whitelaw.

"Do we ride or take a carriage?" Lord Morley asked.

"Carriage," James answered, "We do not have time to get people horses and I do not have enough for people to borrow."

The men headed for the Morley and Whitelaw carriages. The drivers of both snapped to attention and were given hurried instructions. The Morley carriage was the first moving, but the Whitelaw carriage was not far behind.


Leah felt like she was dreaming about riding a horse at speed. Only this time it made her dizzy and nauseous. With everything cloudy already Leah tried to go back into the blackness because it was easier to take. Something jarred her. Why would someone be trying to wake her up? Leah wondered, since I am obviously sick. She crawled back into the blackness in her mind. The next jolt did not disturb her as much.

The motion stopped causing Leah to come out of the blackness a little. Was she being pulled off a horse? Why would she be on a horse? Was it Caleb who was carrying her or was it someone else? What caused her to collapse? Was she poisoned like her father had been? Was it all just a strange dream?

"What happened?" a female voice said. It sounded like Lady Lambert's voice, but Leah could not figure out why she would have a dream with Lady Lambert in it.

"I had to knock her out," Randall's voice answered, "But I only used a small amount." Small amount of what? Is that what was causing this dream?

"Then she should wake up soon," Lady Lambert said, "I will show you where to set her down inside." There were several more bumps before Leah was set down on something. It might have been a bed, but it was not very soft. Leah sank back into the darkness.

The constable and his men caught up with the carriages as they stopped in front of the Lambert Manor. The men got down from the carriages.

"You think Miss Winsand's in there?" the constable asked.

"I know it," James answered, "Along with my wife and the rest of the schemers who will pay for taking my daughter from me."

The door to the manor opened.

"Can I help you?" the butler asked standing in the doorway.

"Yes," the constable answered, "You can get out of the way so we can search the place."

"What is this about?" the butler asked.

"We are looking for Leah Winsand," the constable answered, "Now get out of the way."

"She is not here," the butler said as he stepped outside and to one side.

"What is going on?" Lord Lambert appeared at the door.

"We are here searching for Leah Winsand," the constable answered.

"She is not here," Lord Lambert said, "Aside from the servants I am the only one here."

"Where are Lady Lambert and Randall then?" James

demanded.

"I do not know," Lord Lambert answered, "Jennica just said they were going out."

"Keep an eye on them," the constable told his men, "While the rest of us search the house." The constable went inside followed by James, Caleb and the rest of the men. They searched the house from top to bottom. There was no sign of Leah or Lady Winsand. Lady Lambert and Randall were not there either. The men headed outside again. Lord Lambert and the butler were still standing in the same position.

"I told you they were not here," Lord Lambert said.

"Then where are they?" the constable asked.

"I do not know," Lord Lambert answered.

"Lady Lambert had a meeting this evening," the butler replied.

"A meeting with who?" the constable asked.

"The vicar," the butler said.

"Then they will be at the church," James said, "And we have lost valuable time here." The men got back into the carriages they came in. The constable and his men mounted their horses. All of them headed for the church.

Lord Eglantine had wrapped the reins around a tree branch before moving closer to the church. After the butler had found him and Vivian in a nest of their clothing on the floor he had been decided that it was time to leave. Vivian had gotten dressed before leaving in the Lambert's carriage. Lord Eglantine had to stay long enough to fire the butler and make sure his man's man escorted him off the premises. Then he had ridden over to join her.

The lights of the church showed its location and the carriage. But no one else seemed to be there. Vivian had explained that he was going to help her with anyone who showed up to stop the wedding from happening. Lord Eglantine crept forward to find Vivian exactly where she said she would be. They kissed, but it was interrupted too soon by the sound of horses and carriages coming towards the church. Vivian pulled out the pistol Lord Eglantine had loaned her. He took out the second of the pair of dueling pistols, but figured there would not be much cause to use them if they did this properly.

It took James and his friends longer to get there because of the speed of the carriages. When they arrived they found the church had several candles lit inside and the Lambert's carriage sitting outside. They stopped and everyone got down. They headed into the church.

Inside the church they found the vicar standing at the front talking to Lady Lambert and Randall, who were sitting together in the front pew. All three turned at the sound of the men entering. Lady Lambert and Randall stood up to face the men. Lady Lambert as stylish as usual, but Randall was only dressed in a white shirt and black pants.

"What is this intrusion?" Lady Lambert demanded.

"You have my daughter," James answered.

"Do not be ridiculous," Lady Lambert said, "We are here to visit the vicar."

"Then we will have you stay here while we search the church," the constable said.

"You cannot just riffle through a church," the vicar said.

"Do not worry," the constable said, "We are only looking places a person could be. We will not be going through anything else."

"This is wrong," the vicar said.

"No, kidnapping is wrong," James said, "Attempted murder is wrong. And forcing someone to do something they do not want to do is wrong."

"Men, keep your eyes on these three," the constable pointed the Lady Lambert, Randall and the vicar.

"I will stay here as well," Lord Whitelaw said.

"Very well," the constable said. The rest of the men started to search the church. Two went up and down the rows looking between pews. One person enters through the door on each side of the sanctuary and another through the vicar's door at the back of the stage.

The men checked every room they could find. Caleb found a pile of clothes in the vicar's quarters. Picking them up he recognized them as looking like something a groom would wear when driving someone someplace. James came into the room behind Caleb.

"Did you find anything?" James asked.

"It looks like the clothes Randall was wearing when he kidnapped Leah," Caleb said, "They were on the floor as if someone dropped them before rushing out of here."

"Then Leah has to be here somewhere," James said. The constable entered the room before they could start searching.

"That looks like his clothes," the constable took them and looked them over, "But this space does not look big enough to have a place to hide her." In the pocket of the jacket the constable found a white handkerchief. He sniffed it without getting it too close to his face. He found it had a smell sweet.

"Chloroform," the constable put it back, "This is the kidnapper's clothes, but where is Miss Winsand?"

"Somewhere in here based on the placement of the clothes," Percival answered.

"There does not seem to be much here," Lord Morley said as he looked around. The room was large enough for a bed, a trunk, and a desk. The trunk was open so they could see the clothes scattered inside.

Caleb was looking around the bed when the flooring under his foot creaked. James and the constable looked over. They came over and helped Caleb move the bed out of the way. Caleb got down on his hands and knees to search for a trap door. It took him a moment to find the handle. He pulled it up. Under the trapdoor was a staircase Caleb went down it using only a candle James had lit before handing it to him. He could see a bed set up beside some barrels and Leah was lying in it.

"She is down here," Caleb called up. James came down the steps and saw Leah was there. Leah did not move.

"Is she all right?" James asked. Caleb checked for a pulse and found a strong one.

"She seems fine," Caleb answered, "Probably just the chloroform."

James turned on his heel as he got the musket ready to fire.

"Do not do it," Caleb said. James stopped going up the stairs.

"They tried to take her from me," James said.

"But they did not get her, she is safe," Caleb said, "Let the constable deal with them, it is his job." James's shoulders sagged, but he lowered his gun to his side.

"You are right," James said, "But if this does not work I will do something about them." James started up the stairs again. Caleb lifted Leah from the bed. In his arms she snuggled closer to his warmth. Caleb kissed her forehead. He carried her up the stairs. James and the constable were standing there. The constable nodded and led the way out of the room. They went back to the main sanctuary. Everyone else was waiting there since they had not found anything in the areas they searched. They all looked delighted to see Caleb carrying Leah. Lady Lambert looked like she was going to go red in the face and start screaming, but instead a thought seemed to come to her and she calmed down. The constable took out some restrains and locked Lady Lambert, Randall and the vicar in separate ones. His men led them out of the church. The constable turned to everyone else.

"I will need a statement from all of you," the constable said, "As soon as possible."

"We might as well all go down now," Lord Morley said, "No point in postponing it. Caleb can take Leah home in one carriage while the rest of us go in the other. His statement can be taken later."

"That is fine with me," the constable said. While the rest of them made their way to the door, Caleb went ahead of them so he could get Leah home soon. He was out the door well before everyone else. The constable's men and their prisoners were already on their way down the road in a prison wagon. The drivers of the carriages were nowhere in sight. Caleb figured on putting Leah inside the one carriage before looking for them. Caleb put his foot on the step when he heard a noise from right behind him. It sounded like someone moving in the darkness.

"No one can take my daughter and get away with it," Lady Winsand's words were a hiss. In the corner of his eyes Caleb could see her coming out of the dark. She was holding a primed flintlock. Caleb froze. She could just as easily hit Leah as she could him. A shot rang out in the darkness of the night, but Caleb did not feel any pain. He looked back and saw Lady Winsand slumped over with blood appearing on the front of her dress. James stood near the door to the church with the musket in his hands.

"I knew she had to be around here somewhere," James said. Caleb readjusted his grip on Leah. The other men rushed out to see what happened. The constable saw Lady Winsand and took the musket away from James. James let it go.

"She was going to shoot him," James said.

"That is fine," the constable, "But I still need to investigate it so it cannot be called anything other than self defense."

"Let's go," James said. The drivers reappeared. It looked like they had been tied up on the other side of the carriages, but the person tying them up had been sloppy. They took their places with the right carriages. James headed to the one carriage. Lord Whitelaw did not move with the rest of them.

"I will stay here with the body until the doctor can be called to deal with it," Lord Whitelaw said.

"I will have him sent for right away," the constable said. He mounted his horse while everyone else climbed into the one carriage.

"The Winsand Estate," Caleb told Jack.

"Yes, Master Caleb," Jack said.

"Caleb?" Leah's voice was sleepy.

"I am here," Caleb told her.

"Good," Leah said before she drifted back to sleep. Caleb climbed into the carriage with his future wife in his arms.

Lord Eglantine stayed in the shadows as he watched the scene play out before him. He had tried to stop Vivian from going out and confronting Caleb, but she had been too angry to listen. Now she was dead.

Lord Eglantine figured she was the only thing connecting him to this scene and this plot. Quietly he moved back into the trees to where his horse was tied. Yes, he had lost a lover, but lovers were plentiful if one moved in the right circles.

# CHAPTER TWENTY-SIX

The drive was empty when the carriage pulled up to the step. Caleb opened the door to the carriage before gathering Leah in his arms again. As he stepped down, the door to the manor opened and the butler stepped outside. Caleb went up the steps.

"Lord Winsand is with the constable making a statement," Caleb said, "He said to bring Leah back here."

"Of course," the butler said as he went back into the house. Caleb followed him inside and then stopped while he closed the door. The butler headed up the stairs and Caleb followed. On the third floor the butler opened the door to one of the rooms and stood aside. Caleb went inside. It was Leah's bedroom. Caleb took her over and gently set her down on the bed. Then he tucked the blanket around her. Caleb kissed Leah on the forehead before standing up.

He stood there and watched her sleep. She looked beautiful. He wanted to hold her in his arms and never let the world have another chance to take her away. It did not matter if the threat were gone or not. But the best way to protect her at this moment was to go and give a statement.

Then Lady Lambert and Randall would not be able to get at her and her father would not be charged with her mother's death.

He had been in love with this woman since he saw her up to her knees in the fish pond. Even when she spilled punch on him, Caleb had still been in love with her. He had been serious about eloping, but it did not look like it was necessary. However, looking back he should have suggested it to Leah back when Haines originally gave him that piece of advice rather than letting things get this far.

Haines being right about something was a strange idea to Caleb, but then Percy had been right about things too. And by not giving in for so long Caleb felt like he had missed so much time with Leah. But he was not going to miss any more. He would go and talk to the constable, but he would come back to talk to her after that.

The butler stepped into the room and cleared his throat. Caleb turned. The butler was standing there with a look on his face that suggested Caleb should be on his way. Caleb left the room and the butler followed him out.

Outside the manor Caleb got back into the carriage after giving Jack the instructions to take him to see the constable. The carriage started moving after Caleb closed the door. Caleb's thoughts ran in various directions as he watched the scenery go passed the window. But they always seemed to go back to Leah for he could really think of little else.

The carriage slowed down and then stopped. Caleb looked out to see the constable's office. He climbed down from the carriage. The Whitelaw carriage was not in sight, so Caleb figured they must have finished with the constable and gone home. Going inside the office, Caleb found his father and James Winsand sitting there talking to the constable. James turned his head to look at Caleb. Caleb noticed he looked tired and worn.

"Leah is resting in her own bed," Caleb said.

"Good," James said.

"Now, I need your statement as well as one from the driver of the carriage," the constable said.

"I am ready," Caleb said sitting down in the chair nearest to the constable's desk.

The constable asked Caleb some questions. Caleb went through everything that had happened, from the scream to taking Leah home. The constable asked a few other questions, which Caleb answered. The constable wrote it all down. When he was finished questioning Caleb the constable went outside to talk to Jack. When the constable came back in Caleb followed his father and James out of the office. They got into the carriage and went back to the Winsand Estate.

Lord Morley was about to protest when Caleb got out of the carriage when it had stopped in front of the steps.

"It is okay," James told him. Lord Morley nodded. Caleb closed the door once James was out of the carriage. Roger had the door open for them as the carriage drove away.

"How is Leah doing?" James asked Roger once he and Caleb had stepped inside.

"She was not awake yet when I last checked," Roger answered, "Is there anything you need?"

"A cup of cider would be good," James answered.

"Yes, sir," Roger replied. Then he headed off to the kitchen. James started up the stairs with Caleb following him.


Leah woke up to the sound of voices outside her bedroom door. She sat up and looked around. She was in her own bed. Her party dress was wrinkled and creased with some dirt rubbed into it. She remembered someone grabbing her from behind. She thought there might have been a ride on a horse and Caleb holding her close. It was all fuzzy and very confusing. She could not hear what was being said out in the hall, but it sounded like her father's voice and Caleb's.

The voices stopped. Leah was thinking about getting out of bed to check when someone turned the knob. The door opened and her father stepped into the room. He closed the door behind him.

"It is good to see you awake," James said as he walked over to the bed. He sat down on the edge.

"What happened?" Leah asked, "Someone grabbed me and then everything after that is fuzzy."

"Randall Lambert kidnapped you and took you to the church," James answered, "It was Lady Lambert's intention that you would marry her son as soon as you woke up. With the constable's help we stopped them before it got that far. Now Randall and Lady Lambert are sitting in jail. The judge is supposed to set a date for the trial tomorrow."

"What about Mother?" Leah asked, "Was she there?"

"She was there," James answered, "She was going to shoot Caleb to stop him from taking you away from there. I saw only one way to stop her from killing him. I am sorry Leah but your mother is dead."

Leah hugged her father. Her mind was torn between happiness her mother would not be controlling her life ever again and the sadness that her mother was gone. With the way her father was hugging Leah back she knew that he was not as confident as he tried to appear to be. The hug lasted several minutes as they held each other up.

"The constable told me what he had found out about the poisonings," James said once they let go, "He is going to add that to the charges. He said the Lamberts had a doctor under their employment. He was likely the one who gave your mother the poison and Randall the chloroform that knocked you out. The constable is looking into the possibilities as well as Lord Lambert's involvement."

"Does that mean it is all over?" Leah asked.

"For tonight," James answered, "Tomorrow there will be

a few more things and when the trial happens we will have to go over it again. After that it will all be over."

Leah nodded.

"I have to go," James said.

"You look like you need to rest," Leah said, "It will take time for you to finish recovering from being poisoned."

"I will rest better when I get back," James replied, "I am going to see the doctor to make sure Vivian is buried. We can have a service later, but I want to make sure she is in the ground tonight."

"Do not wear yourself out," Leah said.

"I will not," James said as he stood up. He started toward the door and then stopped. He turned back to Leah.

"I told the guests that the party would continue another day," James said, "I thought it was best."

"It is best," Leah replied.

"And Caleb is waiting to talk to you," James said, "Unless you would rather I sent him away so you can rest."

"I want see him," Leah replied. "Please."

"Very well," James said turning back to the door. He opened it and stepped out into the hallway. A moment passed before Caleb entered the room.

"Are you okay?" Caleb asked as he sat down in the spot Leah's father left.

"I think so although I am not certain I understand everything that has happened," Leah answered, "Hopefully things will get better over the next week or so. Maybe then I will feel like having the party that was interrupted."

"Most of the guests understand," Caleb said.

"Even then it will be lots of rumours about what happened," Leah said, "Especially with Mother dead. It will take a while to pass unless maybe they will find Meghan Kenley and Oliver Borden and this will all be old news."

"They are not going to find Oliver and Meghan," Caleb said, "After their wedding at Greenwich they headed for his father's other country estate."

"How do you know all that?" Leah asked.

"Oliver asked for me and Percy to help him get Meghan out of her third storey room and lay a false trail," Caleb answered, "Apparently they had been seeing each other for months, but knew her father would not approve because Oliver is the illegitimate child of Lord Borden. The fact that Lord Borden does not treat him as such does not matter. Oliver and Meghan being caught at Hilary's party was planned in hopes it would change people's minds, but it did not work."

"I had wondered why Lord Kenley turned him down," Leah said, "Even Lady Kenley did not like the match. But now Meghan does not have to worry about them. I wonder what Margaret will do now."

"Are you sure you are all right?" Caleb asked.

"It feels like these past few months have been a nightmare," Leah answered studying her hands, "And I am scared I will wake up and find today, learning we were to marry, was just a dream."

"It is not a dream," Caleb told her as he pulled her onto his lap and wrapped his arms around her. Leah rested her head on his chest. She felt safe here in his arms. Caleb did not say anything else.

"I think I am going to write a book," Leah said.

"About all this?" Caleb asked.

"Inspired by this," Leah answered, "I started to tell the story to Father. He wanted to know how it ended and now I know."

"And how does it end?" Caleb asked.

"We get married as soon as my father will let us," Leah replied, "The birthday party is to celebrate our wedding. And then we live happily ever after."

"I think the wedding might be a little farther away than that," Caleb said, "The vicar is enjoying being locked up in a cell with Randall at the moment. We will have to wait until another one arrives."

"Or we could elope," Leah said looking up at Caleb.

"Your father would skin me and gut me like a deer," Caleb said, "He already warned me against that. He intends to see you get married."

"I do not want to wait," Leah said.

"I promise you will not have to wait any longer than necessary," Caleb said then he kissed her. Leah wrapped her arms around his neck so he could not move and then put the full craving she had for him into the kiss. She received the same in return.

"I love you," Leah said when they came up for air, "And I want you to hold me as I write the scary parts of the story."

"I will," Caleb promised, "I love you too."

## EPILOGUE

*August 1, 1966*

The gravel path twisted through the hedges that made up the garden maze. The sun was beating down, but the shadows made by the tall hedges provided relief. It made for a nice walk in the garden, and reminded Leah of a similar day she had gone down this path. But that day she had been running from her mother and her life. Today she was not running from anything, just enjoying a walk in the garden. So much had changed since that day. She had met Caleb and fell in love. Her mother had died. Though there were more people at the service out of respect for Leah and her father and curiosity than mourning for Vivian Winsand. A few were disappointed they did not get to see the body, but Leah's father had made sure his wife was good and buried the night she had died. Leah had not minded what her father had done. Lady Lambert and Randall were put on trial for kidnapping, among other crimes like the murder of the cook's helper and the attempted murder of her father. They had been found guilty and sent to prison. If all the information had not come out at the trial there would have been even more speculation fuelled gossip. Leah had testified, along with her father, Caleb and Lord Lambert. Lord Lambert had since sold his estate and moved to London. Rumour had him joining the army and going off to India, but Leah did not know whether it was true or not.

Leah had just spent the morning with her father, who had gotten most of his strength back. He had spent the morning playing with his first grandchild, Rose. Rose was now sleeping on Leah's shoulder and would probably not wake up until she needed to be fed. Leah smiled as she glanced down at the bundle curled up against her shoulder. Rose was only two months old, but Leah now understood what her father meant by a child being the greatest joy a person could have. Of course, he might have recently changed that to grandchildren being better than children, but that was okay with Leah. The strawberry blonde hair and blue eyes could make anyone fall in love with the tiny face. Caleb claimed Rose looked just like Leah, but Leah was not completely convinced.

The rustling of the hedge farther up the path broke into Leah's thoughts. The rustling continued as if there was someone in the hedge. A year ago she hesitated to go any farther, but today Leah knew there was nothing to be afraid of.

"Hello?" Leah called out. The gardener's head and shoulders popped out of the hedge and looked at her.

"Hello," the gardener said, "How are you and the little one doing today?"

"Very well," Leah answered, "Rose spent the morning playing with her grandfather, so she is sleeping. Father said your wife had a baby."

"Two days ago," the gardener beamed, "A boy. He's perfect."

"Congratulations," Leah said.

"Thank you," the gardener said, "Lord Winsand said when I am finished here I can get back to him and my wife."

"Then I will not disturb you further," Leah said.

"Have a good day," the gardener said before withdrawing back into the hedge. Leah smiled as she continued along the path and passed where the gardener was working. A year ago she had asked permission to continue and now she could talk to him. So much had changed in that time. The day after the trial her father had thrown a party for Leah. Everyone was invited. They thought they were coming to the party to celebrate Leah coming into society. They were shocked to find themselves in the middle of a wedding between Leah and Caleb. A new vicar had shown up shortly after the report went out about the last one was taking money to perform duties for illegal activities. The charges of being an accomplice in the kidnapping did not stay, but the church was unwilling to give him back his post. Or any post from the sound of things.

After the wedding Caleb had moved into the Winsand Manor for six months before he and Leah had moved into a suite his parents had renovated. It was long enough for Leah to see her father was doing better and would be okay. Though he was complaining about all the guests he had been getting recently. Many of them were widows or older women who had never married. He had started getting Roger and the new housekeeper to turn them away, as well as not going out socially alone. Melissa had been found. She had run off to the village and was trying to get farther when Roger found her. She was pregnant and did not know what to do. Roger had brought her back to the house and Leah's father had talked to her. Melissa continued as Leah's maid and her little girl, Jem, was going to grow up alongside Rose. Melissa refused to tell anyone who Jem's father was. Caleb claimed he knew, but he would not tell Leah because he felt it was better if Melissa's business.

Leah continued walking. She came to the corner in the maze and went into the clearing with the fountain. The flowers were different this year, but everything else was the same. Leah went around the fountain and through the opening on the other side. This was the part of the maze where if you went off it you would get lost, but Leah remembered the path she wanted and followed the twists and turns.

Despite Caleb's claim, Lord and Lady Kenley had found Meghan and Oliver. But it was several months later and Meghan was already expecting her first child. Lord Borden let them move into his manor. Since his daughters had all married lords and were fine, Lord Borden named Oliver his heir. Lord and Lady Kenley still did not want Meghan married to him, but they could not do anything. According to Margaret, Meghan and her parents talked only on the occasions they meet at someone else's event. Margaret had not been shipped off to London for several months as planned. Instead Lord Kenley had gone to London and found someone for her to marry. He found a viscount, who bought the Lambert Estate. Margaret married him shortly after as her parents arranged it. She never discussed her marriage.

Leah arrived in the next clearing and stopped in front of the statue that stood there. The woman in the flowing dress still held the child in her arms as she smiled down at it. Leah remembered not understanding the sad look in the smile when she had first seen the statue. Now with her own child in her arms she understood, just as she now understood what kept Selena wanting to stay at the convent after her parents took her child from her. And all those feelings made Leah want to hold Rose tighter. Hilary announced she was pregnant months after she and Percival married, but less than a month later she lost the child. Leah had cried with Hilary over the loss. Recently Hilary was looking like she might be pregnant again. Leah prayed she was and that the baby would survive.

Leah went around the statue and through the opening on

the other side. She followed the path the rest of the way to the door. The door was closed and right where Leah knew it would be. The memory of standing there waiting to catch her breath, hoping Caleb would be on the other side for her came back. For a moment Leah held her breath and wished Caleb would be there if she opened the door. But she knew Caleb was supposed to be busy talking business with his father, which was why Leah had gone to see her father for the morning.

She pushed on the door and it opened out into the field. The grass was waving to her, inviting her out. The fish pond glittered just down a slope from the door. But Caleb was not standing there waiting for her. No one was there. Leah knew there would not be, but she still felt the disappointment. She pushed those feelings aside before stepping off the path and into the field. Leah looked around the field. There was no one in sight, which was not unusual. Most people used the road if they were going to travel between estates. Leah had felt like walking this morning, which was why she was walking through the field. It was much faster to get between her father's house and the Morley Estate. Leah closed the door and started for the fish pond.

Her father's book would be out in the next month. He had told her about his next one during lunch. It was going to be a children's book. He had even found someone to do the illustrations. Most of the other books had been written for Leah, but this next one was going to be written for Rose. Leah hoped it would be ready by the time Rose was reading. Leah's book was not going to be ready for a long time. Every time Leah sat down to write something interrupted her. Leah had asked her father how he dealt with all the disruptions and he had just smiled at her without giving an answer. The problem was that writing was not as easy as sitting with a pen in hand putting words together in sentences. That was another thing her father had made look easy which in reality was difficult. But Leah was determined to finish the book someday.

Reaching the fish pond Leah found it as clear as the first time she had seen it. She now knew it had been made because some lord wanted to be able to fish without having to go find an actual lake. No one was sure why the bottom lacked weeds. The water was inviting with the way the sun beat down. Even with her hat Leah could feel it. Being careful of Rose on her shoulder, Leah crouch down and dipped her fingers in the water. It was warm.

Leah looked back at the door. The door was closed. All that was there was the hedge, which went into the distance in both directions. Leah turned and looked across the lake. There were just the trees between the field and the Morley Estate. No sign of anyone, especially since Caleb was busy. Lady Morley and the groom, Haines, were off to look at horses. She knew from being on the other side of them that no one could see through the trees.

Leah sat down at the water's edge. After making a nest in the grass, Leah laid Rose down in it. Then she took off her hat and put it over her daughter to protect Rose from the sun. After another check to see if anyone was around Leah took off her shoes and stockings. Standing back up she hitched up her skirt to her knees and stepped into the water. The water felt wonderful and she continued farther in. When the water level reached her knees Leah had to hitch her skirt up to the middle of her thighs to keep it dry.

The fish were a little bigger this year than they were last year. Caleb had told Leah that people do fish in the fish pond, but only rarely. She had never seen anyone and with the amount of fish in the pond it looked like it had been awhile. Leah watched as the schools of fish swam passed her. It still reminded her of dancers at a party, but this time it brought up the memory of the party to celebrate her wedding. She had been one of the dancers on the floor that night. It had been fun dancing in Caleb's arms without any worries about tomorrow to destroy the happiness of the moment. And she had not run into, tripped over, and stepped on someone else the whole time.

Movement caught Leah's attention and she looked up to see Caleb coming out of the trees on Warrior's back. He saw her and directed Warrior to the fish pond. Warrior was not happy about stopping before the ride had even begun, but he did what he was told. Caleb looked at Leah. Rather than blush, Leah smiled at him.

"I seem to remember this scene," Caleb said.

"I thought it might be nice to see how the fish were doing," Leah said, "While Rose is asleep." Leah pointed to the bundle lying in the grass.

"And how are the fish doing?" Caleb asked as he got off Warrior.

"A little bigger than last year," Leah told him. Caleb pulled off his riding boots and wadded into the water towards Leah.

"That is good," Caleb said as he reached her. He pulled Leah into his arms and kissed her. Leah let go of her skirt to wrap her arms around his neck.

"I thought you were busy talking to your father," Leah said when the kiss was over.

"I needed the break and I was wondered how the two most wonderful girls in my life were doing," Caleb answered.

"Your daughter wore out her grandfather," Leah said.

"And how are you?" Caleb asked.

"Everything is perfect now that you are here," Leah answered. Caleb smiled before kissing her all over again.

# ABOUT THE AUTHOR

Colleen Price was raised in Northern British Columbia. She enjoys writing and drawing. On occasion, she will take out her paints and put brush to canvas.
Colleen greatly appreciates her reader leaving reviews on either Amazon or Good Reads.